Days of Danger

Days of Danger

FRITZ HABECK

translated from the German
by James Kirkup

Collins
ST JAMES'S PLACE, LONDON

Map by Ernst Schrom

© 1960 by Verlag fur Jugend und Volk
English translation © 1963 Harcourt, Brace & World Inc,
and William Collins Sons & Co Ltd
originally published in Austria by Verlag fur Jugend und Volk
under the title Der Kampf um Die Barbacane
First published in Great Britain 1968
Printed in Great Britain
Collins Clear Type Press London and Glasgow

Days of Danger

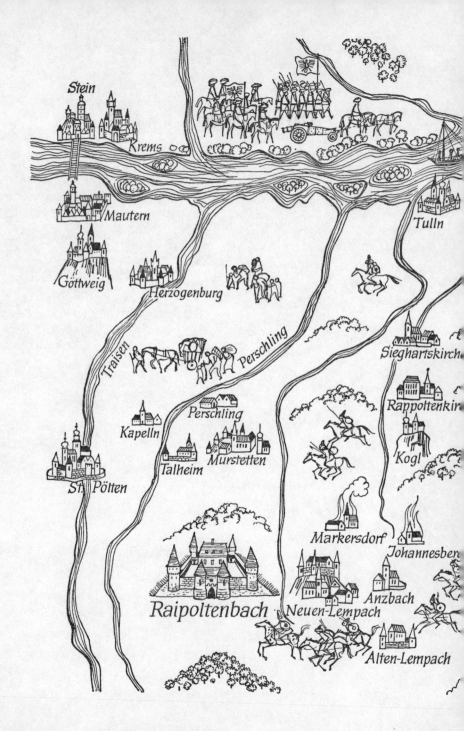

1

I remember now, nearly twenty years after it happened, that my story began on a rainy Sunday in early July, 1683, which was when I first encountered the man with no ears or nose. I was fourteen years old and had just returned home for the summer holidays from my school in Vienna. Home in those days meant Raipoltenbach near the village of New Lempach, a big house where ever since my father's death my mother had been in charge of the dairy. This place was a great mass of dark grey stone, which on the one side was half sunk in the ground, so that the low, massive beams over the doors were on a slant. The high, pointed gable of the projecting thatched roof also stood crooked. From the triangular bit of wall formed by the pointed gable, a long rope hung, running over a rusty pulley, and this was for hauling up bales of hay. At either end of the building were two gigantic linden trees, and in their deep shade the house with its tiny latticed windows looked even more sombre and mysterious, for its appearance was dark enough already, the stone being almost black in colour.

The man came from the direction of Lempach, and when he was still a long way off, I could hear his piping. I was sitting on a carpenter's bench outside the door, whittling a willow wand; when I looked up, I saw, outlined against the grey sky above the flat ground between Lempach and Raipoltenbach, the figure of a man walking, and something about his uncertain gait made me lower my knife and stick in order to watch the stranger's movements better. He was proceeding in a stumbling sort of way but going quickly all the same, and his hands were raised to a fife on which he was playing a marching song. He stopped just beyond our moat, put the fife away in an inside coat pocket, and gazed up at one of the corner towers of the big house. Then he walked on again and came straight up to me.

He was wearing greasy breeches, with ragged stockings, and shoes through which his toes appeared; his blue coat had once been gold-braided, but now only a few shabby gilt threads showed where the glittering braid had been. He had on a broad leather belt, from which hung a hefty rapier and a black three-cornered hat. His beard was red and cut in a circular fringe, and his head was shaven. He had no nose and no ears: in their place shone three smooth bluish scars. He cast a brief glance at me, then let his eyes wander over the courtyard of the big house, its outer fortifications and the great two-towered gateway, the linden trees, the smithy behind them, with a bush growing beside the woodpile; not for one instant did his little bright blue eyes cease their roving.

"The Lord Jesus Christ be praised!" he said, crossing himself. This sounded and looked very strange because to judge by his appearance, one would have expected him rather to whip out his sword and break into a volley of curses. "It does an old soldier's heart good to find himself in such an easily defended place." He pointed stumpy fingers at his scars. "The Turks did that to me when they took me prisoner—may the Lord bring retribution upon them, the heathens!" Once again he crossed himself. "Now would the young gentleman be so kind and tell me whom this castle belongs to?"

Though I was no common farm lad but a student and attended the Jesuits' classes at the Imperial Theological Seminary, I had never before been addressed in such a deferential manner, and I was flattered; so I answered more politely than the dubious appearance of the stranger might have warranted. "It belongs to our gracious and noble lord, Count Palffy."

"To Count Palffy! He owns the whole of New Lempach,

Old Lempach, and Paungarten too! Then is this magnificent residence standing empty?"

"A steward and his family, together with my mother and myself, live on the premises."

He nodded, as if he had suspected this from the start. "That's what I thought!" he declared, slapping the basket hilt of his sword. "The young gentleman of lordly family! I dare say you have a handful of good soldiers about the place too?"

"My father is dead. And we have no soldiers."

He shook his head. "No soldiers! A fortress like this and you have no soldiers—now isn't that a sin and a crime! I know all about this kind of place. If the young gentleman will be so kind as to consider the aspect of those four corner towers and those walls joining them—that's solid strength for you! The layout's almost foursquare, not too big, not too unmanageable, with a broad moat and that stupendous barbican—you don't have to be afeard of the Turks with all that! If I had twenty men, I could keep a whole army at bay here, and by all the saints, I'm telling no lie!" And of course he crossed himself once again.

"Soldiers cost a lot of money, and the Turks are a long way off," I answered.

He gazed at me silently for a while, then broke into a mocking laugh. "A long way off! What does the young gentleman mean by that? How many miles? Six hundred, or sixty, or six? And if I were to tell the young gentleman that the Tartars have already been seen in Neusiedl and Steinbruch, that they have been burning and looting our land for some time now, and that the janizaries—foot-soldier reinforcements—are marching to join them from the rear, a hundred thousand strong—what would the young gentleman have to say to that?"

"I should say that you're exaggerating."

He gave a curt nod. "I'm exaggerating; yes, that's what he *would* say." Screwing up his eyes, he looked across towards the smithy. "If you have no soldiers, at least there must be a few good brawny farm hands about the place. What about the blacksmith and his lads?"

"They've all gone off to Purkersdorf with their drill-master to dig trenches. And as for the Tartars, according to what we've been told in school, they're fanning out over a wide area; the Turks won't get as far as here because the Emperor's army stands between them and us."

"God bless the Duke of Lothringen!" he cried. "I've seen him with my own eyes——"

A few hammer blows were heard coming from the smithy, and the stranger suddenly broke off. With rapid steps he came right up to me, bent low down over me so that I smelled the stale wine on his breath, and whispered menacingly: "Would the young gentleman be after telling me a lie? Would the young gentleman be trying to lie to me, no?"

I wanted to jump up but dared not, for he remained crouched over me. His steely eyes held me fast; we stared at one another for a while, and I was afraid I was going to faint because he looked as if he were going to throttle me. Finally he spoke again, but still in a whisper: "Do you know what happens to people like you what give false information? We knock the living daylights out of 'em; there's not much left of 'em after that, I can tell you, son. Now, who's gone to dig the trenches in Purkersdorf?"

"All of them except the blacksmith and the steward," I managed to stammer.

He gave me a searching look, then stood upright, fetched a deep sigh, and laughed. "The young gentleman will pardon an old soldier: rough ways, but a heart of gold; it's the same with all of us. And I wasn't joking when I asked you those questions, you know. The country's in danger."

That broad smile in the noseless face was almost more terrifying than the angry grimace that had convulsed it earlier. I had to lower my eyes; I looked past the blue coat with the leaden

14

buttons and saw on the hill a carriage that had just come over the top and was now beginning to move down towards the big house. "The doctor!" I said in a voice I found was hoarse.

The stranger swung around and at the same time stepped behind me. "There's a parson sitting in it!" he growled.

"A reverend gentleman in a gown. . . . It could be Father Lukas—yes! It's Father Lukas and the doctor!"

Suddenly I couldn't think why I was sitting there as if glued to my seat and jumped up. "The doctor knows more than me— you must ask *him* your precious questions!" I cried somewhat contemptuously, feeling myself in charge of the situation once again. But when I turned around, the stranger had vanished.

2

The carriage drove past me, turned into the outer gate of the big house, rolled through the barbican, and stopped in the courtyard. I went running along behind it until it stopped; then I made a deep bow to the gentlemen who were getting out and offered each of them my hand to help them down.

The doctor and the priest were a curious pair, for the priest was tall, plump and friendly, whereas the doctor was short, skinny, and bad-tempered; but the two had been together for years, though they never agreed about anything. To us it was an inexplicable friendship. It had been Doctor Voytt who had recommended that I be admitted to the Theological Seminary, because, as he said, "The Jesuits, despite their repellent ideas, are clever and sharp as knives and to-day are, unfortunately, the only decent teachers in existence."

"I've heard you're a thorough lazybones," he said to me now.

"A few years ago I'd thought you might some day take my place in Lempach—but lazy good-for-nothings never become doctors."

Then he turned towards the door of the big house, and Father Lukas, following him, put his arm around my shoulders and drew me along with him. "Probably you know well enough why I'm here to-day," he said to me (in Latin, because this was the only language spoken in the seminary), "and perhaps you're thinking I'm a sort of bird of ill-omen. But that's not so; you've no cause to worry. I dare say you *are* a lazy young beggar and I dare say you weren't very diligent in your studies; and I know for certain you've been up to a few silly boy's tricks. But all the same I like you, and when I've got things moving a bit, all will be well for you. I hope that——"

But he got no further, for my mother came out, bade him welcome, and then led the two gentlemen into the corner room. I followed them.

As the dairy had barely enough sleeping accommodation for my mother and myself and as the big house was only occasionally visited by the gentry, my mother was allowed to make use of two rooms on the ground floor of the fortress; this privilege had been granted all the more readily as she had been born a Khainacher, and the Khainacher knights had a century ago owned this very fortress, losing it later in the struggles arising from their evangelical beliefs. So now the four of us sat down at the round oaken table in the North Room; pewter pitchers of Langenberg wine were set before the men, and the priest gave us the latest news about the Turkish advances in Hungary.

As usual, the doctor disagreed with him about everything. "Far too much idle chatter about what they call the Turkish peril," he growled contemptuously. "The Turks aren't heathens, nor are they monsters and criminals, but human beings like ourselves. If they were such monstrous beasts, why should the Emperor be negotiating with them? Why have we an ambassador at the Sublime Porte? Why was the Turkish Ambassador received with such great tokens of respect in Vienna? Why do we send gifts to the Sultan? Why do the Hungarians prefer Turkish to German domination? Why do Dutchmen serve as volunteers on Turkish vessels? Why is England delivering gunpowder to Turkey, and why has the blessed King of the French placed his siege marshal at her disposal, while we work ourselves up as if the whole future of the West depended on us?"

"Which means, quite simply, that you want the Sultan to be our emperor and to have the janizaries here in Lempach looking after things."

No, that was not what the doctor meant; his face turned bright red and he started talking at the top of his voice about Jesuitical wiles. But the crosser he got, the more merry grew Father Lukas, until finally my mother intervened to stop the dispute and inquire the reason for their visit.

"Frau Thanradl, your respected mother, would never guess what has brought me here," the priest answered and gave me a wink. "It's about this young fellow, as a matter of fact. I had to preach at the monastery in Lilienfeld, and because it was on my way, the Reverend Father who is Director of Studies there asked me to call here on the way back and speak with you." He paused for a moment, then turned and smiled at me and ordered me (in Latin once again) to leave the room.

Despite his friendly attitude, I didn't feel at all happy about his visit; that he would do his best to make things easy for me, I didn't doubt, but what my mother would say was another matter altogether. Feeling somewhat apprehensive, I stepped out of the big house into the courtyard, climbed the steps up to the barbican, and sat down at the little window over the main gate. Below me I could see the houses on my right: the dairy, the stables, the winepress, and the smithy. Away to my left stretched the gloomy pinewoods. The clouds hung low, and it began to drizzle softly.

They were going to expel me from the school; I was sure of that. That would suit me quite well, but I was sorry for my mother, for she had set such hopes upon my going to the university and making something of my life in a respectable sort of way. A pity that what was "respectable" was also so boring.

Heavier and heavier drops of rain kept falling on the grey landscape, and everything seemed to me dreary and wretched in the extreme. I felt utterly forlorn. At last I heard the priest and the doctor coming out of the big house with my mother, and heard my mother call me. I did not let on where I was, but I leaned out just a little to look at the carriage, watched the priest and the doctor finally get in, then followed the vehicle with my eyes until it was out of sight.

Only when dusk began to fall did I go down, and during the evening meal I learned what Father Lukas had said.

It was as I had thought. My results in grammar and rhetoric were so poor that the small amount of ability I was granted to possess in the humanities was not enough to even things out. The Director of Studies said this was because I had rebelled too often against the discipline of school, and Father Lukas himself was convinced that I would do better in some other line. These were the reasons they had used to persuade my mother to take me away from school.

We sat opposite one another in the corner room; there was a five-branched candelabra standing on the table, and in the glow of its fluttering candle flames I saw my mother's eyes bent sternly upon me.

"You really need a good thrashing," she declared.

Experience had taught me that such announcements were no idle warnings. My mother was as big and strong as a trooper, and she had the voice of a sergeant-major. When I was little, she simply used to lift me up in one hand and give me a spanking with the other. Though this was no longer possible, her chastisements had lost none of their vigour.

"I really ought to give you a sound thrashing," she said. "But this is the way things were bound to turn out. Your father—the Lord rest his soul—was not one whit better than you."

My father? But my father had constructed the Iron Frog! The whole of Vienna had gone to see it when it was put on exhibition. It was a mechanical frog, more than a foot high, a real monster of a frog and really frightening when it jumped on your foot, rolled its eyes, and opened its great metal mouth in a hideous croak! The Iron Frog was the sensation of the times, and my father, watchmaker and chief mechanic to the Holy Roman Emperor, had become famous because of it. So he was not one whit better than me?

"He only wanted to work on things that he found amusing," my mother went on, stroking her chin reflectively. "With him it was machines. With you it's painting. Father Lukas thinks you have talent, but the Theological Seminary is not an art academy."

That was unfortunately only too true, and I couldn't think of an answer.

The maid cleared away the dishes and went out. My mother fell silent. After a long pause, during which I felt like a cat on hot bricks, she finally came out with: "So there's no point in your going on with your studies. You're not cut out for a soldier, and you haven't got the wit to make a businessman. Father thinks you're only good for painting and that I should let you have lessons. It's all very well for him to talk—he won't be paying for them, and the Countess, whom he asked to help you, won't hear of it. So it's up to me, I suppose. Come with me."

She stood up and went with the candelabra in her hand to the chest in the corner, opened it, and took out a small iron box. With a key that she took out of a purse attached to her belt, she opened this box, signed to me to come nearer, and showed me the contents. Lying on a velvet cushion was a massive gold chain, together with a sort of tiara set with many big diamonds, a number of gold bangles set with precious stones, and a crucifix covered with rubies and emeralds.

"This is all that's left of the Khainacher fortune," she said, and her voice sounded choked and queer, which made me feel a proper cad and very miserable. "Your great-grandfather wore the chain in Parliament; it is your own inheritance, and when I'm gone, it will be yours. You must promise to hand it on to your own eldest son, as I shall do. But the tiara—that can be used for your painting lessons. I know of someone who a few years ago offered me a good price for it, enough to cover some years of study in Italy."

"Mother!——" I flung my arms around her neck and tried to kiss her cheek. But she shook me off as if I were a playful puppy.

"Now that's enough of that. You're my only child, and you must have the money. But remember one thing: I'm not throwing my money away on a good-for-nothing lazybones. You've got talent, but you've got to work. It's not all play, you know. You've got to learn and work right hard! Really *work*! If you don't—and heaven's my witness—I'll have nothing more to do with you!"

I made another attempt to embrace her and managed with difficulty to plant a kiss on her chin. Then I brought out my drawings, explained each one of them to my mother, and finally went off to bed feeling almost drunk with delight at the thought of the radiant future that stretched before me.

This was how it came about that I didn't tell either my mother or the steward or the doctor or the priest about my encounter with the noseless and earless stranger; if I had thought of telling them, that night would have passed off quite differently, and I should never have experienced all the things that happen in this book.

3

It was long past midnight when I was awakened by a heavy hammering, and it took me some time to realise that someone was banging on the door of my room. "Andreas! Andreas!" the maid was shouting. "The place is on fire!"

In a twinkling I was out of bed, had slipped on my shirt and breeches, and become aware of a strong smell of burning. A few seconds later I jumped out into the courtyard while still fastening the buckle on my belt.

But it was not the big house that was on fire. The glow of the flames came from the direction of the dairy, and the wind was blowing the dense billows of smoke across from there, making it difficult to breathe. The doors were all open; I stood looking about me but could not at once make out anything clearly because the smoke was so thick. A little way off I could see the pale dress of one of the maidservants, who was dashing backwards and forwards like a flustered hen, nattering to herself all the time: "The Turks are here! Lord help us! It's the Turks! O Lord, have pity on a poor girl!" Then someone seized my hand. It was the steward's seven-year-old son, and he hauled on my fingers as if he wanted to pull them off, all the time repeating: "It's the . . . it's the . . ." But he could never get any further.

At last I found my mother standing inside the moat and filling a bucket with water.

"Where's the fire?" I shouted. I had to shout at the top of my voice, so loud was the roaring of the flames, the crash of falling timbers, and the howling of the wind.

"The stables!" my mother yelled back, her voice already

hoarse. "Get in the chain and pass the buckets on to Anni!"

I did as I was told and for the next hour or so did nothing but carry full buckets of water from my mother to Anni the maidservant, who was about twenty feet away; then I would take an empty bucket from her and run back to my mother with it. Each time we exchanged buckets, I made a hurried inquiry, and thus I learned after a while that, besides ourselves, there were two other maidservants in the chain and that the steward and the blacksmith were endeavouring to prevent the spread of the fire to the barns. The horses had been let out of the stables by the blacksmith and had galloped off towards the wood. At that time we possessed only three horses, for the Count had taken the rest with him while he was serving as a general with the Imperial Army. Of almost seven hundred sheep, only fifty had been left; if we had had a larger number of cattle, the blacksmith could not have saved them all, so fast had the fire spread to the byres.

At last, when I could hardly move my arms and legs for weariness, the task of putting out the fire came to an end. The stables and the sheep-pens were burned to the ground, and the glowing ashes still sent out so fierce a heat that I was unable to venture any closer. The barns had been saved from the conflagration. My mother went over to the steward who was lying stretched out, completely exhausted, under one of the linden trees; a maidservant was giving him a drink of wine and bathing his scorched face with cold wet towels. The blacksmith was standing beside a heap of charred beams, using a rusty old halberd to fish out and scatter the still-smouldering timbers in order to prevent the outbreak of a fresh conflagration.

"How on earth did it break out?" my mother asked; her voice had become so hoarse that it was almost impossible to understand what she was saying.

The steward could only moan helplessly, but his little son

came running out of the door of the big house, waving his arms above his head and crying: "It's the . . . it's the . . ."

Meanwhile the blacksmith had thrown his halberd aside and come over to us. His hair, his bushy eyebrows, and the beard on his sooty face were all singed, making the whites of his eyes gleam in a spooky way; his clothes were in charred rags. He was racked by coughing.

"It's the hand of the Lord!" he proclaimed. "It has come to pass, as it is written in Psalm 94: 'They gather themselves together against the soul of the righteous, and condemn the innocent blood. But the Lord is my defence; and my God is the rock of my refuge. And He shall bring upon them their own iniquity'."

"When you say iniquity, do you mean our own lord and master?" my mother asked.

The blacksmith did not reply.

And now the steward's wife came running out of the big house; she, too, like her son, ran with her arms uplifted and waving, and as she ran, she screamed: "They've broken open the chest and stolen the money! They've broken open the chest!"

"It's the . . . it's the . . ." the little boy howled.

"*Who* broke the chest open?"

"I don't know! How should I know?"

"But the Lord 'shall bring upon them their own iniquity'," the blacksmith murmured.

"And shall wipe us from the face of the earth, isn't that so?" my mother panted, speaking in her loud, toneless voice. "My family were once Protestants. I know all those high-sounding phrases, Jakob, so let's have no more of them!"

" 'They gather themselves together against the soul of the righteous . . .' "

My mother and I ran through the barbican, across the court-yard, into the big house and our corner room. It was dark in

23

there, for my mother like everybody else had jumped out of bed without bothering to strike a light. But we didn't need candles. In the middle of the room we stumbled over a piece of wood, and in the dim radiance from the dying fire, which still glowed in the courtyard, we saw that our own cupboards had also been broken open.

The little metal box was missing.

My mother crossed herself. "The Lord's will be done," she whispered.

At my age, I was less inclined to accept the ways of God to man. I wasn't in the least interested in old Khainacher's gold chain or in the other trinkets apart from their money value, which was to have paid for my painting studies. But now all that was already in the past.

The steward rushed into the room shouting that all his money had been stolen; even worse, the Count's money had vanished, too. He would have to leave at once for Lempach in order to break the news to the Countess. "I'm going with you." my mother said.

I stayed behind. I sat down under the linden where the steward had lain and stared at the smouldering embers. So the man with no ears and no nose was also an incendiary and had asked about whether we had soldiers and hefty blacksmith's apprentices only in order to plan the robbery better. Where was he now? Obviously he'd be over the hills and far away to carry on his frightful handiwork elsewhere. He'd be easily recognised by his scars, but how could I, still not much more than a boy, go running after him? And where would I, in this period when the Turks were threatening invasion, find soldiers who would recover the booty from the robber? No, such thoughts were quite fruitless.

And now, what was to become of me?

For a long time I squatted under the linden tree, my arms wrapped tightly around my knees, and watched the fire slowly dying out. Day began breaking; there was dew on the grass, and a few wisps of mist dragged over the meadows. Finally I thought I had found a possible way out. I ran straight to Lempach and asked for my mother but learned that she had departed for Paungarten with the Countess.

I couldn't wait any longer, and as I knew only too well how little sympathy my mother would have for my scheme, I returned to Raipoltenbach, washed, changed my clothes, and wrote a short note in which I said I had gone to Vienna to see Count Alram.

About midday I started.

4

The old Count Alram had been a rich, widely travelled, and highly cultivated gentleman who had held my father in high regard, not because of the Iron Frog but because of the astronomical timepiece that Father had constructed for the Emperor and that showed not only the time of day but also the date, the phases of the moon, the horoscope, and the motions of the planets. So close had the friendship between the two men become that my father had ventured to ask the Count if he would be my godfather. I would not have needed the good offices of Doctor Voytt in order to be taken into the seminary if old Count Alram had still been alive. But unfortunately he had died a few days after my father in the same terrible plague that raged in Vienna all through 1679 and caused over sixty thousand deaths.

The old Count had several daughters and one son, who at the early age of sixteen had already fought against the Turks under the Imperial Commander-in-Chief and later the King of

Poland, Johann Sobieski; he had been taken prisoner and had lain two years in captivity in Turkey until his father succeeded finally in buying his freedom. After his return he maintained a squadron of dragoons. He was quickly promoted and served as a colonel on the Hungarian border until, against the express commands of his general, von Allsberg, he held his troops so much in reserve—instead of sending them forward in battle— that he fell into disgrace and had to give up his regimental duties. Only a month ago I had heard from Father Lukas that Georg Christoph Alram was now once again in his Vienna town house on the New Square; and although, according to my mother's tales, he had always appeared as a high-handed man interested only in war, I wanted to try my luck with him. Perhaps he still had glimmerings of what a boy's dreams were like and would send me—if only because of the friendship that had existed between our two fathers—to Italy to some great master teacher of painting.

I wandered through the valley of the Anzbach and across the range of hills down into the vale of Vienna. Twice I was overtaken by dispatch riders going at a gallop and once by a carriage being driven at a spanking pace, but otherwise I saw hardly anyone, apart from a few peasant women going to their work in the fields. I had taken some food with me, but towards evening I began to feel thirsty, and as the doctor had warned me against drinking water from the streams, I went to a farm-house and bought a beaker of milk. There was no one but a very old man in the house, who had to hunt around a long time before he found the milk churn in the cellar, and all the time he kept up a perpetual lament about the mad times we were living in. "All the men taken away!" he moaned. "All the men taken away because the soldiers is no good at fighting!"

"Caution isn't a bad thing," I suggested rather priggishly.

"Caution! Caution!" he screeched in his wheezy old man's voice. "Caution may be all right, but on the other hand it may not. What's happened to the warning bonfires? Have you ever seen one burning? Have you ever heard one warning bugle blast? What are they there for if they aren't used? But if things had been going really badly, we'd have seen it by the flames and smoke rising from the top of the Eselberg near Lempach."

I hadn't given a thought to the bonfires that were to act as alarm signals against the approach of the Turks, and so the old man's speech seemed to me to bear out what my mother had always claimed, that all war scares were only the result of idle desire for sensational news. And what if the Turks were already on the march through Hungary? There was never peace in Hungary, and our army would see to it that the enemy did not enter our country.

By the time twilight was falling, I had reached Purkersdorf, which had been transformed into a retreat for refugees from the surrounding countryside and was surrounded by trenches. Apart from the earth walls, the palisades, and the strong road-blocks, I could observe nothing very warlike about the place, and when I met pock-marked Karl from Raipoltenbach, who looked after the horses for us at the dairy, he told me that the digging of trenches was a useless humbug, a dreary task that must have been thought up by the Imperial Court in order to plague honest working folk. Rifle drill in particular he thoroughly hated, and when he thought that back at home the harvest was standing waiting to be brought in, he said it made him want to tear his hair out by the roots, he felt so mad.

He took me to his barracks, where I spent the night; the next morning I got some breakfast there and set off again on my walk to Vienna. After about two hours I reached Hägging, which also was intended as a refugee centre; then within another hour I was at Schönbrunn hunting lodge, and soon I could see the walls, bastions, and towers of Vienna in the distance. The weather had turned out fine, the sun was standing high in the heavens, and I could see clearly on my right the vineyards of

Gumpendorf, on my left Krowotendörfel. Not for one moment did I give a thought to the war or the Turks as I went running down into Vienna through the fortifications and through the Kärntner Gate into the city where I was born and where I had spent the greater part of my life until now.

The servants at the town house on the New Square were all unknown to me, and it took a long time to explain what I wanted; then I was conducted upstairs and made to sit and wait on a bench in an antechamber. There it was dark and quiet, for there was only a small window looking out on an inner courtyard; from time to time a footman crossed the room, looked at me a little contemptuously, and then disappeared again. After a while I heard a door opening in the next room, followed by the sound of two men talking. At first I could barely make out what they were saying, but later I was able to pick out a few sentences.

"No, it's always the same!" an angry voice was saying.

The other deeper voice answered more calmly and quietly, so that I could not catch the meaning.

Then the first voice sounded again.

"Nothing but corruption and incompetence! It's not as bad as it was under Sinzendorf, but it's bad enough! Here we've had the Turks for neighbours for nearly two hundred years, and what happened? Nothing! Absolutely nothing!"

The other's murmuring voice was heard again.

"Oh, that!" the angry voice broke in. "The fortifications have been widened and the bastions extended—all right! And what has been going on in the plain? A whole week ago Mechtl's letter informed Scheller: several market towns are almost completely undefended, arms and munitions are lacking, the people are either not being sent by their local lords to dig the trenches or are simply staying away! In Pottendorf the drill-master was paid his six Gulden and promptly disappeared with them. Rodaun, Petersdorf, and Traiskirchen haven't done a thing. The

28

Duke has twenty thousand men; but the Grand Vizier has two hundred thousand! That's why the Court needs a military adviser!"

Again the deep, soft voice was heard, this time sounding rather worried.

Then I heard swift footsteps. The doors were flung open, and a man of about thirty appeared. He stood on the threshold with the doorknob still in his hand and glanced round the ante-chamber as if he were looking to see if anyone were listening to the conversation. He was wearing a scarlet close-fitting coat in the very latest fashion with broad turned-back cuffs and huge pockets, the whole richly ornamented with gold buttons and braid; he also had on black knee-breeches and scarlet silk stockings. Around his neck was a lace collar, and on his head he bore a gigantic ringleted wig whose locks fell around his shoulders. The face that was framed in this cataract of hair was narrow and tanned, the nose long and sharp-hooked. The upper lip was adorned by a fine, thin black moustache as neat as if it had been pencilled on.

"What are you doing here?" the man asked me, and I could tell from his voice that it was he who in the next room had so frankly expressed his opinions on the defence measures taken by the Imperial Court. "Who are you?"

"My name is Andreas Thanradl, and I am the son of Thanradl the clockmaker—your honour's respected father was my godfather and he told my father . . ."

He waved his hand impatiently. "Why have you come here?"

"Your honour, I find it very hard—I have a request, a very important request . . ."

"Important! My dear young man, here we are sitting on a barrel of gunpowder. I can't imagine anything more important at this moment than the fact that the fuse leading to this barrel of gunpowder is already lighted!"

"If your honour would kindly grant me a few moments. . . ."

29

He gazed reflectively at me for a few moments. "Thanradl?" he said to himself, drawling the name a little. "Wasn't that the Iron Frog man?" He laughed. "So you're the little frog! Come back to-morrow afternoon, and perhaps I'll be able to find time for you."

With that he slammed the door behind him.

I had been sure that he would either dismiss me out of hand or grant my request; but that he should put me off until the next day, not taking me into the house and so compelling me to spend the night alone in Vienna, was something that had not occurred to me. I did not want to go to the seminary after they had thrown me out; the families we had known in former days had left their houses, and of course I had no money for a room at an inn.

So I wandered through the streets, with aching limbs and weary feet; I was hungry and dead tired, and besides I was afraid that the watch would pick me up and arrest me if I were out on the streets after the ten o'clock curfew. But what else could I do until morning? It grew darker and darker, and finally I felt I could not walk another step. I sat down on the steps of the Maria Stiegen church, propped my tired head in my hands, and hoped for a miracle.

5

Though such a thing would seem scarcely credible out in the country, here in Vienna it seemed quite natural that no one should take any notice of me among the swarms of people hurrying by. The house windows began to light up all around me, and I couldn't help thinking that other boys were now sitting down to a well-laid table, which made my own hunger worse than ever. I had certainly never lacked affection from my mother; now I felt suddenly wretched and abandoned by everyone. Other boys had beds to sleep in, had a good hot evening meal served them; they could go and study wherever they wished. But I was cast out into darkness and discomfort, a poor beggar boy crouching on the chill steps of a church. These thoughts disturbed me so much that out of sheer intensity of misery I began to feel tearful over my sorry fate, though of course I did not give way to such childish things as tears.

Suddenly I heard a strange dragging sound; I looked up and saw before me the fattest woman I had ever seen. She was so fat that she could hardly walk and had to thrust one gigantic hip laboriously forward after the other in order to make any sort of progress at all. She was leaning her massive weight on a hefty, knobbly stick and kept groaning: "What a life! They call this living! What sort of life is it when you have to drag yourself around like this? Devil take it! This is no life for a poor weak woman!"

She stopped in front of me and stood there wheezing as she looked me over from top to toe, then asked: "What's the matter with you, young man?"

As far as I could make out in the dusk, she had at least five overlapping chins.

"I'm waiting," I answered.

"So that's what you're doing. Having to sit and wait is one of the terrible burdens we humans have to put up with. . . . I know what it is to have to sit and wait. Look at me. Fat, aren't I? Yes, good and fat. And why am I fat? Because I don't take exercise. And why do I not take exercise? Because I'm too fat. There's a reason for everything, and they call that life!"

These rather mysterious phrases reminded me of some of the discussions on logic and philosophy we had at school, and I wished the fat lady could have had Father Lukas for a teacher:

then she would have had to express herself clearly, and in Latin at that!

"And I was always such a skinny little thing when I was a girl," she went on.

After she had moaned and groaned about her tribulations a little longer, she took me along with her. She called me a "prince" and said a prince ought to live in a palace and that her own palace stood just near the city walls, therefore not in the midst of a noisy crowd of city folk. The "palace" turned out to be a four-story house, with two windows on either side of the door, but looking so rickety that I was afraid it would tumble down over our heads at any moment. The magnificent inn that the fat lady had boasted of proved to be only a dim-lit hole of a place with a rather pretentious sign hanging outside— a winged bell. Just as we were about to enter, someone from an upper story threw the contents of a trash bin out of the window, only narrowly missing our heads. It was not a good district by any means.

I was to receive supper and a place to sleep if I would help in serving the customers. The fat lady squeezed herself painfully behind the narrow counter, where her husband, a tiny wizened man who looked like a sick rabbit, filled the tankards with wine from a huge barrel. My job was to take them to the tables. The room was not very big, so I didn't have far to carry the heavy pots; but because the space was so restricted, it was difficult to make my way between the tables, and as it happened, it was the table in the farthest corner that called for the most wine. Sitting there was a fellow as thin as a rake, with a shifty-looking face in which the long, crooked nose kept twitching suspiciously, as if it already smelled the hangman's noose. He was sitting with his hat on, a funny, narrow-brimmed hat, and an old patched set of bagpipes was slung over his shoulder. His companions made no better an impression: on his left squatted a bristly bearded character in a leather jerkin, on his right a squint-eyed dwarf wearing a grubby night-cap. Somehow their very appearance made one think they should be arrested on the spot.

Near the counter sat a young man who had just finished singing a somewhat sentimental song, accompanying himself on a lute, when I set a fresh tankard of wine on the corner table. The man with the shifty, thievish face turned his long nose to look at me and snarled in a shrill voice, so that the whole room heard what he said: "Is that what you call singing in Vienna? That's the sort of song the little girls sing at the spinning wheel where I come from. We menfolk have a different sort of music altogether!"

"Then sing it yourself!" the young man beside the counter shouted.

Shiftyface (for so I called him in my mind) unslung his bagpipes and blew a series of eight notes. Then he took a deep breath, and he and his companions began stamping rhythmically on the floor as they bellowed their song. Shiftyface blew for all he was worth. The others made the floor shake with their stamping, which continued even during the pauses between the verses. The song began with the words: "No emperor, no noble name." How it went on I've forgotten now, and I remember only the final verse, because I was to hear it so often later on:

> "The raven croaks, the gallows creak,
>   And blood down the steps runs black;
>   When the wind blows over the waves, my lads,
>   Your captain'll call you back."

At this last chorus, Shiftyface would lower his bagpipes and sing with the rest. The room became very quiet; we could hear only the very unlovely, rather croaking voices of the men and the rhythmical stamping of their feet. At the end Shiftyface played the sequence of notes once more that had introduced the whole performance, and when he had ended, there was silence in the room for quite a while.

"That's a song for real men!" Shiftyface said, growing uneasy under the weight of the stillness. "If only we'd had Kaspar here with his fife, then we'd have had a proper songfest. The Turks have sliced off his nose and ears, but he can still blow on that fife of his—his bitterest enemy wouldn't deny him that."

I had remained standing by the table. I could feel the blood thumping through the veins of my neck. "Is he a friend of yours?" I asked, almost without knowing what I was saying.

Shiftyface looked at me a little suspiciously. "What's the matter with you?" he snarled.

"Doesn't he wear a blue coat, and hasn't he a red beard?"

"So! Maybe you've met him somewhere?"

"A few days ago I met someone in Lempach who had met a man answering that description."

Now all of them looked at me, and something in their combined stare made me feel anxious. I swung around, squeezed my way back to the counter, and tried to get my thoughts in order. But before I could decide what to do, I found old Stubblebeard in front of me. He put his hand on my shoulder and whispered: "Supposing it was old Kaspar you met, did he not give you any message?"

I shook my head, but then it struck me that my silence would make the men suspicious, so I added softly: "Not here! Later!"

After Stubblebeard had returned to the table in the corner, I snatched up a cloth lying on the counter, started drying the dishes with it, and gradually worked my way towards the door. As soon as I was close enough, I shot quickly through the half-opened door into the street. As no one raised a hue and cry after me, I was hoping that my disappearance had not been noticed, and I ran as fast as my legs could carry me to the square, where there was a section of the night patrol whose task was to enforce the curfew. I had got no farther than

34

Wildwerchen Street when I encountered a contingent of three soldiers belonging to the night watch whom I implored to come with me to the Winged Bell hostelry and arrest the jailbirds, one of whose band had robbed and set fire to the big house in Raipoltenbach.

They laughed me out of countenance and began to question me, asking me where I came from and what I was doing on the streets so late at night. I refused to answer them but begged them to follow me.

"We'd better take him along with us," one of them said.

Only by giving an address could I save myself from arrest, and so in my predicament I gave the name of Count Alram. That is how I was brought back to the New Square, where I spent a very unpleasant night half dozing on the dirty wooden floor of the porter's lodge.

6

The Count was busy getting dressed the next morning when I was called by a tall, strapping guard to go and see him. He was sitting on a low, plush-covered chair while a manservant drew on his long stockings and put on his shoes; another, with a little scented cloth, was washing the Count's hands, which he allowed to hang limply over the arm-rests; and in the background a hairdresser was carefully brushing a long wig that was placed on a mahogany stand.

"Why do you go running around the streets at night?" the Count asked, and he didn't sound very pleased with me.

I related my adventure, but his surly mood didn't seem to be improved by it.

"First of all, you should have told me you didn't live in

Vienna; then I could have given you somewhere to sleep," he retorted crossly. "And secondly, you've behaved just as one might expect a student from a Jesuit school to behave. If you'd told these fellows that you would meet them somewhere to-day in order to give them a message from this Kaspar, then we could have laid hands on them. Now your escape has probably alerted their suspicions. And why did you come to Vienna anyhow?"

I had to explain all over again and did my best, but he gave me not the slightest sign of interest or encouragement. His dark eyes rested their deep, piercing stare upon me the whole time, and I had to take my courage in both hands to prevent myself from stuttering or losing the thread of my discourse. When I had said my say, the lackeys had also finished their labours; the Count rose to his full height, allowed himself to be helped on with a blue silver-embroidered coat, and then slowly and ceremoniously sat down again so that the hairdresser might put on the full-bottomed wig. "That's all nonsense," he said. "The sort of young fellow I like has only one thought in his head—fighting. I simply cannot comprehend how someone of your age, nearly fifteen, could find the remotest pleasure in sitting indoors with his nose in a book or daubing paper or canvas with pastels or oil paint. Heaven knows we have parsons and pen-pushers and paint-daubers enough—and you can become whatever you like to be, according to your tastes. But I won't lift a finger to help you in that direction."

He rose once more, a servant buckled on his sword, and another handed him his three-corned hat.

"To-day a messenger came with a note from your mother," the Count went on, without deigning to look at me. "She asks me to send you to Josef Langseisen at Katzensteig; there you are to wait for her, for she will come herself to Vienna to-morrow or the day after. Now as far as I can make out, the Langseisen family is no longer in Vienna. So for the time being you are to stay here until your mother comes to fetch you." He turned to the tall guardsman. "Michel, you will show the young fellow his room!"

Upon which he proceeded to the ornate double doors and swept out of the room without bestowing a second glance upon me.

Michel was nearly six and a half feet tall and had shoulders like an ox. He took my arm in a rough, friendly way, and we went up the stairs to the fourth story, during which he explained to me that I shouldn't take the Count too seriously, that he was always in a foul temper whenever he was in town, but that as soon as he was out on the battlefield or in camp, he was the best fellow in the world.

"I shall never see him at his best, then," I answered, "for I have no intention of being in camp with him."

By then we had reached the fourth story, and Michel showed me the room, in which there were a bed, a chair, and a cupboard. Then he sat down on the bed, which creaked ominously beneath his weight, and began to tell me how he had found his way into the army. I listened to his entire life story. I not not only listened but looked, for as he described his exploits, he pulled up his sleeves, hauled down his stockings, opened his coat and bared his chest and body, and lifted his hair up and pointed to his scalp. Everywhere there were scars, and every scar had its legend. Michel's whole body was a mass of scars, which he had received in the wars with the Turks. Then he told me about being taken prisoner and also about a number of quite incredible happenings, for he was convinced that the world was peopled by demons, invisible gnomes, witches, and warlocks of every shape and size. He told me about a lake in Hungary that had turned its waters into blood overnight, so that if you dipped a neckerchief into it, the cloth turned red and, despite repeated washings, never became white again. He related tales of sulphurous rain, of toadstools as big as a man,

37

of crystal balls that walked on human legs, of mists with voices and phosphorescent trees. But he spoke most of Asmodeus, the limping devil, who at night would lift the roofs off houses because he liked to watch people's private lives and so was able always to spread dissension and misunderstandings among ordinary folk, which he thought was a great joke.

"It was Asmodeus who sent you the man with no ears and nose and then whispered to you that you should come to my lord and master. That devil's lurking around somewhere up there, lifting a corner of the roof a little and laughing over your predicament."

I think we sat close on two hours in the low-ceilinged room while the words poured out of Michel in a never-ending stream. Finally he declared he was hungry and took me to the kitchen, where I was given a huge portion of boiled mutton and cabbage. I had just wiped my platter clean and was going to hand it to the cook for another helping when the door burst open and in rushed a dwarf wearing a vast slouch hat as big as a cartwheel, enormous riding boots, and a scarlet sash around his waist, in which he had stuck an ancient pistol.

"It's the Turks!" he shrilled, threw his hat on the floor, snatched the tin platter out of my hand, and put it on his head, pulling frightful faces all the time. "It's the Turks!" he shrieked again and went dancing around the kitchen.

"Baron Blunderbuss!" said the cook with a laugh.

"Baron Blunderbuss!" The kitchen boys laughed.

"He's not quite right in the head," Michel explained to me. "Our master brought him from Hungary and offered him to the Emperor as his court fool or jester, but the Emperor wouldn't have him."

"The Turks are coming!" yelled the dwarf, pulling the old blunderbuss out of his sash.

Michel seized hold of the little chap and lifted him high above his head with one arm, while the dwarf struggled helplessly, waving his arms and legs in the air. "What's all this about the Turks?" Michel roared.

"Beaten the army—army gone—army *kaput*!"

"Baron Blunderbuss!" yelled the cook.

"Baron Blunderbuss!" shouted the kitchen boys.

They all burst out laughing at the sight of the dwarf held so comically aloft in Michel's giant hand.

But it was no joke on the dwarf's part. When we went into the street and spoke to the passers-by, we heard the rumour that was already spreading throughout the city: there had been a battle at Petronell, and the Turks had beaten the Imperial troops into an ignominious retreat. For a while we hoped that the report might be a false one, but towards evening the Emperor left the city, drove in his carriage to Rotenturm, rumbled across the drawbridge over the River Werd and across the bridges over the three other tributaries of the Danube to Corneuburg, from which he drove on to Linz and Passau.

A stream of refugees followed him for six hours after his departure; the whole Court and almost the entire nobility, apart from the army officers, took flight, just as in 1679 they had all run away from the plague. Coachmen and ferryboat owners were asking exorbitant prices and kept raising them even higher when dusk fell and bonfires were seen burning their warning lights on all the mountains round about—bonfires that had presumably been lighted by the Tartars.

The cook and the kitchen boys were laughing on the other side of their faces now. In fact, the smiles had been wiped off every face in the city.

For a full six hours, coach after coach drove over the draw-bridge. We wondered how the city had been able to feed so many horses. And we wondered what sort of fate was awaiting us. The army was beaten, the Emperor, the nobility and their costly possessions vanished. . . .

"We'll just have to sweat it out alone," a tanner standing

near me said. "And the water we drown in'll be pretty foul."

Six thousand people had abandoned the city. The skies were red with fires.

How was my mother faring?

7

The next day the refugees no longer formed a regular stream, but people were still leaving the city through the New Gate and the Red Tower Gate, and I even saw a finely dressed lady sitting on a dirty dung cart drawn by one of her menservants; formerly such an equipage would certainly have been too lowly for her. Through the three other gates, the City Gate, the Scotch Gate, and the Carinthian Gate, refugees were streaming in—above all, the winegrowers of the district who felt it would be too unsafe to stay on in hamlets such as Odakring or Heiligenstadt. As every person who came looking for refuge had to bring his own provisions with him for several weeks, most of them were carrying big sacks on their shoulders, were shoving handcarts and driving cattle along before them. All the same, they had had to leave the better part of their possessions behind for the Tartars to seize, and so nearly all the women were weeping and the men looked dismal and despairing.

I, too, felt just as wretched. I kept running from the City Gate to the Carinthian Gate, always hoping to recognise my mother among the hordes of refugees, yet waiting for her arrival in a state of alarm and despondency. I should have preferred to run back to Lempach, but Michel warned me against this quite severely and told me I would certainly fall into the hands of the Tartars, in which case neither my mother nor I would be any better off.

My mother did not come, but at noon the Duke of Loth-ringen's dragoons rode through the city in order to set up camp on the other side of the Danube, and from them I found out that at Petronell there had indeed been an engagement but that there was no question of a battle having been lost. With the approach of the chief Turkish forces, there were only a few more days left to us; meanwhile, we were to receive infantry and artillery support from the army, and Count Starhemberg, who had just arrived and who was to take over the direction of the army as commandant of the city, could now begin to make haste with the preparations for defence.

To begin with, every household had to supply only one worker on the defences, but the time was short, and soon there was another demand for able-bodied men. Liebenberg, the mayor, lent a hand with the work, and in the end nearly all the men were hauling stones and timber so that the defences might be ready before the Turks arrived. We had to get the protective screens ready, build the palisades, haul the 312 pieces of artillery into place, dragging them from the arsenals on to the bastions and ravelins, construct cradles for them, and wall up the gates. To this end, many houses had to be pulled down and many roofs taken off for fear of fire; the houses also had to be provided with fire-extinguishing implements.

The whole city slaved away for a week, the men labouring on the trenches, defences, and palisades, the women working on munitions and loading gunpowder into the mines that we intended to use against those of the Turks. A thousand hundred-weight of gunpowder, to our great joy, arrived as late as 12th July on ships that had sailed from Salzburg to Vienna. Apprentices filled barrels with earth to serve as breastworks, while soldiers instructed student and citizen companies in the handling of weapons.

To me, this week seemed to pass in a fevered daze. I knew nothing of the troubles besetting the commandant or the Duke of Lothringen, who had to meet a force ten times greater than their own. I carried timber, I carted earth, and from time to time I would run back to New Square to ask if there was any word of my mother's return to the city. Refugees were still coming in, and they told hair-raising tales of the horrors perpetrated by the Tartars. We couldn't help believing them, for not one night went by without an angry, fiery glow appearing in the heavens, and when I thought of the doctor in Lempach who had spoken of the Turks as if they were the easiest people in the world to get on with, I was filled with anger. From what those who had escaped told us, it appeared that the things soldiers had reported about the enemy were quite true.

My mother did not come all that week. It was just possible that she might not have set out on her journey or that, on receiving word of the danger, had taken cover somewhere along the way; but it was just as likely that the Tartars had seized her and taken her prisoner. The worry would have kept me awake each night if I had not been so worn out every day by the hard work we had to do; every evening I just collapsed on my bed and slept like a log.

"It's only the Tartars out there," Michel used to say when he noticed how worried I was. "Tartars are like flies: when you swat them, they fly away. Now it's the janizaries that are dangerous—and they're not going to Lempach; they're coming to us here in Vienna. They know their business, they do. But if Vienna falls, then the whole Empire will fall, and with the Empire, the whole of the West. God can't want that to happen. We'll put up our fists, my lad, and let them run against them till they knock themselves out!"

8

On 13th July the commandant had the outlying districts of Vienna burned down so that they would not be used by the approaching Turks as protection and sleeping quarters. On the fourteenth the main part of the Turkish Army had reached there and set up camp from the Hundsturm through Odakring and Währing right up to the Danube in a gigantic, brightly coloured half-moon of strange costumes and white tents. From Krowotendörfel, however, the janizaries dug approach trenches in the direction of the City Gate, and by making use of these, they could come up to within two hundred paces of the walls.

In the afternoon there was suddenly a fire alarm. At the time, I was having a belated lunch at the house in New Square, and I ran with Michel and Baron Blunderbuss across to the Scots convent, from whose courtyard thick waves of smoke were pouring. A great crowd had already gathered on the Freyung, our big public square—though it's really a long wide street—and they all wanted to lend a hand with putting out the fire. But the doors were locked, and no one dared burst them open until the mayor appeared and smashed them with an axe. In the meantime, the flames had spread farther, and as in the neighbouring arsenal there lay eighteen-hundred hundredweight of gunpowder, we all thought, while we were helping to put out the fire, that we might be blown sky-high at any moment.

As before at Raipoltenbach, I formed part of the chain of people passing buckets of water; Michel was busy up in front, but Baron Blunderbuss kept running like a mad thing all over the Freyung, screaming incessantly: "Feurio! Feurio!" As the Turks had still not fired their cannon, we knew that they could not have caused the fire. We were all convinced that the conflagration had been started by an incendiary, and several people who seemed to find the hard work of fighting the fire a bit too onerous for them set themselves to discovering the culprit. I don't know who had the idea of giving Baron Blunderbuss powder and shot and persuading him to put a fresh flint in his ancient pistol; anyhow, the dwarf baron flung off his slouch hat, jumped up and down several times on the same spot in his great riding boots, jerked out the pistol, and fired at the smoking building, in which he obviously suspected an enemy to be concealed. With the complete lack of common sense that distinguishes any large crowd, the mass of people roared that he was the incendiary and rushed upon the dwarf.

I dropped my bucket and did the silliest thing that anyone in my position could have done: I tried to persuade an angry mob that it was mistaken.

"That young lad's in it as well!" screeched a haggard woman with strands of grey hair falling across her face.

"Get him! Hack him to bits!" snarled another, in whose gaping mouth only a single tooth gleamed unnaturally white like a witch's.

The rest of the mob turned upon us at once, but Baron Blunderbuss saw an opening and raced down the Freyung and away. Later I learned that the crowd had caught up with him at Petersfreithof and had literally torn him to pieces, although he was as innocent of starting the fire as a new-born babe. The same fate befell a boy about three years older than I simply because he was wearing a Hungarian hat, and a lackey who was bringing all sorts of things out of a house threatened by the fire—among them a pyrotechnic set piece—was only saved from the raving mob by the intervention of his master, a lieutenant-colonel in the Imperial Army.

44

I didn't know all this then and never gave a thought to the fact that now it was a matter of life and death; I was only afraid I might get a good beating and so ran as fast as I could down the Renngasse to the Elent and down towards the goldsmith's, behind me a raging horde of women and numerous apprentices. I might be able to shake off the women, but the young apprentices were hard upon my heels, and I was just thinking I would have to give myself up through lack of breath and the stitch in my side when I saw a fat innkeeper standing with straddled legs in front of his tavern door. Quick as a weasel, I slipped through his legs, and while my pursuers tussled with the innkeeper's almost immovable mass, I dashed through a smoky kitchen, crawled into a dirty, damp yard, where I stumbled up a flight of worn stone stairs, flew through two or three rooms, and then leaped through a window into another yard, where I hid myself in a burst, half-rotten rain-water barrel.

A long way away I could hear the innkeeper's scolding voice and the shouting of the apprentices. I caught the sound of doors banging and the wild shrieks of the women pursuing me but no one entered the yard where I was. Inside the rain-water butt it was anything but pleasant, because it was damp, it stank, and besides it was crawling with spiders, wood lice, and horrible thick white worms. The yard's smell of decay laid itself upon my face like a stinking wet cloth, so that despite the July heat, my teeth began to chatter; but I stuck it out until it was dark, and only then did I leave my place of concealment.

As I slunk across the courtyard towards an old, rusty-iron back door, I noticed a chink of light coming from a tiny window. When I heard from within drunken voices and the stamping of heavy feet on a stone floor, I decided to go and peep in. A voice was singing:

45

"The raven croaks, the gallows creak,
And blood down the steps runs black;
When the wind blows over the waves, my lads,
Your captain'll call you back."

Seized now by a nameless dread, I turned away at the end of the refrain, rushed to the door, tore it open, and ran full tilt back to New Square.

9

I met Michel in the kitchen, where he was recounting to a small group of footmen how when he was at Choczim, he had seen a green, shimmering ball rise out of a marsh to a height of fifty feet, where it burst and rained down millions of flying ants on the Turkish Army below. As soon as he noticed me, he asked where I had been all this time, and I told him of my flight, of my hiding place at the goldsmith's, and then about the singing voice coming from the lighted window.

"Let's go and have a look at these lads," he said, standing up. "Are you frightened?"

Of course I was, but on the other hand, I was full of curiosity and a longing for adventure, and so I led Michel to the place from which just half an hour before I had fled in such terror. The iron door was still standing open; we groped our way across the dark yard to the little window and peeped in.

The room had obviously been used earlier as a stable, for there were mangers in the background and stalls strewn with straw, which now served as sleeping places for several ragged fellows who were lying or sitting there. One of them was picking over his shirt for fleas, a second was exploring his nose with a grubby finger, and the third was just dozing. In the centre stood an upturned box with a lantern on it; around the box were four men playing cards. One of them I recognised as having been among the men at the corner table in the Winged Bell.

"Is that them?" Michel whispered.

"I know the one opposite us, not the others."

"Right! Let's go in!"

We opened the creaking stable door; we entered a passage made of slippery stones. On our left was a break in the wall covered with horse blankets; we pulled them to one side and went through. The men all looked up. One of the card players reached for a full tankard of wine, and the man who had been looking for fleas put a hand under the straw; then they sat looking at us without moving.

"Good evening, all!" said Michel cheerily. "Lovely night to-night."

They were silent. He looked about him.

"Nice place you have here. Better than up on the ramparts." Then, turning towards me, he said: "You see, it's not only the big nobs who are able to take things easy. There's some of the lower classes as can find themselves a bit of comfort. When things look black, those with money run away, and those who haven't any take their ease in empty stables."

They still made no move.

"Well, you can all stay here and live like pigs if you want—I want only one of you." He pointed to the man who was sitting opposite the window. "You there. I want you to come with us and have a little chat."

For a moment there was silence; then the man slowly stood up. The other card player threw his full tankard, the man with the fleas flashed a knife from under the straw and flung it at Michel, and the others were all suddenly on their feet. Michel turned his head aside; the knife whizzed past him and stuck quivering in a door-post behind him, while the tankard merely struck the horse blankets from where it fell clattering to the ground.

The first man tripped over Michel's outstretched leg, the second got it in the stomach, and the man I had recognised stopped only an inch short of Michel's sword tip. The others made no attempt to grapple with us.

"I can't invite you all along with us," Michel explained, smiling. "But I'd gladly send you some of the night watch."

"What do you want?" the man from the Winged Bell asked surlily.

"I'll tell you that later. Just now I want you to come with me!" With this, he took a step backward and jerked his head towards the exit.

Our opponents gaped at each other and seemed to be pondering what move to make next. Finally the knife thrower shrugged his shoulders and fell back on the straw; the others also relaxed. But our man gave them all one more look, nodded at them, and went out into the passage.

"If you try to run away, I'll catch up with you at the next corner and break every bone in your body," said Michel in the pleasantest and friendliest manner possible.

The man gave no answer and walked out in front of us. We escorted him safely to the New Square house, but there Michel told me to wait in the kitchen, for their interview might take a form unsuited to my eyes and ears. After an hour he rejoined me, sat down beside the hearth, and gazed thoughtfully at his gigantic fists.

"You can say good-bye forever to your jewellery and stuff," he said at last after a long pause, which as a practised and emotional storyteller he had allowed to elapse in order to increase the suspense. "Your Kaspar is no ordinary Kaspar but the great Kaspar Fetz, well known by every man, woman, and child in Steiermark. I myself was once or twice in Graz and heard talk of him there—people spoke about him just as we here speak about the plague or about Satan himself. He had the best band of ruffians ever collected together in Austria. The man with the bagpipes whom you met in the Winged Bell was his second-in-command, the little chap wearing the night-cap was his secretary, and the big fellow with the stubble beard his treasurer. He stole the most beautiful Arabian steeds from the Pasha of Esseg; he seized, in broad daylight, a field gun from a Turkish fortress and intercepted and made off with a great sum of money that the Emperor was having transported to Venice. Ten years ago the Turks caught him but didn't realise who he was; they thought he was just a petty thief and to punish him only cut off his ears and nose. The next day he escaped, and within the same year three Turkish guards found themselves minus ears and nose. This year the Emperor's secret service smoked him out of hiding and captured him with most of the rest of his band. But those three you saw slipped through their fingers, and old Kaspar, the night before he was due for execution, overpowered his guard, jumped out of the cell window, and despite heavy fire managed to make his way across the moat and the walls and away. The three cronies heard of his escape, were waiting for news, and took you for a messenger. After you had disappeared, they—with another member of the band—went at once to Lempach, and only one of them stayed behind there because he suddenly got cold feet—he's a mere beginner, a pickpocket rather than a true robber; he wasn't with them in Steiermark and only joined up with the other three here in Vienna."

I had listened with bated breath. I, too, knew the name of the dreaded Kaspar Fetz, because in Vienna also there had been many tales told about him, and I saw at once that Michel was only too right when he said that we would never see our property again. But after all, were our little bits of jewellery all that important? Was my painting all that important? At the moment I found myself in a city that was surrounded by

Turkish forces ten times as strong as ours; the Turks were masters at laying siege to a place, and if they took the city, my fate was settled: with most other young people I would (if I were still alive) be taken to Turkey and sold there as a slave.

No, everything was changed now, changed utterly. What had seemed so important yesterday was to-day of no consequence whatsoever.

It was Kaspar Fetz's fault that I had walked to Vienna and got into this predicament. That was that: he was no longer a part of my life, and I was honest enough to admit that I didn't feel in the least bit angry about it.

10

By the next morning the Turks had advanced their approach trenches to within thirty feet of the walls and had started to fire on the city defences with cannon, which they had set up between Krowotendörfel and Rotenhof. The commandant went at once to the defences and a little later was wounded. I was there when they carried him away, and many people were shaking their heads sadly, but the old soldiers just grinned and said the old man was a tough bird and would soon recover. Indeed, only a few days later he had himself carried up on the ramparts and remained there several days until he was stricken with dysentery and was wounded a second time but remained at his post.

About that time the work on the fortifications was discontinued, and the repairs to breaches and the isolation of burning houses were attended to by the guild companies, so that there was no call for the assistance of a fourteen-year-old boy. As long as I had been kept busy, I had been able to endure the excitement and suspense; but now my enforced idleness and my worry about my mother drove me half out of my wits, and I would have given a great deal to have been able to serve as a soldier on the ramparts. As civilians were forbidden to stay up on the fortifications, I, who was bursting with curiosity to know what was going on, had found a little spot high up on our roof from which I could look right over the houses to the Rotenhof. In order to get up there, I had to climb out of an attic window on to a narrow ledge, along which I would creep on all fours until I reached the ornamental gable end at the front of the house. For a good three yards my path overhung a sheer drop to the street, and my mother wouldn't have been able to watch such a performance at all; but once behind the gable end, I was safe. I could lean against the wall and observe everything that went on over at the ramparts. In addition, there was a balcony just below, and so it happened that I was able to overhear two conversations held by the Count with his advisers, from which I gathered that he had offered his services immediately after the beginning of the siege but had been refused by the commandant.

"What terrible thing have I done that I am given this lack of encouragement!" he cried, slapping the edge of the balcony again and again with his hand.

I leaned carefully from my hiding place and watched him— that is to say, I watched the gigantic full-bottomed wig and under it a purple-red coat and an arm lying along the balcony's balustraded edge. Beside him stood a short fellow whose voice I already knew because he often paid visits to the house. He was von Aichbichel, the Court Chamberlain.

"He was always an obstinate man," he said.

"I can be obstinate myself when occasion calls for it. But this idiot von Allsberg," he went on, apparently referring to the event that had brought him into disgrace, "gave an order that might have brought half the regiment into the graveyard and the hospital! And no reason for it! No need to squander my men's lives like that!"

"Such questions are difficult to answer afterwards. But it is a fact that you refused to carry out an order. . . ."

"And by so doing saved my regiment!"

"You refused to carry out an order and found yourself faced with a charge of cowardice. . . ."

"*Me*! A coward! Then why am I offering my services now?"

The Court Chamberlain was silent for a while, and the Count stared at him without speaking. "I can see one possibility," the Chamberlain began again hesitantly.

"And what is that?"

"We have received no recent messages from Kuniz, who is still unfortunately in the hands of the Turkish Army but tries to keep us informed by dispatches sent through his servant. This connection is very much imperilled by the course of events and could stop at any time. We have absolutely no other contact with the Duke, and messages can only be entrusted to someone who speaks Turkish and knows how to live with the Turks. Now you were once a prisoner of the Turks . . ."

"How could I, a colonel . . ."

Aichbichel laid his hand on Count Alram's arm. "Naturally it is the sort of commission that formerly only a lieutenant would have been asked to undertake, but it is now more important than any sortie could be and even more dangerous; and besides, your name need be known to no one apart from the commandant and His Majesty."

"That's impossible! The Duke, too, must sooner or later hear about it, then Dünewald and probably also the staff officers. When more than two people share a secret, it is a secret no longer."

"And what if it doesn't remain a secret? It all comes to the same thing in the end: you get your regiment back!"

The Count thought for a moment. "Perhaps you're right," he said. "What do you suggest? How shall I . . ."

With these words he drew the Court Chamberlain from the balcony back into the room and left me in a very divided state of mind up in my observation post.

11

The night was uneventful, but the next morning the cannon fire increased, for now the Turks were using guns of the heaviest calibre. Towards noon I succeeded in making my way unobserved to the City Square and there concealed myself behind an old mortar piece, from which vantage point I was able to watch a group of men repairing the shattered sections of a twelve-pounder's gun carriage. Suddenly a high-explosive bomb whooshed overhead, exploded right in the middle of the group, and killed them all. Six infantrymen who were standing nearby were gravely wounded, windows were shattered, stones and bricks went flying everywhere, and I thought the whole city must have been blasted into the air.

Then, when the dust and smoke cleared and I saw the dead lying there and heard the wounded screaming and groaning, when I saw with my own eyes, right in front of me, someone's torn-off foot, the great pools of blood and the destruction wrought in the square, I was overcome with disgust and loathing and very nearly vomited on the spot. During the last few days it had seemed to me sometimes as if my mother had been wrong when she used to say I hadn't the least makings of a fighter. But now I agreed with her; I was obviously unsuited to violence and war and would never have a warlike spirit. It suddenly appeared to me that war was utter madness, was indeed a crime and a sin against humanity, against God and His entire creation.

Feeling heartsick, I went back to New Square. I wanted to speak about my experience to Michel, who was hewing wood in the yard, but he himself had news he was dying to tell and so he began to speak as soon as he caught sight of me. During the night, two Christians had come across from the Turkish camp and reported that, first, the Turks had received reinforcements, and, second, that Mödling, Baaden, and Perchtoldsdorf had unfortunately surrendered.

"Surrendered!" he shouted, and swung the axe deep into a block of wood. "Surrendered their faith, their loyalty to the Emperor! You know Perchtoldsdorf—the church there is strongly built, and the tower stands detached just nearby, a tower made of great blocks of stone; it has guns placed up at the top and a well with marvellous fresh ice-cold water! If you had enough provisions, you could hold out for a year in there! But as our lord and master says: were we in fact prepared? There was no food, no ammunition—instead, just faith that things wouldn't turn out too badly! But when things *do* happen to turn out badly, what then? You can't fight with charm, and muddling-through won't fill your belly. The Turks and Tartars were camped outside the place, and the Pasha buttered up the people there, saying what virtuous folk they were and how their fame had spread even to Constantinople and how proud he was to welcome them as his new subjects, and if they would kindly just pay him a certain vast sum of money, there would be no burning of property and not a hair of anyone's head would be harmed. . . ."

He heaved a deep sigh and went on. "And because the people had so little ammunition and because they were such lily-livered dolts, they upped and carried their money out of the church into the square and laid down their arms beside it. But then something happened that only goes to show that he who bites the dust quickest is the one who's got the least guts. Barely was the last weapon laid on the ground than the Pasha drew his curved sabre and lopped off the head of the market superintendent, with whom up till then he had been on the most excellent, friendly terms. Then within a few minutes, without any chance of offering resistance, more than three hundred men were slaughtered, simply slaughtered like cattle!"

He spat with contempt and disgust. "The women and old folks and children had stayed in the church and in the tower. Well, the Tartars locked them in, set fire to both places, and roasted them all alive! Mountains of charred corpses are still lying inside. That's what happened in Perchtoldsdorf; and in Mödling pretty much the same sort of thing happened."

I shook my head in bewilderment. "But if they did not try to defend themselves," I began hesitantly, "if they did not try to defend themselves—then why—why did the Turks do such things?"

Michel gave a mocking laugh. "Because war is war, and if we have war, we must expect all kinds of horrible things to be done. Also, because they're our enemies –not only enemies of the Emperor but also enemies of our religious faith. Above all, they're *your* enemies, *my* enemies, *our* enemies, and no amount of fair words can talk *that* away. It's either kill or be killed: conquer or die like cattle."

"Have you heard anything from Lempach?"

"No, I've heard nothing from that quarter."

"But are the Turks in that region, too?"

He shrugged his shoulders. "Who knows? They're everywhere. So far they've destroyed over sixty places in the neighbourhood of Vienna, plundered the houses, taken the people prisoners, and dragged them off to Turkey."

I looked hard at him. "I must speak to the Count," I said boldly.

He gave me a searching glance. "What do you want with the Count?"

"I want to ask him something. Now. Ask him if he'll see me. At once."

One hour later I was conducted to the master's study. The Count was standing at the window with his back to me and only turned around when the door had closed behind me.

"Well, what d'you want now?"

"Your honour, my mother has not come to Vienna. I don't know where she is; I don't know whether she is still alive or whether the Turks have sent Lempach up in flames—Raipoltenbach too, perhaps. I can't bear to stay on here in the city, where I can do nothing but sit and twiddle my thumbs. I beg your honour—please take me with you when you go."

"When I go?" The Count wrinkled his forehead. "Take you with me? What put that idea into your head?"

"I was up on the roof, and I overheard. . . . Up on the ramparts there are soldiers aplenty, but for what your honour has in mind, a boy can be of some use, because he doesn't attract attention and could more easily bring through a dispatch or a message than a grown soldier. And I promise your honour . . ."

"You will promise me to hold your tongue about this," he broke in. "That's the one thing I ask of you. I cannot take you with me, for in the first place I don't like people who listen to other folk's conversations, and in the second place, carrying dispatches through the enemy lines is no sport for boys, as you perhaps imagine. You have your bed and board here. Wait until the city is relieved. You can't do anything more."

And he indicated that the interview was at an end.

12

So I had to stay on in Vienna. The Turks kept up their fire and destroyed more and more houses and killed more and more people. They also set up a battery in Leopoldstadt and bombarded us from the island; they shot fireballs into the arsenal on the Seilerstatt, and it was only through God's grace that the whole district was not blown to smithereens. A bomb hit the great cathedral, the Stefanskirche, during the sermon, and blasted off a poor woman's leg, and on 23rd July in the evening two Turkish mines went off under the walls at the Burg and Löbel bastions, killing ten men. Immediately after that the Turks stormed the ramparts three times, but our men were ready for them with muskets and scythes and beat off the attacks.

The commandant gave orders that the great bell of St. Stefan's Cathedral should only be rung as an alarm signal. Whenever it was heard, everyone who could carry arms was to hold himself in readiness: the soldiers had to be at their posts, the student companies outside the Schottenkirche, the citizenry on the City Square, and the rest in the New Market. Besides this, he commanded that, because of the losses through mines, new mobile palisades on wheels were to be built, for which the timbers from burned-down and derelict houses were to be used.

Most of the time I spent crouching on the roof. If I saw a house hit anywhere and severely damaged, I would run there and help with the evacuation of the tenants and the salvaging of their possessions. I also went once to the arsenal to lend a hand, and there I met a boy, scarcely a year older than myself, with whom I made friends for an afternoon. He was called

Karl and came from Swechat; his father had been killed by the Tartars. Hidden in a dung heap, he had been compelled to witness helplessly the flogging of his mother and sisters by the Tartars, who later bound them and dragged them away.

"Everything's at sixes and sevens in our house," he said, as we bound sharp stakes together for the anti-invasion fences we called Spanish Riders—I suppose because they looked like the lance-carrying picadors in a Spanish bull ring. "House, byres, and stables are all burned down, the cattle driven away, the fowls eaten, the fields trampled and devastated. I'm not going back."

"What will you do?" I asked.

He laughed. "As long as we beat the Turks, that's all I want; you'd never guess what piles of stuff I got from outside!"

"From outside?"

He gazed around him circumspectly and then went on in a whisper. "The things people left behind them out there! And not everything has been spoiled by the fires. There are scores of rooms that still stand intact, as if nothing had happened! There are cupboards in those rooms, and in the cupboards there are boxes, and in the boxes there are things . . ."

"But that's stealing!"

He laughed again. "Stealing! And what about the things we lost from our farm? Who has our cattle and our corn? The houses are empty; they were set on fire. Anything still left inside them doesn't belong to anybody!"

"And do you get there by climbing over the walls?"

"I simply walk through the gate! You have to know the guards and give them a little something, of course. Every night there are at least ten to twenty of us outside there, picking things up. I found embroidered cloths, fine shoes, and even a bit of jewellery and some ready cash!"

"Where do you get out?"

"Across the bridge by the new bastion."

"And when you've got outside?"

"Then I creep along the walls as far as the Danube and from there into the Rossau. That way I don't have to pass through the fortifications."

"What about the Turks?"

"There's not many of them in the Rossau; not many at Schottenburg either, and anyhow they're mostly asleep. But if they do happen to be awake, you hear them soon enough, and in the dark it's easy to hide from them."

We went on working together without speaking for a while. Then he cast a glance about him again and said, this time even more quietly: "Besides, they're not such bad sorts. They're not all Turks! They're men from Moldau and Hungarians and Bosnians and Serbians, and a whole lot of them speak German. . . ."

"Then have you talked to them?" I asked in a shocked whisper.

He was going to reply but stopped for a second. Then he shrugged his shoulders and whispered: "Not me. Other chaps. And they told me they're quite friendly, that you don't need to be afraid of them at all, even if they don't withdraw and the city falls. You just have to know how to handle them and use your wits. . . ."

That night as I lay in bed, I was unable to sleep. If Karl and others were sneaking outside, then I should be able to do it also! And if the Schottenburg was not entirely overrun with Turks, from the Schottenburg it was easy to reach Währing; between Währing and Döbling there were very few Turkish encampments, as I knew already from my roof-top observations. It should be possible to sneak through that way, go by Weinhaus to Gersthof and Neuwaldegg, and then by way of Heuberg and Satzberg strike through towards Hütteldorf and Hägging. Once in Hägging I would be on the road that my mother must have taken when she set out for Vienna.

Here in the city I was being treated like a child. The Count couldn't bear the sight of me and still looked upon me as the boy from the Jesuit seminary who wanted to be a painter. I'd show them. If Karl could do it, so could I.

And perhaps I could do even more.

13

I had no packing to do because apart from the clothes I was wearing, I only intended to take a knapsack for food and also a kitchen knife; all the same in the morning I had plenty to see to. First, I sewed a sort of rough sheath for my knife out of an old piece of leather and gave it a strap so that I could carry it under my coat, hanging from my belt. Then there were various other things I had to attend to that seemed to me important if my flight were to be successful. An expedition to the arsenal where I committed a small theft played a great part in my plans.

At noon I was sitting with Michel in the kitchen and was wondering whether I should say good-bye to him or not. He had been a true friend to me, and I was reluctant to leave without saying farewell; but I was afraid he might reveal my plans to the Count and so I kept my own counsel, which was not very difficult, as he hardly let me get a word in edgeways.

He was telling me that in Bosnia he had encountered a very powerful devil with three heads: the first head had spoken Latin, the second German, and the third Turkish, and all at the same time. But when he chopped off the first head, without any resistance on the devil's part, masses of books gushed out of the stump, flapping their covers, and the sight of these books had been even more horrible than the three-headed monster, though the two remaining heads now no longer talked but merely laughed mockingly.

In the afternoon I was dispatched with a note from Count Alram to the city defences, where it had to be delivered to Count Guido Starhemberg, the cousin of the commandant. I think he must have been asking in this note that he might be provided with the uniform of a dead or captured Turk, for young Starhemberg only laughed when he read the note and told me to inform my master that he would do what he could but that it all depended on the Turks.

Shortly after that we heard from the direction of the Turkish trenches, which were barely fifty paces away from where we stood, a sort of wailing and a kind of music with a lot of drumming and clashing of cymbals. Count Guido went up in front in order to look down and see what was going on. He paid no more attention to me, and as I had now at last managed to reach the battle area, I made no haste to return home but squeezed myself into a corner and kept my eyes open for whatever I might see.

The defensive position, or ravelin as it is called in military language, stood like a three-cornered mass of stone in the middle of the moat; behind me rose the city walls, which at that section joined the Burg and Löbel bastions. But I could not see what was going on in front because I was keeping in the background and the breastwork in front of me blocked the view. But I could see the top of the ravelin towards St. Ulrich's Church, and on the top there stood a cannon; nearby soldiers from the Starhemberg regiments were leaning on the breastwork of the ramparts.

"Come on, give us a tune, and we might dance with you!" one of them shouted.

The next instant a terrific explosion made the ground shake; everything seemed to sway and totter, and I flung myself to the ground. A vast cloud of smoke rose up before us while great clods of earth and shattered stones rained down upon us, and there was the most terrible stench of gunpowder. I hardly dared raise my eyes, but I could hear Count Guido shouting: "They're coming! Up, men, and at 'em!" I realised that all the others were at their posts while I lay with my trembling body pressed hard against the ground.

But I'm no coward, I told myself, and remembered how we had always laughed to scorn any cowards in my class at school. Perhaps I'm no soldier, but I'm not a coward. "Pull yourself together, man, and show them you're no coward," I said to myself.

I slowly picked myself up. The air was still full of smoke and flying debris, but I dashed across to the breastwork and looked down. The rows of palisades were shattered, the cover on the walls blasted to pieces. Later I learned that the Turks as well as the Christians were staggered by the force of that gigantic mine, but at that moment all I could hear was the weird music of the Turks. Then I saw them clambering out of their trenches; janizaries with white peaked caps, swinging their sabres and carrying hand grenades in their free hands.

An artilleryman trained a loaded cannon on them without waiting to adjust it to the correct range, stepped back, and gave the signal to fire. His fellow artilleryman lit the fuse, the shell spat out of the cannon's mouth, and the cannon itself jumped back nearly a yard.

Then I saw a second lieutenant running down below, but suddenly he stopped and grabbed with his left hand at a lance that stuck quivering in his chest. It seemed to me to take an eternity before he slowly fell to his knees, but in the meantime a captain rushed forward, followed by soldiers with drawn swords, and from the ravelin they started firing muskets at the janizaries. Count Guido was down there, too, and the command of the ravelin had been taken over by a man I knew:

it was the chief engineer, Rümpler, one of the best German builders of defence works.

The janizaries had reached the gaps blown in the palisades; they came to grips with our own men, and at the same moment the Turkish artillery started bombarding the bastions in order to put our cannon out of action. Whether our cannon were able to fire back or not, I can't say because I hadn't the faintest idea at the moment what was going on; I could only hear the deafening crashes and the yelling infantry and the weird music wailing from the enemy trenches. The stench of gunpowder became worse every minute, so bad that it almost made me spew up, but I gritted my teeth and swallowed hard several times. I was determined to prove, if only to myself, that I was no coward.

In the meantime, our men had dragged some of the wheeled palisades into position, but they were too late: the janizaries had already broken through. Fortunately, the cannon on the ravelin had just been reloaded and was able to fire a blast at the Turkish trenches, firing far enough out not to injure our own troops and yet close enough to scatter a freshly emerging wave of janizaries, who were thus unable to charge the breaches in the defences.

For a brief while it looked as if the worst of the danger were over, for Count Guido stood with his men holding the breach, but then a Turkish bomb exploded in front of the ravelin, I heard piercing screams, and immediately afterwards another wave of janizaries leaped out of the approach trenches and stormed the breach.

Never from my observation post on the roof of Count Alram's house had I seen events so clearly, nor had they ever appeared to me so terrible. Formerly it had seemed like a play acted out, like the actions in a puppet theatre or in a picture book: brightly coloured and exciting. But now I could feel the ground shaking, smell the bitter stench of gunpowder, hear the whistling of bullets and the shrieks of the wounded, and see the blood pouring from the bodies slaughtered in the front ranks; and that is why I understand so well now what the defenders of Vienna had to go through when they held out a full two months against a Turkish army many times greater in strength.

The present encounter lasted only an hour, but that hour seemed to me like an eternity, and when I later learned that it was only a fairly minor skirmish, such as the besiegers had often started—though many of them were much worse—I could hardly believe it. I had been convinced that at that place and time the whole fate of Vienna lay in the balance and that if it passed off all right for us, the city would no longer be in danger. But for the others that frightful battle only had the significance of any everyday occurrence.

The lieutenant colonel and the captain had fallen; Count Guido Starhemberg and Chief Engineer Rümpler were wounded (the latter died of his wounds a week later). These facts are recorded in the chronicles of the war. Of the soldiers who perished in that encounter, the exact number, let alone the names, is not known; they were about fifty. One of them died at my feet, lying bathed in his blood; in the place where his left arm should have been was a gaping wound pulsing blood. He never stopped shouting in his agony: "Oh God, help me, dear God, don't let it happen, oh God, stand by me, dear God, I don't want to die, oh, mother, mother, mother . . ."

Yes, it was as Michel had said: we had to defend ourselves.

But whoever does not fight only in self-defence but fights for the sake of war and fighting: that man is evil.

14

Dusk was already falling when, down in the kitchen, I finally managed to catch one of the five cats that were usually running about there during the day but that on this particular evening had decided for some reason to go into hiding. I took it in my arms, stroked it, and carried it up to my room, where I placed it in a basket I had comfortably furnished for the purpose. It was a basket with a lid that could be fastened down, and in it I also put my knife, a short leather belt, a dark lantern without a candle, a tinder-box with flints and wick, and a well-tied snuffbox full of gunpowder: that was my entire equipment.

Towards eight o'clock I was at the gate, and when the porter asked why I wanted to go out at such a late hour, I told him that my cat was sick and that I was taking it to Frau Langseisnerin, who knew how to treat cats; however, I would be back before ten. He grumbled that sick cats ought to be drowned and not taken for walks on a dark night, but he let me through, and I went with my basket to the Big Market near the Fools' Pound, where once they had put drunkards in a cage as a free entertainment. At that part of the square, the Fools' Pound and Fish-Spring House formed a dark corner where I could sit unnoticed and wait for a favourable moment to begin my undertaking. Once the night watch paced by within a few feet of me, and of course the cat had to yowl in its basket just then, but as yowling cats on warm nights are nothing very unusual, the guard just walked on without discovering my hiding place. About midnight I slunk down Crab Alley, turned left at the Great Press, and found myself outside St. Rupert's Church in the Old Square.

Nothing was stirring; the only thing to be heard was the pacing of a guard on the ramparts that ran between the Danube bastions. I put down the basket, laid the snuffbox on the topmost step of the church, unrolled the fuse, and unravelled the end. Then I carefully opened the basket and felt for the cat's tail. The moon had not yet risen, and though it was a clear, starry night, it was still so dark that I couldn't see very well. The cat scratched, yowled, and bit, but finally I had it well jammed between my knees and with the leather strap tied the tin lantern to one of its hind legs.

"I'm sorry about his," I whispered to it. "This is no silly schoolboy's prank, pussy. I'll have to hurt you a little, but you'll soon be rid of this thing. But not too soon: that's why I've tied it on with a leather strap that you can't bite through."

After the lantern was made fast, I kept the cat firmly under my coat, took the snuffbox and the tinder-box into a niche in the wall, and after some difficulty managed to light the end of the wick to a satisfactory glow. Then I put the box down on the steps, carried the cat under my coat to the top of them, and let it go. It bounded away down the steps, and at every leap the lantern banged against a stone, making enough noise to rouse the whole neighbourhood. I shouted "Help! Help!" and immediately ran back into Press Alley, through Star Alley, and down to the little gateway over the cliff that stands in the left bay of the Gonzaga bastion. When I got down there, the two guards were standing fairly far off arguing whether they should run up the steps of St. Rupert's, where the noise and the cries had come from. At that moment my snuffbox exploded, and that decided them. The guards raced up the steps, I raced to the gate, unloosened the two crossbeams, and was away.

The bastion towered high over me, but the men up there were paying too much attention to what was going on inside the walls to notice the creaking of the great wooden gate. I slipped unobserved along the wall, then ran down a small slope and hid among the reeds and burdock fringing the little brook that links the moat with the Danube. I lay for a while listening to the noises from above, then carefully slipped into the water and hauled myself to the other bank by grasping the stakes of the small wooden bridge that led from the city to the ravelin.

Once on the other bank, I groped my way along the wall, which here descended precipitously to the Danube, until I felt myself on level ground. Then I began to run, following exactly the route that Karl had described to me, proceeding bent double all the way to the Rossau. When I had left the big gardens behind me and reached the first house, I took a deep breath, walked through an open door, and found myself in a room where I rested for a while.

After a few minutes I took off my shoes, stockings, and breeches, wrung them out, and rubbed myself with a bit of cloth that I found by groping about in the blackness, until I was fairly dry. It was decidedly unpleasant to put on the wet things again, but I had no other choice. After I had made quite sure that everything was quiet outside, I left the house and looked back to the city, whose walls rose grey and grim out of the blackness of the ground and stood darkly against the starry sky. Not a soul was to be seen, not a thing to be heard.

I knew in which direction to go, so I walked through the outskirts of Vienna towards the west, up the Schottenburg and then on towards Lichtenthal, where I followed the brook towards Währing. The Turks had so far attacked the city only from Sankt Ulrich and Leopoldstadt, and—though their encirclement stretched far out over the outlying towns and villages—I had not encountered anyone so far. The moon began to rise, and I saw their white tents on the hills to my left. I found the way through near Döbling, which I had noted from my roof-top post, and cautiously slipped between the two groups of tents, making for the mountains. By dawn I had reached the wood.

"Count Alram can think himself lucky if he brings off his plan as well as a Jesuit student has done his," I was proudly thinking to myself when I sauntered gaily around a bush and bumped right into a Turk sitting on a tree trunk and obviously sound asleep.

His cat nap was my salvation because in that first second we were both so startled that neither of us shouted out. Apparently he was on guard there, had made himself a little too comfortable, and now thought he had been surrounded or caught out by an officer. At any rate, it occurred to him too late that he ought to lay hands on me, and before he was yet properly awake, I was already dashing away into the undergrowth. I didn't stop until I had no more breath left, and then I rested only a few minutes before trotting on gently again. I ran so far and for so long that in the end I realised that I had completely lost my way and must now creep back to the edge of the wood to get my bearings again. As that would certainly mean capture if I emerged in daylight, I trotted on a bit farther and finally found a small dale, deeply cut by rain, right in the middle of the beech wood. At the bottom was a hollow full of old leaves. I rolled myself in the leaves, covered myself with twigs and light boughs, and huddled there, completely hidden.

Although I felt more exhausted than ever before in my life, for a long time I could not get to sleep. My experience with the sleeping Turk only now presented itself to me in its full significance and danger. I still seemed to see him before me in his blue, baggy breeches with his short red jacket, his cap pushed back on his head, a long, dangling moustache around his mouth, a curved sabre in his fist. I still seemed to be running uphill and downhill, hearing pursuing feet pounding along behind me.

At last I knew no more as I fell into a profound sleep.

15

When I woke, the sun was shining down on me through the branches of the trees. I didn't know how late it was, but I gathered that I had certainly slept longer than two or three hours. If my judgement was correct, the slanting rays indicated late afternoon, and the sun must be in the south-west, that is, in the direction I had to take in order to reach Hägging.

After I had wandered slowly for an hour or so through the wood, which here was thick with undergrowth, the ground began to slope downward, and soon I reached a small valley. The trees thinned out, and before I moved into the open, I looked all around me. All I could see, some way off, was a farm-house that seemed to be abandoned. I weighed whether or not I should risk crossing the valley by daylight, decided I would, and ran up the other side of the valley until I had reached the wooded land again; there I lay down for a while to get my breath back before striking out in a south-westerly direction again. About an hour later I did the same thing once more— only this time the bottom of the valley was substantially wider, and I saw at once that I should need at least ten minutes to reach the concealment of the trees on the other side. Here there was not just a single farm-house, but a hamlet where there seemed to be nothing stirring but where there might easily be Turks in occupation. A few clumps of bushes behind which I hoped to find cover and the onset of dusk finally persuaded me to take the risk; soon I was creeping from one clump to another, keeping a good lookout for possible enemies all the time.

I discovered them soon enough: two riders on small, shaggy horses who were trotting down the valley. At once I ducked under a bush, allowed the pair to pass me by at a distance of about thirty paces, and was about to continue on my way when suddenly another three horsemen appeared and soon after that two more. They all wore long brown cloaks with a cord around the middle, so that they looked almost like mendicant friars; but on their heads they sported a kind of turban. They disappeared into the hamlet on my right, where there must, therefore, obviously be an encampment. I decided to wait for nightfall behind my bush; but as no one else appeared during the next quarter of an hour, I grew impatient, crept out of my hiding place, and had almost reached the other edge of the valley when a figure stepped out of the trees and shouted at me in a hoarse voice.

I couldn't turn back, and escape into the wood was cut off, so I made a sudden veer to the left. As my course now lay at an angle to the wood's edge, I had farther to run than the stranger, who despite his long smock was progressing at an astonishing speed. I turned on my heels and sped off to the right, but this dodge didn't do me any good either. . . .Then as luck would have it, I stumbled over a mound of sand and sprawled full-length on the ground.

Before I could pick myself up, the Tartar was upon me. In my desperation I completely forgot about my knife, which I had taken with me for use in such eventualities; but I remembered a simple means of self-defence that we had sometimes used in our boyish battles. As the man was bending over to get hold of me, I dug both my hands in the sand and threw two good fistfuls in his slant-eyed face. The Tartar jerked back as if he'd been hit by a bullet and rubbed at the sand in his eyes. In the meantime, I got up and within seconds had disappeared again into the wood.

I heard him cursing and then panting along behind me, but at once I turned left and after a few paces lay down in the undergrowth so that the cracking of twigs would not betray my whereabouts. He, too, stood still for a while, listening. It was quite silent and also fairly dark where I lay under the trees. Almost a minute passed like this before he began systematically to search his surroundings, but he was more than fifty feet away from where I lay. While he went stumbling among the bushes, I kept shoving myself a little farther away from him, taking good care not to move when he stood still, but crawling on at once whenever I heard him making a noise as he blundered about. In the end, I managed to creep so far away from him that I was able to stand up and, stooping, grope my way through the dusk.

Suddenly I heard voices and guessed that others had come to help him, so I hastened my steps until I could hear no more. I came to a deep hollow under a rock covered with moss and creeper, slid down into it, and endeavoured to calm my agitation. My whole body was shaking, and my breath was coming so loudly that I feared it might betray me, and it took some time before I finally managed to bring some sort of order into the confusion of my thoughts. But one thing was clear: I could not stay here, for in the morning the Tartars would certainly start their hunt again. I had to go on farther into the wood, even at the risk of losing my way. So after I had rested for about half an hour, I set off in the direction I had already taken, without knowing where on earth my path would lead me.

In the meantime, it had grown dark, and after a while it began to rain softly. I couldn't see a hand's breadth in front of me, kept slithering on wet roots or damp foliage, stumbling over creepers, stones, and fallen tree-trunks, banging my head against low-hanging boughs, scratching my face and hands on thorns and brambles, and several times measuring my full length on the hard, wet ground. After only an hour I was so exhausted that I began to feel like bawling with weariness and rage. At last I tumbled down a steep drop more than eight feet deep at least, wrenched an arm, and lay where I fell because I quite simply couldn't move another foot and couldn't therefore stand up.

Apparently for a short while I lost consciousness or fell asleep; but, in any case, I did not rest soundly enough to replenish my wasted strength. How I managed to get on my feet again I do not know; I only remember that in a state of semi-sleep or fever I went stumbling and falling through the blackness of the night forest, whimpering with pain and from time to time even crying out loud. I was soaked to the skin, and soon there was no place in my weary body that did not silently scream in an agony of pain.

My childhood had been spent mostly in the city, so I didn't know the lore of the woods and forests, especially the forest at night with its uncanny outbreaks of weird noise. Here something would creak; there something would whimper and chatter; at another part I seemed to hear someone—or some thing—smash through the undergrowth, while from overhead came a sudden wailing cry or else a queer groaning and griping; then to my left something started to shuffle heavily, making funny thumping knocks, while from my right came the shrill, hysterical tittering of an unimaginably horrible creature. . . .

In the state I was in, Michel's grisly tales suddenly took on a new and more real life; I thought I saw the three-headed demon swerving through the air ahead of me, seemed to glimpse reddish glowing eyes staring unblinkingly at me from all sides, eyes that slowly moved away, blinking, if I ventured to approach them. Balls of crystal fire, giant insects with hairy, spiky spider legs and eyes on long horns, endless, waving soft feelers, floating jellyfish with stinging tentacles, luminous worms, transparent yet bleeding white horses, green-chinned witches vigorously astride filthy broomsticks or dancing obscene little rounds with black-magic relish—all these things, and many more, much worse, hovered and swerved before me in the sinister dark and all but choked me with terror. . . .

72

After fighting my way despairingly through a clump of clinging thorn bushes, I found all at once a white-clad Turk facing me, gazing at me mockingly with his deep black eyes.

This time I wrenched the knife out of my belt and stuck it right into my opponent's body. But it was no enemy, only a dead, withered tree-trunk that had gleamed whitely and eerily in the blackness of the forest.

Never shall I forget that awful night, the first night in which I encountered alone the grisly forces of unfriendly nature and thought I was going out of my mind with horror and fear.

At last, dawn began to glimmer. I staggered across a meadow and reached a farm-house that lay there forlorn and grey in the sad morning light. In every room one could see with what frantic haste the inhabitants had left the house: the cupboards, chests, and drawers were all wide open, many objects lying scattered on the floor. I should gladly have lain down on one of the abandoned beds, but I dared not, in case I were discovered during the daylight hours by wandering Tartars; and so I merely looked for something to eat, for my knapsack had long been empty. In a corner of the cellar I found some shrivelled old turnips, ate two or three, and drew a bucket of water from the deep well. Then I scouted around for a dry hiding place. Behind the stables I found a loaded hay wain, climbed up, dug a deep hole in the hay, so that I was lying almost in the middle of the load, pulled the hay back over me, and though I was bitterly cold in my wet clothes, was very soon sound asleep.

16

The wagon was moving.

I could see nothing and could sense nothing but the jolting of the wheels, the squeaking of the axles, the plodding of the horse's hoofs, and from time to time a barking shout that sounded like the cry of an animal. After a while we stopped, and more voices were heard. But now they did not bark; I could make out a phrase here and there but did not understand the speech. Men were jumping down from horses and moving about. A smell of smoke reached me through the hay.

I was in a Tartar camp.

They'll be unloading the hay, I thought: I hope they don't take it all off at once.

If I could manage to stay concealed until evening, I could perhaps escape under cover of darkness. So I slowly began to squirm my way deeper into the hay. But as it was rather dry stuff, I stirred up a lot of fine dust, which forced itself into my nose and mouth. For a few minutes I fought against the desire to cough; but then I simply had to sneeze, and after that it was impossible to restrain my coughing. The voices approached and seemed to be discussing what to do. Someone laughed. Then a lance was thrust through the hay—above me, under me, and finally met my thigh and pierced it. I gritted my teeth, but the Tartar knew well enough that he had discovered me, dug deeper, and I screamed out loud. The lance was withdrawn and the hay pulled off the wagon. A filthy hand seized me by the neck and dragged me into the air.

The wagon was standing at the edge of a brook in a meadow where a few horses were cropping the grass. Somewhat to one side I saw a circle of about fifty small huts constructed of twigs and leaves; in the middle of the circle a small fire was glimmering and smouldering, and over its embers were steaming and stinking a number of bits of meat. There were five Tartars surrounding me, grinning as they witnessed my discomfort. Their brown cloaks were splashed with mud, their slit-eyed faces shiny with dirt, and they all stank like old billy-goats. The one who had hauled me out of the hay gave me a shove that sent me sprawling, while another tied my hands together with a long leather strap. He pulled the belt between my legs and fastened the other end around my neck. Then he felt me over, took away my knife, drove me with kicks and prods to one of the leaf huts, sent me flying headlong with another ferocious kick, and finally tied up my legs, too. This all happened so quickly that I hardly had time to realise that—for the present at any rate—they were not going to take my life. I was once more alone. The Tartars outside crouched over their fire and tore at their lumps of meat with bare hands, gulping them down half raw, like famished beasts.

"Where did you come from?" someone behind me whispered.

Painfully I turned a little to one side and only then discovered a young man lying beside me who was tied up just as I was. The Tartars had apparently shaved off his hair and beard but had not gone about their job very carefully because there were many cuts all over his face and head, from which the blood had run and dried. None of these cuts could actually be called a wound, but all the same he looked frightful, and at first I thought he must be half dead.

"From Vienna," I answered.

"And why didn't you stay in the city?"

"I want to get to my mother's place in Lempach."

He thought for a while. "Don't tell them that you've come from Vienna," he finally advised me. "They'll take you for a spy if you do and torture you. And be careful what you tell the boy."

"What boy?"

"You'll be seeing him."

One of the Tartars had heard our whisperings; he came up to us, threatened us with his fist, and gave each of us a hefty kick. Behind him there appeared a young boy about the same age as myself; he too was wearing a brown cloak with a cord around the middle and his head was shaven.

"Are you from the farm-house up there?" he asked me.

"No. I've come from Währing."

He nodded. "You should be thankful you're here. Perhaps it won't be very pleasant for the next few days, but if you behave well and do everything you're told, we'll untie you; then you can come along with us and become a real Tartar yourself."

"Did they take you prisoner, too?"

He laughed, showing two rows of blackened, decaying stumps. "No—I knew right from the start what was best for me. The right man in the right place: a bow and arrow, no popes and preachers, no lords and masters, no farm work! You can just take for yourself anything you fancy, don't need to beg or do book learning and ciphering, don't even need to wash yourself; you don't have to doff your cap to any man; you can curse and swear and drink as much as you like. Is there anything better than that in all the world?"

Though I myself had not gone willingly to school, had not paid overmuch attention to my prayers, and often had used soap and water on myself only with the greatest reluctance, this view of life didn't appeal to me much. I didn't want to turn into a smelly Tartar, but I was cautious enough to appear to agree with the boy. And then I asked him if he couldn't find me a bite to eat.

He shrugged his shoulders and was about to answer when a Tartar shouted to him. He turned, ran across to the fire, and apparently received orders to cut some grass or corn, for the

Tartar thrust a sickle into his hand and sent him away. The boy shouted something back and jerked his head towards me; the Tartar thought for a moment and then nodded.

"You can mow a bit of wheat," the boy told me when he came back. "There's nothing else; we've only enough meat for ourselves. But when you put the grains in water, they grow soft —we usually eat nothing else." He led me to a small field of wheat that lay at the end of the meadow, loosed the strap around my wrists, and tied my feet together as one does a horse's so that it may not wander too far away while pasturing. Then he pushed the sickle into my hand and sat down at the field's edge to keep an eye on me.

Thinking of the ears of grain I would need for myself, I guessed that with one sweep of my sickle I had cut enough; but my watcher indicated, as soon as I paused, that I had to go on working and only allowed me to stop when I had cut at least three sheaves. As I was unable to bind them, he called me an idiot, heaved a deep sigh, bound them himself, and loaded the first one on my back. I had to lay it down beside the wagon, then beat handfuls from the other sheaves against the shafts until the grain fell out. The Tartar apprentice handed me a dirty old cloth in which to gather and tie up the grains, giving me a handful of them with the advice that I take them to the brook and hold them under water. I laid the sickle near the hut, bent over the brook, and held the grains of wheat in the running water for a long time. My hands grew so cold that I hardly had any feeling left in them, but I didn't see any change in the state of the grain.

With great difficulty, I swallowed a few of them and slaked my thirst. Then I went back to the hut. The sight of the sickle gave me an idea. I hobbled across to the wagon, gathered up some loose hay, and dropped it on the ground near my hut, covering up the sickle. During all this time the Tartar boy had been elsewhere, and when dusk came, one of the Tartar men bound me more securely. This time he tied the strap as a noose around my neck, pulled it between my legs, and knotted it around my hands so that I would throttle myself if I tried to lift my hands to my chest; and he tied the thongs around my feet to the strap binding my neck and hands. He made the young man next to me bend back like a bow and drew the straps binding his ankles right up to his neck; he tied him to a saddle and threw a few coverings over him. I also received some coverings, but they stank so dreadfully that I thought I would suffocate until I succeeded in pulling them slightly aside and getting a little fresh air.

I waited and waited. Although it had grown dark long ago, the Tartars were still sitting around their fire drinking. I had heard that the heathens drank no wine, and so I was very astonished. Later, however, I learned that many of these Tartars were not Mohammedans but really almost wild men who didn't even believe in a pagan god and only howled for mercy when there was a thunderstorm; otherwise, they knew no form of prayer or worship. It was nearly midnight before everything was quiet, and I turned cautiously in order to seize the sickle under the hay.

After a long tussle I managed to get it out, but then I was unable to wield the sickle because of the way I was tied. It took another half hour before I worked the sickle around to my face and could take it in my teeth. Then I shoved the point between the straps tying my wrists, but as the bending forward of my head drew the noose tight, I thought I was going to faint, so deeply did the thong bite into my throat. This choking feeling at every movement I made seemed to last forever, but I had to keep my hands moving up and down because only thus could the straps be cut through. I was just going to give up in despair when one of the thongs loosened and I felt my left hand able to move a little. I soon had it free, sliced quickly through the other bonds that tied my right hand and those around my feet, and was just going to throw off my malodorous coverings when suddenly someone snarled a command and I heard footsteps approaching. I froze with horror.

It was the Tartar apprentice. He pulled the coverings back, but as it was dark, he did not notice that my bonds were loosened. "Keep still," he growled, "or you'll get a whipping."

"I've got a stomach-ache," I muttered.

"It'll be better in the morning. Get some sleep now!" His breath smelled strongly of wine.

He drew the coverings back over me and staggered across to the fire. I now knew that one of the Tartars was always awake, that they had perhaps even posted sentries; and I waited a long, long time before I ventured to raise a corner of the blanket and look about me.

The fire had burned down and now showed only a few glowing ashes. The Tartars were apparently sleeping in their huts, for only one of them lay by the fire, with the boy crouching nearby; but he, too, seemed to be asleep. Slowly I inched over towards my neighbour, shoved my hand with the sickle under his coverings, found the thongs binding him so painfully, with his back arched like a bow, and cut him free. Then I sliced through the bonds around his neck.

"Thanks!" he whispered. "But if they catch us, they'll mow us down with their sabres, and I don't know if I can run. I've been tied up now for three days; my feet have gone quite dead."

Nevertheless, I loosed the rest of his bonds that tied him to the saddle and asked him whether he couldn't attempt to crawl. Once we were sufficiently far away, he could do a few exercises with his legs, and they would soon be able to function properly again.

We gathered together the coverings under which we had lain so that they looked as if we were still lying underneath, and then we crawled cautiously across the meadow towards the field of wheat. It took almost an hour to cover this small distance, which normally would have taken only a moment. Behind the field stood a wood of scraggy alders, after that a clover field, and then a dense fir forest. We rested under the alders while I massaged the young man's legs; when he was finally able to stand upright, we crept away and succeeded in reaching the forest.

"God will reward you for this," my companion said when we reached the top of a hill and felt we were safe at last. "Tomorrow morning they were going to send me to Vienna and hand me over to the Turks there so that I might be sold into captivity as a slave." He told me that he was from Mauerbach and had been overtaken by Tartars on the way to the refugee village of Hägging. He and his brother had escaped, but the Tartars had seized his wife and taken her away. He and his brother had lived for a week in the woods, but then intense hunger had forced them back into the valley. They had found something to eat, but his brother had again fallen into Tartar hands, and when he had tried to set him free—and succeeded— he was captured himself.

I then asked him where we were now, and he told me we were making for Hadersdorf. He preferred to stay in the forest and live off leaves and berries and herbs and roots rather than venture into the valley again. "It would be better for you to do the same," he advised me. "The Tartars are everywhere, and I don't think you'll ever get to Lempach."

"From Hadersdorf it's barely an hour's walk to Purkersdorf," I replied. "And Purkersdorf is a refugee village."

"Yes, so it is, and the Turks still haven't got it. But the road to Purkersdorf is swarming with them; and it's likely that they won't let us in to Purkersdorf anyhow but shoot at us, as has happened before. Better to stay here!"

As dawn began to break, he built two nests for us in the forked branches of an ancient tree, and there we slept until evening. Then, however, I took my leave of him and walked off into the darkness, full of faith that God would bring me safe and sound to Purkersdorf and that old pock-marked Karl from Raipoltenbach would have the gates opened for me.

17

During the first two days of my escape, I had often felt hungry, but it hadn't bothered me much because the tension under which I was living scarcely left me time to think about it. Now hunger came upon me with such fury that I should certainly have run to the nearest farm-house without any thought of danger if I had only been able to find one. Walking became extremely painful, although I could not have wished for a finer night. It was warm, the sky was cloudless, and the moon was almost full. Not a breath of air was stirring and not a sound was to be heard all around me—no noise of animals or birds, not a voice, not a cry. Even in the depths of the forest it was not completely dark; the moon shone here and there through the branches, and I made my way forward without much difficulty.

Before I descended into the valley, I sat for a while in a clearing and gazed at the meadow, whose grass was long and pungently sweet-smelling. At the opposite edge of the forest a deer came into view, sniffed the air, and then stepped out into the moonlight. There was a dreamlike loveliness in the night and an almost unreal sense of peace; I would have been happy if I had not been so hungry.

But as one misfortune often engenders another, so pleasant things often come in sequence. Down in the valley I reached a dam on which stood an abandoned wagon that had obviously been overtaken by the Tartars and plundered. Its shaft, jaggedly splintered, pointed to the sky, the backboard had been torn off, and objects that the Tartars had apparently considered worthless and therefore left behind lay scattered far and wide. In a clump of nettles I discovered a well-secured knapsack that had apparently escaped the eyes of the Tartar robbers.

I opened it. It contained a loaf of bread, a pot of dripping, a piece of salted beef, a jar of pickles, a prayer book, and a knife. In an outer pocket there was a small pistol with a roll of bullets and a bag of dry powder.

I should have liked to cry aloud for joy and do a dance of triumph, but I allowed myself only a delighted chuckle—something I couldn't repress or I might have burst with happiness. At once I fixed myself a thick slice of bread and dripping and a hunk of meat, fastened the knapsack again, slung it on my back, and began walking southward, chewing contentedly all the time.

In about half an hour I came to a wall, which I followed until I reached a gate with latticed doors that had been wrenched off their hinges and cast aside. I went through the gate and found myself walking between the ancient maples of a dead-straight avenue towards a brightly moonlit edifice I soon identified as a castle. To right and left between the massive tree trunks stood statues on lofty pedestals, but they were all broken and often smeared with filth or otherwise defaced. A Greek goddess sported a moustache wiped on her upper lip by someone's dirty finger; a Roman general wore for a laurel wreath a large cow pat; a nymph held her own smashed head under her arm; and there were other unmentionable and disgusting jests perpetrated by the barbarians.

The castle itself no longer had any roof—it had been destroyed by fire. Otherwise, it seemed in a fair state of preservation, and as I could see no signs of any tenants and from my previous experience guessed that the Tartars preferred to camp in the open, I entered the place and began ascending the broad ornamental staircase. The night was clear and bright, and the great windows let in enough light for me to find my way around and observe the extent of the depredations that had taken place here.

Valuable old Gobelin tapestries were hanging like faintly coloured rags from the walls; the magnificent parquet floor had been hacked up with axes; and in the middle of the great gallery I saw the ashes of a camp-fire that had been made from chopped-up furniture of the most exquisite quality. In the library, books were strewn about the floor, and the barbarians had used the place as a communal lavatory. Beautifully upholstered seats and couches and silken carpets were slashed to pieces.

In the next rooms, I trudged through great drifts of shattered delftware and Venetian glass. In the picture gallery were piled the smashed gilded frames of paintings; of the priceles paintings themselves there remained only an evil-smelling heap in a dark corner: they had been burned.

A few of the rooms had been relatively untouched; yet I felt I didn't want to stay in any of them. But as I was groping my way along a corridor, I felt a ridge in the wall that seemed to me to indicate the presence of a secret door. I sought for a hidden spring or bolt but could feel only the ornate carving of the panelling; I persisted and pressed hard on the knobs and whorls of wood, and all at once, to my intense delight, I felt the wall give way. The door opened of itself and gave me access to a chamber that obviously had not been discovered by the Tartars, for it showed no signs of having been plundered. There was a four-poster bed with fresh bedsheets and pillows; beside it stood a trunk and a wardrobe; in the centre of the room was a table with two chairs—the whole in perfect condition.

This must have been a room belonging to some attendant who had always to remain close to his master's bedroom, since the appointments seemed a little too simple for a noble person.

I was no nobleman and was well accustomed to simple living; moreover, I felt as if I had been wandering about now for weeks without once enjoying the bliss of sleeping in a proper bed. The longing to lie down on those smooth white sheets became so overwhelming that I cast all caution to the winds. I decided first to make myself a hot meal, if possible, to take a bath, and then to sleep my fill.

I went downstairs again, found the kitchen, lit a fire, put a pan on the hearth, and heated up my salt beef. It was a sumptuous repast. After I had washed, I returned to my secret chamber, undressed, and wearing only my shirt, lay down on the bed. The sheets felt so delicious against my bare legs that I tried to stay awake as long as possible in order to enjoy the sensation to the full. Finally I could hold out no longer, and hardly had I said Amen to my drowsy prayers than I was fast asleep.

I dreamed I could hear the sound of a distant harpsichord playing and connected it with the image of a beautiful young girl at an exquisite instrument until I suddenly awoke in bed in a strange castle. For a while I succeeded in retaining the memory of that delicious dream; then, sighing, I opened my eyes. There was no more harpsichord music, and I clambered shivering out of bed to put on my breeches. In the trunk I found an unused pair of long stockings, which I put on although they were rather too big for me; then I loaded my pistol, slung the knapsack on my back, and left the chamber.

Once out in the corridor, to my great astonishment I heard once more the playing of the harpsichord, and now I recognised the piece of music: it was the same as the piece the old Countess in the Walichgasse (where our house had been in my father's lifetime) had always played—the saraband from a suite by Froberger. I crept softly in the direction from which the sounds came, peeped through a half-open door, and saw between two windows on the far wall of one of those rooms that had been left almost untouched a perfectly preserved harpsichord I had not noticed before. But there at the harpsichord sat a janizary in his white cloak, a white peaked cap on his head, his curved sabre hanging at his side! He sat there playing the saraband, as if it were the most natural thing in the world to be doing.

Although I already knew that janizaries were men who were born Christians, captured in their earliest youth, and then brought up as heathen Turks, I had not heard that their Christian heritage included the art of playing the harpsichord, and I stared at him as if at some overwhelming miracle, lost to the world, until I realised the danger I was running and prudently withdrew. I stole on tiptoe to the staircase, raced silently down the steps, and was just going to slip through a side entrance into the garden when I felt myself all at once hoisted into the air from behind. While my legs kicked helplessly in the void, I flashed an angry glance behind me. I was hanging suspended from the fists of a gigantic Turk who was holding me at arm's length and looking at me mistrustfully.

18

My pistol was small, so small that it could be carried in my pocket; but in its construction it differed in no way from a large pistol. I had taken dry powder with me, had pressed the bullet firmly into the barrel, and tested the flint. Then I had stuck the weapon in my belt. All I had to do was to pull it out, raise the hammer, aim and press the trigger.

I pulled it out. I raised the hammer. But I could get no farther because at that moment the pistol was in the hands of the Turk.

He was laughing at me.

He was wearing pointed, turned-up shoes, wide yellow

breeches, a red sash around his waist, a yellow shirt, and a red turban.

"You little devil!" he cried delightedly, in German.

It was only then that I recognised Michel.

"Yes, it's me," he said, grinning, when he saw that I had finally realised who he was. "And upstairs it's our gracious lord and master playing the harpsichord; he's dressed up as a janizary. But not for much longer. Come with me!"

We went back up the staircase. Michel called to the Count, and the latter came towards us along the corridor. "It's Andreas!" Michel cried; Count Alram, the janizary, laughed and slapped me on the back so hard that I nearly fell down, shook my hand, drew me with him into the harpsichord room, set me a fine chair to sit on, and asked me to tell him all that had happened.

I did so as well and as quickly as I could, and they both listened attentively to what I said. The Count smiled sometimes or burst out with: "Good! Very good!" He was particularly struck by the fact that I had thrown sand into the first Tartar's eyes but even more so by my account of how I had used the sickle to escape. "And the best of the lot is that you succeeded in breaking through the ring of tents, that you found the gap in the Turks' encampment—not just by seeing it from your observation post on my roof but actually by finding your way through the gap in darkness!"

Of course he had not taken as long as I had to get through. He had set out only the previous night, had made his way straight across the Turkish encampment, wearing Turkish clothes, and by noon he had reached this castle—all exactly as he had planned. He was to rest here until evening and then, having changed into Christian garments, was to continue his course westward.

"If you like, you can come with us," he said. "I wasn't able to cross the Danube at Vienna, so in any case I must pass

86

through Lempach on my way to Krems. Is the roast ready, Michel?"

"Just about ready. I'll put it back on the spit for a moment." Michel turned to go, but the Count called him back.

"Another thing! Among the smashed plates next door I saw one very fine piece that was almost untouched; serve me on that plate. And find me as crisp a wine as you can for the sauce. I had a look around the cellars—the Tartars of course destroyed nearly all the bottles, but you'll certainly be able to find a few glasses of wine in the bottoms of the smashed bottles. I'd prefer to drink a Wachauer, if you can find some, with the meat—and after that a Jerez!"

When he had seated himself again at the harpsichord, Michel and I went down to the kitchen, where there was a roast hare waiting to be warmed up again on the spit. But first we had to look for the wine, and this was not easy, for not very many bottles had been left unharmed. We trod cautiously among the splintered glass in order not to overturn any fragment that might contain a few last drops, and as very few of the remaining bottles were labelled, Michel could only distinguish the different sorts of wine by tasting them. When we finally had gathered a little to make the sauce and got together a big jar of Wachauer and a flask of Jerez, he had already become very merry, and we shouted and laughed in the kitchen until the rafters rang. At last, with the meal we had prepared, we went upstairs where the Count was waiting impatiently for us.

In the meantime, he had changed his clothes, but now he was not wearing a wig or a gala uniform but a simple set of breeches and jerkin resembling those worn by officers in the field. He had also laid aside the curved sabre and buckled on a magnificent rapier.

I asked him how these clothes and particularly the rapier had been brought through the enemy lines.

"I carried them," the Count answered simply. "Carried them

under my arm; and if anyone had asked me what I was carrying, I should have said it was booty stolen from the Christians. But I couldn't proceed on my journey now carrying such a repulsive weapon as this sabre."

Michel spread the table with a white cloth, laid out the one good plate for the Count and two broken ones for us, placed the knives and forks, and brought two metal tankards. The Count sniffed the wine, cast a contemptuous look at the tankards, and said it was unworthy of a nobleman to drink such excellent wine out of metal containers. So we all three went into the room strewn with broken glass and china to try to find a goblet of some kind. It took some time, and the roast hare was getting cold, but in the end the Count discovered a rummer that was only slightly cracked, with its stem and base intact. Now we had to put the roast back on the fire a second time, and while Michel was tending it, the Count looked at my pistol.

"It lies easy in the hand," he said. "The silverwork on the lock is wonderfully fine, but beauty doesn't make a weapon fire any better." He weighed the pistol in his hand again, turned it over, lowered it, raised it, lowered it, looked for a target, and noticed in the next room a small bell such as is used to call servants. A swift arm movement and the shot rang out and hit the bell, which fell over and rolled loudly on to the floor.

"Not bad. You must have some practice with it. A small pistol like this doesn't need such a quick eye; it depends more on the feel, and that you can get only by practice."

"But what if the Tartars should have heard the shot!" I gasped in horror.

A careless wave of the hand was his only answer.

Michel brought back the roast hare.

"Hotting it up doesn't make food any better," he commented as we sat down to table.

"It makes it neither worse nor better," the Count declared. "The important thing was to find the glass." And as he noticed my glance of astonishment, he added: "A nobleman is distinguished by a certain style of behaviour he never abandons, even under the most unfavourable circumstances. My own principle is to pursue a refined and cultivated life out here but to live in the utmost simplicity in the town. In Vienna I am called a mere fire-eater, but in the field I am a true gentleman. The former attitude evens things out a bit and prevents me from being either a drawing-room hero or a boor. If the people in the city have become so attached to art that they've forgotten what real life is, then I like to refresh their memories—which I do. If the people outside forget that human beings should also be creatures of civilised refinement, then again I like to show them what is meant by that. That is why in the drawing-rooms of Vienna I talk about twelve-pounders, frontal attacks, and camp-fires; but here, among the ruins and the Tartars, I play a suite for harpsichord—if there happens to be an instrument available, If there were none, I would compose and recite a sequence of sonnets. *Bon appétit!*"

We devoured the meal with relish.

When the Count was sampling his Jerez, we heard galloping horses; I dashed to the window and saw about twenty horsemen racing towards the castle.

"The Tartars are coming!" I shouted.

The Count finished his wine calmly, wiped his lips with a linen napkin, and leisurely stood up. "How tiresome," he said. Then he walked out of the room. Michel took two pistols, and we followed him. I must admit that I was entertaining mixed feelings, the chief of which was fear.

The Tartars had reached the front entrance when the Count appeared on the threshold. They saw him at once and hurriedly reined in their horses. The Count spoke two sentences in Turkish. One of the Tartars took his bow and arrows from his shoulder.

"Michel, a pistol, if you please," said the Count.

Michel handed him one, the Count unhurriedly raised it and fired, and the Tartar fell from his horse.

Again the Count spoke two phrases in Turkish. No one moved. The Count drew his sword.

The Tartars turned around; one of them took the fallen man's horse, and then they galloped back down the avenue to the front gate. They left the dead man lying.

We climbed up to the first floor. "What did your honour say to them?" I asked.

"That I was still at dinner and did not wish to be disturbed —that my servants were also at dinner and had no time to spare!"

"And is that why they rode away?"

The Count shrugged his shoulders contemptuously. "Tartars burn and pillage; they keep alive through the terror they cause. If you face up to them, they're as cowardly as dogs. There were simply too few of them—only twenty or so. Any one of us could deal singlehanded with twenty Tartars—you know that."

"But if they had attacked . . ."

"Yes—*if*! That's what it always boils down to, and you have to know that. This great 'if' can turn one man into a great general and another into a corpse. Well, the Jerez is waiting. It is excellent. We must finish the bottle."

19

After the meal the Count lay down on the floor, shoving his janizary uniform under his head as a pillow, and fell asleep, with firm instructions to Michel to wake him as soon as the sun's rays touched the tops of the maple trees. Michel also put on Christian clothes, and we both sat out on the balcony commanding the approach to the castle. Michel told me of the unfortunate battle at Gran where the Count had had his horse shot from under him. Eight Turks had set upon him, and all eight of them had had their heads chopped off.

"It's quite different here from in Vienna," I replied, not wishing to go too deeply into this little fable of Michel's. "Here he offered me his hand, he smiled at me. . . ."

"Didn't I tell you so!" Michel cried triumphantly. "You wouldn't believe me then. But now you are seeing him as he really is!"

"Is he not himself in Vienna?"

Michel took exception to this question and warned me that I would come to a bad end if I was perpetually carping and splitting hairs. "Forget your Jesuits and school and Latin! If you'd had to sit and wonder whether a sickle was for cutting corn or for cutting your bonds, then you'd still be lying tied up among the Tartars!"

When the sun's rays touched the tops of the maple trees, he awoke the Count; the latter arose and was at once wide awake, as if he had hardly slept at all. We left the castle and set off down the avenue; but after we had passed through the main gate, the Count suddenly halted and shook his head. "I've made a mistake," he said.

"What, your honour?"

"Well, I should have shot three instead of just one of these Tartars and kept their horses. Why should we have to go to Krems on foot?"

"All the same, the horses would be no use to us in the forest," I pointed out.

"You're right, but firstly a nobleman goes on foot only in case of absolute necessity, and secondly the woods now don't come into the question. They are still passable all around Vienna; but in this region we'd need a day to cover a mile, so many fallen trees block the way and the undergrowth is so thick—not to mention the bogs. After Purkersdorf, theVienna Woods turn into a primeval forest."

For a while we stood silent beside the gate wondering what to do. "Only the Tartars have horses in these parts," I said at last. We all looked at one another. "We must steal them from the Tartars," I concluded.

"Steal them!" the Count cried wrathfully. "I don't steal. Get this into your head, young man: life is a battle; it's kill or be killed. If any parson tries to teach you anything different, then he's either mistaken in his ideas or lying. Life is a battle, and even a nobleman has to adapt himself to life under such conditions. While the Church and the apostles of humanity try to avoid the battle—which is impossible—we enter the fray and through knightly rules of conduct raise it to the level of an art. A nobleman does battle, but he is no deceiver, no traitor. He robs; he never steals. I shall not steal my horses from the Tartars; I shall relieve them of their mounts. And I shall do so because I need them for myself."

He gazed searchingly about him, but as there were no Tartars to be seen anywhere, he fetched a sigh and set off on his way. Michel and I followed him.

The sun was still shining and the Count wandered carefree over the countryside, as if there were no question of danger. He did not go through the forest but along its edge. He sought out no cover behind clumps of bushes: he marched straight across the middle of fields and meadows and all the time whistled the same tune from the saraband that he had played at midday on the harpsichord. Suddenly he stood still, sniffed the air a bit, turned away from his path, and strode across to an old willow tree from behind which a ragged peasant was hauled out.

"Why are you hiding?" the Count asked his captive.

"Because I'm afraid," the peasant answered.

"You're not all that young any more; you must be a grandfather by now. So why are you afraid? Granted, the Tartars might put you to death. But you'll have to die in any case, and for a grandfather that's only natural. Anyhow, there are no Tartars to be seen."

The peasant's hair looked like a hangman's cap: obviously someone had put a basin over his head and snipped around the bottom. He had a white beard and two watery blue eyes and a red, warty nose. He scratched himself, squinted up at the clouds, and then looked past the Count. "I'm a grandfather all right," he replied slowly. "And the Tartars are here, though your honour may not have noticed them. A mile away upstream there's a camp with over three hundred men and many horses."

"Are they good horses?" the Count inquired.

"They burned down everything," the peasant went on. "The farms and the barns, the churches and the big houses. They murdered the men, took the women away by main force to live with them in their huts, and sold the children as slaves. Every night the Mother of God stands behind the white oak and weeps."

"Where is the white oak? And why does the Mother of God weep? She must be used to such things by now."

"They stole away all our stores and provisions and trampled underfoot the fruit of the fields. They have poisoned the waters with corpses, and the wells are filled in with dirt. The sun is red, the moon is red with blood, and the fair land becomes a wilderness. The martyrs are sitting up in their graves and watching us."

"You should be a parson."

"And the Rappolten church they have made level with the lowest earth, and Old Lempach and New Lempach, and Anzbach and Johannesberg and Murstetten and Inprugg and Asperhofen and Paungarten and Totzenbach and Sankt Christophen. 'And He opened the shaft of the abyss; and from the shaft smoke rose like smoke from a great furnace, and the sun and the air were darkened by the smoke from the shaft.'—that's what it says in Revelations."

"It may well be so—although I think that was Luther speaking and not St. John. Over three hundred men, did you say?"

"Yes, your honour."

"Go with God—He is the best companion."

We went on over the fields quite calmly, as if what the old man had told us was all nonsense. However, on reaching a small mill that stood under a gigantic ash, the Count suddenly turned off to the right, followed a row of bushes up to the forest, went along the edge of the trees, stopped by a tall bush, and pointed silently down to a bend where a great deal of shingle and sand had piled up, standing out bone-white against the green of the meadows. Six horses with lowered necks stood gravely drinking. Beside them six Tartars were waiting.

Michel nodded.

The Count raised an arm and pointed to the left, and Michel nodded again. He indicated his pistols; Michel nodded once more. Then the Count looked at me and with a quick head movement motioned to me to follow him. "You take the horses," he whispered.

Michel jumped from bush to bush, going always to the left, while the Count and I went straight up to the Tartars; as I was no nobleman, I should have preferred to remain behind the bushes with Michel. The Tartars only noticed us when we were about ten paces away; at that point we stopped, and the Count called out to them in Turkish.

I did not understand what he said, but I saw how the Tartars drew their daggers and how two of them laid arrows to their bows—obviously they were going to be discourteous enough not to allow the Count's modest request to pass without contradiction. That was their undoing, for just then the first shot rang out from the meadows to their left, and one of the bowmen reared back, then sank to the ground. The second was on bended knee already; his arrow whizzed towards us and slit the Count's coat. Immediately after that the second shot rang out, and the second bowman slowly toppled over. Of the remaining four three came at us, but the fourth turned on his heels and fled.

The Count drew his rapier and got ready to parry, taking up an attitude as if he were in a fencing class. I clutched the little pistol and murmured a swift prayer.

The three men stopped in front of us but seemed undecided whom to tackle first. At last one of them made for the Count; the Count took a step backward, feinted to the right, then shifting his balance to the left foot, lunged and ran the Tartar through. Meanwhile, the second had come up to the attack, and as the Count had in his move to the left come considerably nearer to this opponent, the latter's sabre swipe missed the Count by only a hair's breadth. He drew his rapier back; then the weapon described a half-circle downward and, as it came up, struck the right hand of the Tartar, who gave a loud cry, let his sabre drop, and ran. The third followed him.

"The horses!" snapped the Count.

I obeyed. Although I had never had much to do with horses and felt rather nervous of their hoofs and teeth, I succeeded in capturing two of them by their bridles. Michel had meanwhile run up, caught another two, and the Count seized the final pair.

If I had imagined that now we would all spring into the saddle and ride away, I was sadly mistaken. The Count thrust a number of bridles and reins into my hands; then he released the first horse and commanded Michel to lead it around in a circle. He behaved as if he were at a horse sale, while just behind us three men were in their death throes, while we knew there was a Tartar encampment in the vicinity; and while, also, two escapees were running to seek reinforcements that were perhaps already leaping into their saddles, about to fall upon us like a swarm of hornets.

"A little weak in the hindquarters," he said. "Take the chestnut with the white blaze next."

Five times Michel had to parade around with the horse before the Count had decided if the chestnut with the white blaze would do for him.

"The Tartars' camp is just over there!" I couldn't help whispering in my agitation.

"That's their fault, not mine," the Count retorted. "They should have stayed in Tartary—that's where they belong, not in the Vienna Woods. I need three good horses. When I've got them, we shall be safe. But if I let myself be flustered by that band of cut-throats and pick out the wrong horses, it could be the death of all of us."

With the greatest sang-froid he inspected all six horses, made his choice, and let the three remaining horses go free. Michel helped me into the saddle, and then we rode back the way we had come. After about five minutes we crossed the stream, trotted along the upper edge of a wood, passed through a plantation of scraggy young trees that hid us from sight, and finally reached an elevated point from where we could observe about a hundred Tartars down in the valley, galloping towards Vienna.

"Silly donkeys," Michel said, grinning.

The Count merely shrugged his shoulders.

20

Many of the men I knew were more or less good riders, and I had often read and heard about the art of riding; it was something taken as a matter of course. One sat on the animal, pressed the spurs against its sides, and rushed away like a cloud of dust in a gale. In so many of my boyhood dreams I had seen myself galloping through the night on a foaming black charger; but the charger had always been an imaginary one, gentle as some helpful sprite in a fairy tale.

Now I was really sitting on a plunging steed, sitting on a real Tartar saddle, and both were, I thought, extremely unpleasant. The saddle hurt my legs as if it had been created for this express purpose, and the black horse moved with such terrifying forward lunges that after a few minutes' trotting I thought my stomach was where my head should be. Again and again I tasted a burning sourness in my throat, kept losing one stirrup or the other at every violent movement, and when I tried to hold on tightly to the reins, the horse snorted, lashed its tail, and threw its head back so sharply that I was cringing and ducking all the time. Once it caught me on the chin, and although I already had one hand on the pommel of the saddle, I had to let the reins go entirely and hold on with both hands —otherwise a fall would have been inevitable. After I had relinquished the reins, things went a bit better, and the trot, thank heavens, lasted only half an hour; but in that awful halfhour I felt I had atoned in full for all my sins.

When we drew near Purkersdorf, the Count allowed his horse to fall into a walk, and my own did the same, although I had given it no signal to do so. We approached the defences and were soon being shouted at from the walls, being requested not very politely to go to the devil—otherwise we'd be shot down. The Count shouted back that he was the bearer of a message from the commander of Vienna to the Duke of Lothringen and wished to parley with the captain of the place.

"We don't take any notice of that kind of nonsense!" came the mocking reply from the walls. "We've seen people like you before, and they were nothing but common incendiaries!"

"Your honour," I whispered. "Ask them for news of my mother!"

"Is there a Frau Thanradl among you?"

"Anything else you'd like to know? We know no one of that name, so now be off with you or we'll pump you full of lead!"

"So you know how to load a gun?"

"We'll show you!"

The Count made his chestnut rear, turned it about, and called derisively: "Don't forget to look under the bed before you go to sleep—there might be Tartars underneath!"

With that he galloped away, and again my black horse followed his without any urging from myself, adopting the same uncomfortable gait that had caused me so much misery and pain. A single shot whistled over our heads, and then we were riding into the cover of the bush; we fell into a trot and then into a walk. Michel began cursing the lily-livered fools of Purkersdorf who were afraid of two men and a boy. For a while we rode on gently and quietly; meanwhile, evening had begun to fall, and I no longer felt quite so unsure as before on my high horse in the open countryside. While I was wondering if the Purkersdorf people had simply kept my mother's name quiet or if in fact she was not there, the Count stopped all at once, listened, and turned towards the wood.

"I hear wagons," he said.

Now I also could hear a strange noise approaching from the west, a grinding and creaking and jingling of heavy wheels and harness. Then several riders appeared down on the road, but they were not Tartars: they were wearing brightly coloured capes and turbans, and Michel whispered that they were Turks. There followed at some distance more riders and then the wagons. But at the same time a group of five men trotted by nearer to us—they obviously were the outriders. After the wagons came more riders, then nothing, and then a small group again as rearguard.

"A baggage train," Michel muttered as they disappeared, leaving us again with only the sound of wheels and harness and hoofs. "They're not Tartars but real soldiers. We can't play around with them."

The Count waited a very long time, longer than I thought was necessary. He no longer seemed so carefree but almost too cautious. Once he appeared about to ride on, but he hesitated, rode his horse back into the cover of the wood, and soon afterwards I heard the sound of galloping hoofs making the ground throb. Three spahis raced across the fields.

"We shan't take the way through the oak groves. We'll turn off right and ride between Stiefelberg and Buchberg towards Kogl."

I didn't know the hills and thought that I would have to make my way south-west from Kogl to reach Lempach and allowed myself to be carried on through the night by my wild black steed. Since I let him have his head, he had stopped snorting and tossing his mane, and if my progress in this manner looked somewhat different from the ideal horsemanship of my dreams, I did not feel too unhappy about it and only dreaded the moment when the Count might judge the light to be good enough to break into a trot.

After about an hour our path began to climb steeply and became so narrow that we were constantly brushed by the branches of trees on either side. Great stones cluttered the ground, and there was a strong smell of burning. The Count took the lead; I went next, with Michel bringing up the rear. Suddenly the Count's chestnut reared.

The Count halted. "Are you seeing ghosts?" he asked his mount.

As my own horse was restless, too, I seized the reins, but Michel called: "Perhaps it was a wolf, your honour."

Then someone laughed right in front of us, and that sniggering laughter rang so eerily through the darkness that I made a hasty sign of the cross and thought in all seriousness it must be Satan in person lying in wait for us here.

"Who's there?" Michel shouted.

"Me! Only me!" came the answer.

"And who may *me* be?" the Count demanded.

"Black Kate. You're the only Christians on horseback I've seen around here for the last three weeks. Would the honourable gentleman have a little time to spare?"

"What for?"

"I'm looking after a refugee, a reverend gentleman who's had a nasty cut from an axe on his arm. Maybe you could take him to a doctor."

There was silence for a moment; only our horses stamped impatiently in the stillness, and in the distance a screech owl hooted.

Then the Count asked: "Have you got a light?"

"I usually never have one so as not to attract the Tartars, but I can make one if you want to look at the reverend gentleman."

"And have you got sewing things?"

After a pause, the voice answered. "I've got those, too—but the arm doesn't need stitching. Just come a little way with me, only a few paces, then the path branches off towards my hut."

We accepted the invitation, turned off left, and soon after reached an open space where it was lighter so that we were able to make out the shape of a black cat and beside it a charcoal kiln from which thick smoke was pouring. A shadowy figure brushed past us, a door squealed on its hinges, and after a time there flickered behind the tiny window a small, dim light. An old woman appeared on the threshold with a lantern in her hand. She looked exactly as I had once imagined witches to look: a cloth around her head, a long, hooked nose with a wart on the end, a sharply pointed, up-curving chin, and a mouth in which only a single tooth glinted. Under her smock her skinny bare legs were black with grime; her feet were loosely encased in huge wooden clogs.

"Don't touch anything or you'll be black," she said in her croaking voice. "A charcoal burner is black, his clothes are black, his house is black, his bed is black, and his food is black. Bakers are white, but we are black." She tittered shrilly. "Now you can dismount. The reverend gentleman is in the goat's pen. The goat's black, too." She tittered again, and while we were dismounting, she went to a small lean-to that was built on to one side of the hut and opened a door; even she, with her humped back, had to bend low to enter it.

"My son, his wife and children are in Purkersdorf," she was telling us. "But old Black Kate stayed behind; she's not afraid of the Tartars. Somebody has to stay behind and look after the house. And here's the reverend gentleman. Come in, kind sirs!"

The Count and I bent our heads and entered the stall; Michel stayed on guard outside. The hag held out the lantern at the end of a grimy, emaciated arm, and the hairs sprouting from the wart on her nose gleamed in the radiance.

In the light from the lantern we saw a black goat, which gazed at us inscrutably with yellow eyes. Beside it, sitting on a brushwood couch, was a man in ragged clerical garb, his left arm roughly tied up with a rather unclean bandage. Although he was covered with dirt and in a very bad way, I recognised him at once.

It was Father Lukas.

21

After I had given him my overjoyed greetings and explained to my companions who he was, the Count said: "Good. We'll take you with us, Father, and set you down at the nearest village in which we can find a surgeon."

Father Lukas raised his undamaged arm imploringly. "Please, your honour, not that! I must either go to a castle or stay right here!"

"Why to a castle?"

"Because—oh, it's a long story."

The Count brought the lantern closer, drew a watch out of his pocket, and looked at the time. "Past ten," he said thoughtfully. "From here we have about ten miles to Haspelwald—that means five hours at the most. If we rest here for an hour, we can still ride through the valley before dawn." Then turning to the witch, he said: "Haven't you any chairs in your cottage?"

She nodded, grinning. "Fine chairs! Black chairs!"

"We'll sit down in there, and you can mend my coat; it is torn."

He bent his head and went outside again, while I helped Father Lukas to his feet and supported him as he walked as best I could. The witch with her lantern followed us, while the goat, feeling left out of things, bleated plaintively.

In the scantily furnished sitting-room of the hut with its low, smoke-blackened beams, the Count drew off his coat, showed the old woman the hole that had been torn in it by a Tartar arrow, sat down on a chair, and crossed his long legs. The priest sat opposite him, the old woman on her bed in the background. Michel and I squatted on the bench behind the table. Michel drew a field flask of wine from his knapsack, gave the priest some to drink, and the latter began his story.

On Sunday, 4th July, he had been in Lempach at Doctor Voytt's and had spent the night in the Franciscan monastery. On Monday morning he had started off for Vienna and reached there early in the afternoon.

In the meantime, the first news of the approaching Turks had reached the city, and as there were still some matters that had to be cleared up with his colleague in Innsbruck—matters it was advisable not to postpone with the imminent danger of siege—Father Lukas, because of his excellent knowledge of the country, was sent with two other priests on Wednesday to the Tyrol. He was provided with a coach and coachman and two horses; in addition to the papers destined for his Innsbruck colleague, he was entrusted with a small chest containing gold plate used in the celebration of Mass, together with five hundred ducats tied up in a waistband.

He loaded the chest on the coach and tied the belt under his gown. He intended to start at eight but was unable to do so because he had to wait for a letter from the Prefect of Studies, and the Prefect of Studies had been called to see the Bishop. It was midday before he finally left the capital, and shortly afterwards the rumour spread that the Emperor's troops were suffering defeat all over the land.

As bad luck would have it, at Hadersdorf one of the horses fell sick with colic, and as at that time there were no replacements to be had, they had to wait for hours while the coachman tried quack remedies on the horse and kept walking him around in circles. Towards evening Father Lukas decided to spend the night in Hadersdorf and to carry on with his journey the next morning.

That same evening the Emperor left the capital, followed by an almost unending stream of nobles and wealthy people. Although the mendicant orders, as in the time of the plague, stayed behind to give whatever help and comfort they could (in 1679 thousands of them had died in the performance of their duty), the anger of the people was directed at the nobility and the Church and particularly against the Jesuits because they opposed most fiercely the popular trend towards Protestantism. In the opinion of the peasants, their friendly attitude towards the Turks in Hungary had been responsible for the whole war. Father Lukas was to experience this prejudice the next morning when he asked for his bill and learned that he was being charged ten times the usual price.

"Why so dear?" he asked angrily. "We arranged quite a different price yesterday!"

"Why?" the innkeeper answered in a rage. "The reverend gentleman will soon discover why when he rides farther on. And now let's have your money or I'll call my men, and then the reverend gentleman can proceed barefoot and without his coach!"

Father Lukas wanted to put up some resistance, but his two companions advised him to be calm and circumspect. After all, the most important thing was that they had escaped from Vienna in good time, and a meaningless quarrel could ruin everything. They paid the price requested and travelled on westward, but they had only got as far as Purkersdorf when a crowd of armed peasants stopped them.

"Down with the servants of the Pope!" cried their leader, a gigantic man with a long black beard and fists like great rocks.

"Have they got the tonsure?" squeaked another man as thin as a rake.

"Tonsure!" howled a third. "They're Jesuits, aren't they? Come on out and let's get at you, you rotten, monkish rogues!"

"What have they got in their coach! No prayer books, I'll be bound!"

"Look and see what's on top!"

"Unharness the horses!"

The coachman doggedly tried to protect his horses, but he was soon pushed aside. "You hold your noise, you lickspittle of the Pope and his thievish crew! Are you on our side or on the side of those bloodsuckers? Make up your mind quick or you'll get this hayfork down your gullet!"

He hurriedly said that he was on the peasants' side; the band drove the horses away, swarmed over the coach, discovered the chest, and howled with glee.

"It's gold! Naturally it's gold! While we sweat and slave, they pile up gold! And now that the Turks are coming, they're running away! But we have to stay behind and protect their gold so that they can come back and skin us again later!"

The skinny man pointed to Father Lukas and shouted: "Just look at him! As big and strong as a bull! I have to go and fight the Turks with a sickle, while this overfed ox runs away before the first shot is fired!"

"And horses and coach, which we could use in self-defence, they are taking away from us!" the bearded man added. Then he gave Father Lukas a shove. The priest defended himself but was kicked by someone in the crowd, sent sprawling on the ground, and beaten until he lost consciousness. When he came to again, one of the other priests was bending over him, rubbing his wrists to bring him back to his senses. From him he learned that the third priest had been taken away by the peasants, together with the chest. "They searched you, too, but found only your empty purse."

The papers were unharmed, and he still had the belt containing the five hundred ducats around his middle, so Father Lukas and his companion made their way westward again on foot, hoping that they would soon emerge from the panic zone to a calmer place, where they could be given lodging and food and fresh horses. But the pair had hardly been on their way half an hour when they encountered a peasant who threw stones at them and cursed them so fearfully that they had to cover their ears. The man must have told others, for soon afterward about twenty other peasants came after them, stoning them and threatening to kill them if they did not stop. Father Lukas was swift-footed enough, but his companion wrenched his ankle and crawled behind a bush, where the peasants found him and dragged him away.

It got worse, not better. Although Father Lukas had given up travelling on the roads, he preferred to go along the edge of the woods and forests. He had hardly proceeded another mile westward when he was set upon by peasants wielding flails, scythes, and axes. They were pulling a tree-trunk down into the valley to use in the defence works they were building.

"There's another of them damned black crows!" one of them yelled.

In an instant the priest was surrounded. "I have to deliver a letter," he stammered, pulling out of his robe the writing from the Prefect of Studies.

"A letter!" The peasants shrieked with laughter. "A letter! How is it that suddenly thousands of letters have to be carried westward? Why didn't you stay behind in Vienna? Why don't you stay and defend Christianity against the heathens? The peasants are good enough for fighting your battles, but otherwise you spit upon us and take our harvests and dismiss us from our farms if we don't say our prayers exactly as you wish!"

"My brothers, I have never taken anyone's harvest nor sent him away from his farm. I am simply a teacher in a school in Vienna. . . ."

"Simply a teacher! You're a Jesuit!" a short, stocky woodman roared, and swung his axe. "It's you with your reforming who are guilty of making this war! Because you tyrannised over the Hungarians, that's why they brought in the Turks, and now we have to suffer for it! You've betrayed your Jesus Christ, you've falsified the Bible, you've talked round the Emperor with your crafty wiles and speeches, you've corrupted the young folk—you're the plague attacking the healthy body of good Christians!"

"How many ducats have you got on you?"

"Give us the money—we'll give you our old iron in exchange!"

One of them seized the priest by the arm and swung him around; another slit open his robes with a sickle; a third thrashed his shoulders with the heavy flail. Father Lukas didn't know the next thing that happened, but suddenly he saw an axe flash and come down towards his head. He jerked backward and felt the blade enter his arm. At the same time the flail hit him again, and he fell to the ground and once again lost consciousness.

When he came to this time, it was quite dark and there was no companion bending over him. He couldn't get his bearings; everything seemed to be swimming around him. He realised he must have a high fever, and the wound in his arm burned like fire. It was a long time before he noticed that there was sand in his mouth, that his face was covered with mud, and that leaves and brushwood were heaped on the ground around him. Painfully he sat up and shook the earth off his garments. He was lying on leaves and brushwood in a wet grave: he had been left for dead and hastily buried with all the informality of a wartime funeral. Dizziness made him fall back, but once again he struggled upright, grasped the twigs of a bush, and slowly hauled himself up.

I must find someone, he thought despairingly. Are there any human beings left or only beasts? A human being. I must get to a human being somehow. A human being, a human being, a human being. . . .

He staggered from tree to tree, from bush to bush. Again and again he fell to the ground, then stood painfully again and stumbled on. One path led to the right, into the hills, and he followed it, for in the villages there were peasants, and peasants wanted his life because he belonged to the Society of Jesus, which seemed to be hated throughout the land.

He didn't want villages and peasants . . . he wanted a human being!

He prayed: "Oh, God, send me a human being!"

It was getting dark when he smelled the smoke of the charcoal kiln. He had almost no strength left; on all fours he crawled to the open space in front of the charcoal-burner's hut. Black walls, black beams. A door opened, and a witch stood on the threshold. She lifted him up, bound his wound, and put him to bed. When she heard his story, she hid him in the goat's pen so that any peasant who might come along would not discover him.

"Everything's black in our house," she tittered. "Even our hearts is black. . . ."

Her father had owned the big farm down in the valley and the big farm on the hill with the five larches; a farm with three barns, two stables, a bakery, a mill, and two hundred acres of ground. But he had turned Protestant, and the Jesuits had driven him out. He had died in Saxony, a penniless vagabond.

"Words fly away like smoke. All that remains is black soot. . . . Drink your goat's milk, Father."

22

The old woman had long since finished mending the Count's coat, had put it down beside her, and listened quietly to all that was said. Now she stood up, handed the Count his coat, and placed the lantern, which she had hung near the bed to light her work, upon the table.

"The priest drank goat's milk," she said with a little soft, chuckling laugh. "He drank it because there's not much else in my place except goat's cheese. Might the gentlemen care to try it?"

The Count shook his head. "We must be going."

"Might the gentleman be riding towards Kogl?"

"Yes."

"Last night a fellow from Epping came here and told me that the Tartars have set up a big camp between Kogl and Sieghartskirchen. If I were the honourable gentleman, I should not take the road leading to Sieghartskirchen."

"There's nothing else for it," the Count replied. "I know no other way out of the forest."

"If the gentleman cared to get in the saddle and ride back again, he would reach a spring about two thousand paces from the top of the hill. My husband, of blessed memory, dug it out, and you can hear the water running through a hollow trunk. Right behind the spring a path leads downward. It is narrow and stony and certainly not very good for horses, but almost no one knows about it, and it will bring you to the smelteries. If you turn right at the smelteries, you'll come out of the forest near Pentzing, and you can ride around it to Johannesberg."

At first the Count gave no reply, put on his coat, took a ducat out of his pocket, and laid it on the table. "For the goat's milk," he said. "But the goodness of your heart is something I cannot repay—nor would it be any honour to you if I kissed your hand. I've already kissed many worthless women's hands, simply because they had long and noble names." He went up to the old woman, placed his hands on her shoulders, and kissed her on both cheeks. Then he turned and left the room. We stared after him dumbfounded.

"That's just the way he is," said Michel, shrugging his shoulders. "And in Vienna he has the beggars driven from the doors with horsewhips."

We also went outside. Michel held the stirrup for the Count. We mounted; Father Lukas took my horse, and I rode along behind him on the crupper. After we left the room, the witch immediately extinguished the lantern, and as our eyes were not yet used to the dark, we couldn't see anything. We could only guess at a shadow moving somewhere in our rear and heard the old woman's voice crying: "When you've got a bit of black on the end of your nose, think of the charcoal burner! Anyone who touches him gets black, too!"

Then she laughed. It no longer sounded so spine-chilling as it had an hour ago; all the same, it sent a shiver down my back.

We rode in silence back up the hillside, reached the top, and silently began to count our paces in order not to miss the spring—an unnecessary procedure because we heard it from a long way off. After we had watered our horses there, we turned off to the left. The path was really very bad and so stony that we thought it must be the bed of a stream in wet weather and that rain had swept all the earth away. The horses hesitated time and again, feeling with their hoofs for safe footing. I did not feel at all well stuck up on the smooth crupper while the horse made such uneven and stumbling progress. Again and again I thought the horse was going to fall, sighed with relief one minute and the next had my heart in my mouth because it would have been no soft fall into the thick thorn bushes or on to the hard stones.

Finally we reached the smelteries, but the path did not become any wider; it simply grew muddy in the extreme, and now the horses sank at every step up to the hocks in a porridge-like mess of wet soil and dead leaves.

The Count stopped suddenly. Somewhere to the right of us something cracked in the trees. The moon had gone down fairly soon after the fall of darkness, and as the sky, moreover, was clouded, I could see almost nothing; I merely noticed that this cracking sounded different from all the other noises one hears in a forest at night. It was made not by the trees themselves but by a living creature. Was it a fox or a wolf?

The Count rode forward a few paces, then again reined in his mount. This time the cracking noise came from both left and right but stopped at once, as soon as we stopped moving. After a long pause I heard a strange dragging noise in front of me and at the same time behind me. . . . I recognised this dragging noise at once: the Count and Michel had drawn their swords.

Another seven steps and halt again. We could hear the movements of animals or people on either side of the path—then stillness.

This time the pause lasted a long time, but all the while the forest remained silent. Whenever we moved forward a little and then suddenly stopped, we heard the cracking.

"What do you think, Michel?" the Count asked abruptly, in a loud voice. "There's someone creeping through the bushes there! No need to whisper; they were on our track long ago."

"It can hardly be game."

"Game flies. It's people. The only question is: are they Christians? I'll ride on as softly as possible. Keep turned around in your saddle and keep a watch behind: I'll keep watch in front. If anyone attacks, don't nick him, run him through."

Now we were moving forward so slowly that we could hear the cracking sounds quite distinctly on either side of us despite the noise of the horses' hoofs. The sound followed us and stayed around us all the time.

All at once the bushes and trees on both sides thinned out, and we came to a clearing, where it was a little lighter so that we were able to see that we had arrived at a camp. About fifty cattle were standing with their forelegs tied together, cropping the grass by the edge of a small stream, and in the centre were ten carts shoved so closely together that they formed a kind of protective fence. Shadowy figures moved out of the trees and formed a circle around us.

"Dismount!" commanded a deep voice.

"I only take my orders from my superiors," retorted the Count.

"Have we got to pull you out of your saddles?" someone called in a hoarse voice from the other side.

"Just try."

For a while there was silence. "If you think you're superior to me," said the first voice, "then I beg of you, dismount. I would also beg of you not to attack me if I approach you. If you should do so, I have thirty men standing ready here to avenge my death."

"I don't see why I should dismount in order to speak to you, but as your request was expressed so graciously, I shall do so."

The Count dismounted; immediately a shadowy figure detached itself from the circle and came and stood in front of him.

"I am the Mayor of Kogl. We fled from our village and found a hiding place here, which we are keeping to ourselves and will defend in case of necessity. Its situation must not be revealed. If you are Christians, then stay with us. We shall not allow you to proceed farther because the Tartars may capture you and then you might betray where we are if they torture you."

"I must go on."

"I have told you who I am. If you think yourself higher than I, you might at least have the decency to tell me who you are and where you are going."

"I am Count Georg Christoph Alram, former colonel of His Majesty's forces and still a loyal subject to him who is the Emperor of Rome; I am on the way to Stein, to confer with Count Leslie, master of ordnance in the field."

"You must have some sort of letter that confirms the nature of your mission, your honour?"

"I do not know what authority you have to ask me for such a letter."

Just then we heard a suppressed murmur in the circle of shadowy figures that moved nearer now, and one of them cried: "Don't waste words on the blackguard, Kreutzperger! He's only another runaway! We'll show him just how polite we can be to nobles who run away!"

"Perhaps I have not the authority to ask for it," the deep voice went on, ignoring the interruption, "but I would ask you to oblige me by showing me the letter."

"Have you a light?"

"There's a hut over there, built by our woodmen. We can light a lantern inside it."

"Take the reins of my horse," the Count instructed Father Lukas. "We're all going together." The priest obeyed wordlessly and we followed with our three horses as the Count and the mayor proceeded to a small blockhouse that stood to the right near the ring of carts and at the edge of the wood.

"Andreas!"

"Yes, your honour!"

"Come with me. Michel, you dismount and stay by the door." To Father Lukas he added: "Take the bridles of both horses."

I let myself slide down from our horse's crupper and went and stood beside the Count. The mayor opened the blockhouse door and vanished into the darkness inside, where he lit a candle. When he turned to us again, I saw in the candlelight a thickset man with a thick grey beard and bushy grey eyebrows.

"If your honour will condescend. . . ."

We went in; the mayor shut the door behind us, and the Count pulled out of his pocket a flat leather bag from which he took a letter. He laid it on the roughly carpentered table without letting it out of his hands, and the mayor bent forward to read it. I peeped over his shoulder and read:

His Imperial Roman Majesty doth hereby declare to each and every loyal subject that the bearer of this letter doth travel on weighty business and in the cause of Christendom and that he shall be allowed to pass, though disguised as a Turkish messenger, and given all hospitality and consideration according to his just commands.

Signed, Vienna this 27th day of July, 1683,
by His Imperial Roman Majesty's most Privy Councillor, Chamberlain, Vice-President of the High Command, Master of Ordnance, Colonel and Director of the Government of the Imperial Residences in Vienna,
C. Z. Capliers.

"But you're not disguised as a Turk."

"I was until we reached Purkersdorf."

The mayor looked closely at the seal and then raised his head. "I thank your honour and hope that your honour understands in what a painful position we find ourselves. I must confess to you that you would have already departed this life if I had not been able to keep my peasants in check. On the one hand, we are threatened by the Tartars; on the other hand, everyone is running away from them and leaving us behind. The warning fires failed, and we were found unprepared. The Emperor, the nobles, and the rich have fled. The army is over on the other side of the Danube, watching our villages burn. The people are full of rage against the Emperor, the nobility, the Church, the rich; it is almost as bad as in the Peasants' Revolt. Everyone believes that this was was brought about only by the Jesuits and that it has reached its present desperate state only because of the government's inefficiency. Excuse these very frank words, but I must explain to you why it is so difficult for me to allow you to proceed from here."

The Count put back his letter. "I don't mind frankness," he

replied. "Only I won't let myself be ordered about. I have been given a commission to ride as far as Stein, and that as quickly as possible. That I intend to do, and no peasant, I don't care how bitter he may feel, can stop me."

The mayor was silent for a moment and considered the Count in a thoughtful way. "I am convinced that your mission is an important one, your honour," he said after a pause. "But my authority, too, has its bounds. I cannot let you go now, and the more important your mission is, the more important is it that you should put yourself in my hands. The city of Vienna will be no better off if you massacre a dozen or so of my peasants before they finally manage to smash your head in. It is now long past midnight, and you wouldn't in any case be able to cross the Tulln Valley before dawn. Stay with us until tomorrow evening; by then I'll have arranged things for you."

"I am not accustomed . . ."

The mayor broke in. "I am not giving you an order, your honour. It is merely a courteous request." He gave a deep bow.

"A request backed up by thirty bloodthirsty peasants who will murder me if I don't comply!"

The mayor bowed once more. "Unfortunately, that is only too true. But a request is merely a request; the decision is left to you. It's only that in the interests of His Majesty and of the city of Vienna, I should deeply deplore your death."

There followed a few seconds of silence; then the Count abruptly laughed. "You're a comical chap, my dear Mayor. I have a weakness for people with a sense of humour like yours, and so I shall not attempt to demonstrate how to subjugate thirty bloodthirsty peasants. We shall stay until to-morrow evening."

"I thank your honour. Now if you will call your people in here, you can spend the night in this hut . . ."

"That's too kind of you. Not even your exquisite manners

could persuade me to walk straight into prison like that and abandon my horses. No, thank you. We're sleeping outside."

He strode out of the hut and took the first watch. Michel was to relieve him after four hours; Father Lukas and I were to sleep as long as we wanted—which I did.

23

The horse blankets in which I had rolled myself were wet with dew when I awoke. The sky was covered with cloud, and it looked as if it would begin to rain at any minute. I crawled back under the coverings again; they smelled strongly of horse sweat, but it was warm underneath, and I still felt wretchedly weary. Nevertheless, I was unable to get to sleep and finally got up, stretched my arms, yawned, and so gradually came back to life. Of the Count there was nothing to be seen but the outlines of his body under his covers. Father Lukas was awake but simply lay there with closed eyes and moved only his lips; apparently he was praying. Nine peasants were seated in a circle around us; they had obviously been ordered to guard us.

Michel was missing. I turned around and saw that only two horses were tied up at the hut, looked farther around and saw finally that Michel had been watering the third horse at the stream and was now leading it back. This emboldened me to go up to one of the peasants and ask if I might not have a bowl of milk; he gave no word of reply but merely pointed with his thumb to the ring of carts and wagons in the middle of which the smoke from a small fire was rising. The peasants' wives were standing around the fire, and they gave me milk not only for myself but also for my three companions.

While Father Lukas, Michel, and I were breakfasting, the Count awoke. Without paying any attention to the peasants, he strolled between them, yawning loudly, until he reached the stream, washed, took a comb from his pocket, and dressed his hair. When he returned to join us, Michel had to brush his coat and breeches with brushwood and clean his shoes with dry grass. Milk he refused but took two mouthfuls of wine from Michel's flask and nibbled a crust of dry bread. The whole time he gazed pensively at the nine peasants; suddenly he signed to me.

"Sit here and listen carefully," he told me in lowered tones so the peasants could not overhear. "I want to talk to you about something. Even when I was in Vienna, I knew that the people on the land were discontented; that they were prepared to murder and assassinate was something I didn't realise. My main concerns were the Tartars and, in certain circumstances, the Turks. It did not strike me that our own people might be enemies, too. Yesterday we just managed to talk ourselves out of it, but the danger is still not over!"

"But you . . ."

"Don't speak too loud," he warned me. "You see, if I'd for one instant behaved as if I were not absolutely sure of myself, they would have hacked us to pieces. They could still do it. If they do take my life, I can assure you they won't get it cheaply but whether I leave this camp alive or dead is somewhat doubtful."

"Yesterday you scared away twenty Tartars with a single shot!"

"They were just Tartars; they weren't these desperate and angry peasants. On the whole, they are slow-witted and pig-headed, and even the worst aristocrat can treat them badly for a long time without their flaring up. But once they break loose, they're like wild beasts."

"So we're still in danger. . . ."

117

"Well, it's not the first time our lives have been in danger, eh? And when you're a soldier, you must always be prepared to bite the dust one day or another. But I have a mission to perform; I must take this message to the army. It's urgent and can't be held up all this time with me here. I've already told Michel that he should take the leathern satchel you saw yesterday to Stein if I should by any chance not be able to do so. But now it's equally possible that something might befall Michel, too. The priest is badly wounded and a reverend gentleman—I cannot use him. On the other hand, you don't seem to be such a bookworm as I took you for at first, and though you're still not a grown man, you've got a good share of courage and cunning. So you shall carry out my commission for me if neither I nor Michel is able to do so. If ever I shove the leathern satchel into your hands, you'll know what it means, and you'll take it to Count Leslie in Stein."

"I don't know the way, your honour."

"You can ask the way, can't you? You must know the way at least from here across the Tulln to Haspelwald, because Raipoltenbach lies close to Haspelwald. After Haspelwald you go on to Kapelln and Herzogenburg. From there on you won't meet with any more Tartars, for Field-Marshal Dünewald is protecting Sankt Pölten and Count Leslie the Danube bridge at Krems. If you meet soldiers, have yourself conducted to a commanding officer and get him to give you an escort to Stein. You are not to let the leathern satchel out of your possession. Do you understand?"

I nodded. "But what if the Tartars catch me and take the satchel away from me?"

"If they are about to capture you, you must throw the satchel away beforehand. And throw it somewhere where it can't be discovered."

"Then I won't be able to deliver the message."

"That's better than that I should read it to you now and that you should betray it later if you're tortured. The contents have nothing to do with you."

"All the same, I should like to know more or less where the Hungarians and the Turks are and what they have in mind."

The Count looked at me and pondered. Then he lay down again on his cover, put his arms behind his head, stared up at the grey sky, and began his explanation. I didn't follow everything he said but merely gathered that there were only two men who could save our country from disaster, namely, the Duke of Lothringen and Count Starhemberg.

"There's a lot of talk about this Johann Sobieski, the King of Poland," he muttered, shrugging his shoulders. "I know him well, for I've fought under him. He is brave and ambitious, but as a leader of men, there's not much more to him. He doesn't know one tenth of what Lothringen knows about strategy; I would call Sobieski a faultless colonel-in-chief, but Lothringen is a born commander of men. In addition, Sobieski is on the make—he likes money and he's what one might call a hero in carpet slippers."

He gave a faint laugh, slightly contemptuous, before going on.

"No, if the King of Poland really marches with us against the Turks—which is highly doubtful, considering his eternal tergiversations. . . ."

"What's that?" I asked.

"It just means ditherings and shilly-shallyings. As I was saying, if he comes over on our side, that will mean only one thing: that, as king, he wants to have complete command and that, therefore, we lose the war. Let us assume that his command is only a formality and that it's Lothringen who is really leading the army. In that case, we will obviously win, but Sobieski and not Lothringen will get all the credit."

He gave a deep sigh.

"Believe me, Andreas, only Lothringen and Starhemberg can save us, and these two men know too little about one another.

Starhemberg is stuck in Vienna, while Lothringen is in March-feld preparing plans for the relief of the capital. They *must* know what is going on in each other's mind. Therefore, couriers are needed. That is why I am making this journey."

"What do they have to know?"

"Everything a general bases his decisions on: the strength of the opponents and of his own troops, morale, discipline, supplies, munitions, enemy movements and the movements of our own forces. How long the city can hold out; how long Lothringen needs to get his army together. From which direction he will come and when and where he will attack; whether the city garrison should make a sortie or not, and so on."

"And where is our army?"

"Starhemberg is in Vienna, Lothringen in Marchfeld. Leslie is defending the Danube bridge at Stein and Krems. Schulz is in Korneuburg, Dünewald at Sankt Pölten. Bavaria, Franconia, and Saxony come after Krems—and must join us sooner or later."

"And what about the Turks?"

"They are outside Vienna and Raab in Hungary. Moreover, they have here an encampment at Tulln, from which they intend to capture the Danube bridge at Stein; but they can't do this because Dünewald has stopped them. Then there are the Tartars, who accompany the Turks like a swarm of flies; they are moving south from Vienna into the lesser valleys of the Vienna Woods, and from Tulln they will proceed farther south towards Lempach."

"Towards Lempach!"

"Yes. Now their job is to sow disorder and confusion in the rear of the enemy's advance which they are succeeding in doing very well; but I think they're burning too much. Yesterday we met a Turkish baggage train. Why, do you think, was it on its way? In order to bring fodder for the horses, mules, and camels belonging to the Turkish Army outside Vienna: Vienna, which is well known to be surrounded only by vineyards. But if the Tartars burn everything, where shall the Turks obtain their fodder?"

At that moment the mayor came up to us, bowed to the Count and said: "I trust that your honour has rested well?"

"You'd have been terribly upset, I'm sure, if I hadn't been able to sleep for worry."

"I should have deplored such an eventuality for the sake of His Imperial Roman Majesty, who requires the services of a fully rested and not an exhausted courier. I have come to speak to you because I notice that your honour has a wounded man with him. Perhaps we can help him."

"Have you got a doctor here?"

"No, but we have an old woman who understands how to heal wounds and can brew an excellent balsam of herbs and roots."

I was glad for the priest's sake that at last he was to receive better treatment than in the charcoal-burner's hut; but the Count shook his head. "We prefer to wait for the services of a qualified doctor. Has Lempach been taken by the Tartars?"

"The village has been burned to the ground; the fortress has been besieged but is holding out. At least that was the latest news we had yesterday."

"Then we'll ride to Lempach this evening."

The Count gave a nod of dismissal, and the mayor withdrew.

"Of course, you'll remain under your coverings until darkness falls, Father," said the Count when we were at last alone again. "It's a pity I'm a nobleman and may not move in on the enemy but must take the opposite direction. But if you get up and the peasants recognise your Jesuit robes, we can say our final prayers."

"I know that," answered Father Lukas. "And because such a covering can be easily pulled away, I have been praying for our safety ever since last night."

24

All that day we had nothing to do but sit in front of the block-house and talk. The Count explained to me that the French King had a particularly sound Minister of Finance and therefore had a lot of money that he was using to buy up half the princes of Europe; that he had also employed this money in Turkey in the war against the Emperor and had now finally reached his goal. "Perhaps he's a great King of France," the Count said contemptuously. "But to my mind he's a traitor to the Christian West and therefore no person of good birth and breeding."

For every twenty minutes the Count spoke, Michel went on for three hours. He began by stating that every three days outside Vienna the Grand Vizier Kara Mustafa had himself carried in a bullet-proof palanquin around the approach trenches, which only went to show the laziness as well as the cowardice of the Turkish leaders. He went on to inform us that the rank of Turkish commanders in the field could be estimated from the number of horsetails carried in front of them and declared that horsetails were black magic and that there were all kinds of things that could be used to counteract the effects of black magic according to the circumstances—especially effective being the blood of a black dog, the right eye of a wolf, and the heart of a hare. In the host of weird tales that followed, a large part was played by crossroads, midnight bells, clouds of sulphurous smoke, powdered witches' bones, boiled dogs' dirt, demons with six tails, and phantoms surrounded by a strange blue luminosity.

Late in the afternoon the mayor appeared again, made a deep

bow, and said: "Everything has been seen to. If your honour will condescend to depart after nightfall, we shall provide your honour with a guide."

"So that I may not depart before darkness falls?"

"No. Your honour yesterday declared that he wished to remain here until this evening."

"So the provision of a guide does not depend upon the time of departure."

The mayor bowed. "Your honour might have decided to stay."

"You have a strange way of putting things. All the same, thank you for the offer of a guide. We shall instruct you when we are ready to depart." Obviously the Count considered the conversation at an end, for he turned away. The mayor, however, did not bow and go.

"There is just one other small matter, your honour," he said. "The peasants have suffered a lot—they have lost their houses with all their worldly goods and the harvest for this year. We should appreciate it as a sign of your noble mind if your honour would reward the guide for his services."

"That goes without saying."

"We thought of a sum of thirty ducats."

When the mayor named this sum, we all four gazed at him speechlessly.

"But that's ninety Gulden!" the Count cried.

"We'd rather have ducats," the mayor answered politely. "But if those were not available, we would take one hundred gulden."

"One hundred Gulden! But that would buy ten cows or twenty-five pigs! And you call that a tip for your guide!"

"I did not mention a tip, your honour. Unfortunately, our losses at the hands of the Tartars are great, and what my men were thinking was that, if your honour should have happened to bring along a little ready cash with you from Vienna, your honour might condescend to leave it with us in exchange for our willingness to fight on your side."

The Count was silent for a moment. "So it's a ransom," he said.

"That's not a nice word and might give rise to a wrong impression. Let's say rather that it is a reward for your guide."

"I don't need your guide."

"But we must give you one, nevertheless, so that you do not fall into the Tartars' hands. We should not be so presumptuous as to require your honour to abide by our decision—your honour came here of his own free will and not through any wish of ours and therefore has compelled us to take these measures. The guide will assure your honour's safety. Is your honour's life not worth a hundred Gulden?"

"And what if I don't have them?"

"I should at once believe your honour's word on the matter; but my men are uncultivated folk. Many of them, I regret to say, are somewhat uncivilised louts, and it might well be that they would be so lacking in common respect as to go through your honour's clothes as proof positive that your honour did not possess one hundred gulden."

"Just let them try!" the Count shouted.

"I shouldn't let them. You need not worry. But you are not alone. Your wounded man has until now declined the healing services of our old woman; he has stayed hidden under his coverings, although it must have been inconvenient for him sometimes. Even the most brainless peasant begins to wonder at this. Even the most brainless peasant comes to the conclusion that underneath the covering there lies perhaps a priest's costume, and under the costume perhaps a priest. But the monasteries are very wealthy; if they send one of their sons westward, they must certainly have given him a little something that it would be better not to allow to fall into the hands of thieves and plunderers. If, therefore, your honour would be so good as to speak about it to the gentleman under the blanket, then we could possibly reward your guide in a suitable fashion and the gentleman could put aside his coverings once darkness had fallen with the greatest confidence and mount his horse and ride away. Not a hair of his head would be harmed—I give my word for that."

"This is highway robbery."

"If your honour sees fit to insult me, he may, if he so wishes, attempt to come to terms with the peasants. I shall withdraw the offer of my unworthy services. If your honour should find himself willing to pay his guide an adequate reward without referring to it as highway robbery or ransom money, your honour only has to call me."

He bowed and went. We gazed in desperation at one another.

"That's just about the most cunning rogue I've ever come across," the Count said after a long pause.

"We'll not give him a penny!" Michel growled.

"Easier said than done. The fellow's guessed that we've both got money on us; it could be less than a hundred Gulden, but he knows it might well be more. He would like to avoid a murder and so has decided upon a hundred; but if we give him nothing, the peasants will kill us in order to see just how much we really do possess. They're in this state not merely out of lust for money but also because of their rage against the nobility and the Church. Of course, we could put up a fight, but in the end they would overpower us. Nobody apart from the charcoal-burner woman knows we have come here, and she will never learn of our death. Everyone will assume that the Tartars captured us. And so our greatest danger lies in a fight that could only be started in anger. And besides the likelihood of being murdered, we'd stand to lose much more than a hundred Gulden."

Father Lukas lay silent for a while, then shrugged his shoulders and said: "You're right. It's bad luck that I haven't got a penny left. The peasants took my money belt when they gave me that rather premature burial."

The Count nodded. "I know. I shall pay the thirty ducats myself."

As it was getting dark, he sent for the mayor and gave him a bag of gold pieces. "The reward for the guide," he explained dryly. "And now we'd like to be on our way."

The mayor shook the contents of the bag on to a cloth and counted the ducats carefully. "Your honour is a true nobleman," he said with a deep bow. Then he turned around and called: "Men, the honourable gentleman has given us a present of thirty ducats for our trouble and for the safe conduct we promised him! Three cheers for the noble gentleman—only not too loud; we don't want the heathens to hear!"

The peasants raised their arms and muttered an enthusiastic cheer: "Long live the honourable gentleman!"

We mounted, and as we rode behind our guide, the peasants waved farewell to us. They were still shouting long life to the Count.

25

I had no idea where the narrow path our guide had taken was leading us, but after three hours we reached the village of Johannesberg on the Buchberg; I knew the place. It was destroyed. We rode to the left past the burnt-out houses and along the edge of the wood, taking the road that links Johannesberg and Markersdorf; about two hundred yards outside the village stands a wayside cross, and as we were riding past it, a figure suddenly dashed out of the darkness and rushed up to us with wildly waving arms.

"Heaven be praised! Christian men at last!" screamed a young woman's voice.

"Shush!" the guide hissed. "Can't you keep your voice down, you goose!"

The silly goose was a young woman in a white dress with a white shawl; she at once saw that the Count was the most important person and so paid no heed to the guide but turned to say, though now in quieter tones, to Count Alram: "My good lady is sitting over there on her hamper! We fled from the house yesterday, and now the butler has run away and left us sitting here alone. Please help us to get to safety!"

The Count reined in his horse. "What is your mistress's name?" he asked.

"Eleonore von Hauenstich."

"Lead me to her," the Count said, dismounting. He disappeared with the girl into the wood but in a minute called for Michel, who dismounted and followed his master. A little later they reappeared. The Count was leading by the arm a lady clad in a light-coloured dress; behind them Michel was hauling a huge wicker hamper, and the maid brought up the rear.

"I shall do everything I can," the Count was saying. "If you wouldn't mind sitting in front of me on the saddle."

"I can't thank you enough! And what about the hamper?"

"We'll bring that along, too."

Michel let fall the end of the hamper he had been pulling. "Excuse me, your honour—but we have a mission to carry out! If you want to take the lady with us—I don't see, begging your honour's pardon always, what the safety of the city of Vienna has to do with *her*. Anyhow, granted we take her with us. But what about the hamper and the young maid?"

The Count laughed. "You'll set the young maid behind you on the crupper, and you'll fix the hamper in front of you against the pommel of your saddle. Just try to imagine it's full of ready money!"

"It's not money," said Frau Eleonore. "It's my clothes."

"Dark ones?" Michel asked.

"Why?" Her voice sounded surprised. "Yes, there are dark ones among my dresses."

"Those are the ones you should have put on, Lady: in the bright stuff you're wearing now, you can be seen a mile away!"

She shook her head. "I just put on what I thought was most suited to my escape. The brown brocade would have been quite impossible!"

"On your horse, Michel!" the Count cried. "I'll help you up with the hamper and the maid."

Michel obeyed; the Count lifted the maid up on the crupper and the hamper on the pommel, then helped Frau Eleonore into his own saddle, climbed up behind her, and held on to her with his free hand.

"You're a true knight-at-arms," she said. "I shall never be able to thank you properly for all you're doing."

As we wound our way towards Markersdorf, she went on speaking without a pause: "My husband is captain of horse with the army," she informed us vivaciously. "I was alone, for we have no children, but I thought to myself: whatever Balthazar can do, his wife can do also, and if he stands up against the dreadful Turk, I, too, can stand up against them and stay on in my castle, not move a hand's breadth away from the horrid heathens, but show them what we women are made of and prove that Christian firmness is greater than heathen Muslim barbarity. But they took my ranger away to Purkersdorf because he was supposed to go to battle there—in Purkersdorf of all places! My own ranger! Oh dear!"

She paused for a second to give a sniff.

"The next day the manservant ran away, something I had never expected of him and—the shame of it!—towards evening the stable-boys left with all my maidservants on the same cart. Everyone advised me to fly, too. But a Hauenstich never runs away—that's what my husband always told me. So was this Hauenstich going to run away? I stayed on. After the stable-boys had left, I was sitting down to my evening meal, was just putting my spoon into my soup when I happened to raise my head—and there, at the window, what did I see? The most frightful face! Oh, Count! The most frightful face with slit eyes and a shaven head and a long, trailing moustache—a really devilish-looking man! I swooned. Fainted clean away. After-ward, I learned that the butler—he was the last man left in my house—had fired his pistol. Now there was nothing left for us but immediate flight. I took only the most essential things in my basket, my turquoise-blue velvet, the shoes to match, my brown brocade and my yellow silk with the . . ."

At this moment Michel's horse stumbled, and the hamper fell to the ground. As Michel could not at the same time hold it in the saddle and remount and as I was not strong enough and Father Lukas was too ill and our guide refused to take on the "silly goose's" load, the Count had to dismount and shove the hamper back against the pommel of the saddle.

"Do you know who is defending Lempach?" the guide asked Frau Eleonore. "Countess Palffy with her maids. She stands there with her musket at the ready, trained on the enemy, and has girded on a sabre. That's some woman for you! She's not concerned about clothes and finery when the Turks are in the land!"

"What with the clothes hamper and the girl up behind me, I'll be in the same position as Countess Palffy if I don't look out," growled Michel.

"We must take our wounded friend to Lempach. Until then, you must do the best you can with the hamper and the maid."

We rode on, and Frau Eleonore kept on talking: "Well, in Johannesberg the butler suddenly puts down the hamper and refuses to carry it any farther! Just think of that! Poor Resi here had to carry it. The butler wouldn't go any farther with us.

'And who's going to protect me and look after me?' I asked. 'Are you not a man? Would you let a poor, weak serving maid carry that great hamper?' And what, sir, do you think he said? That we could just leave the thing there! Fancy! Coming from a trusted servant . . ."

She went on and on. The Count was silent. Outside Markersdorf we overtook two ox-drawn carts with refugees riding on them; they spoke to our guide and told him that they had started from Tulbing and were hoping to reach Sankt Pölten. The guide for his part told them that he was taking a courier belonging to the city of Vienna and dispatched by its commandant to Tulln, that he was carrying important messages, which, after they had been delivered, would result in the army's moving to attack the Turks and thereafter driving them from the land. About the thirty ducats he said nothing.

"Do you know the way to Raipoltenbach?" one of the refugees asked him.

"Straight over there past Tulln, then carry straight on. But why aren't you going by way of Lempach?"

"The Tartars are there; we were warned against going that way only a couple of hours ago. We want to get to Wolfsbach and Totzenbach."

"Are there no Tartars outside Raipoltenbach?" the Count broke in.

"We haven't heard of any."

When we reached the first houses in Markersdorf, our guide took leave of us, thanked the Count once more for the reward, and set off home. Behind us the wheels of the ox-carts creaked and groaned; before us lay the village, and behind it stretched the unwooded valley of the Tulln; above, we could make out the dark slopes of the Haspel woods.

We rode at a walk through the village and over the bridge across the Tulln; but when we reached the open fields, the Count ordered a trot in order to cover more quickly the wide-

open spaces where there was no protection. I had the greatest
difficulty in holding myself on the smooth crupper of the horse
and held on as tightly as I could to the priest's waist, putting
my arms around its vast circumference as far as I could reach.
Michel had not only the weight of the serving maid behind
him but also that of the hamper to support, and as both kept
tending to slide off, I often heard him muttering curses. Nevertheless, all went fairly well and we had already reached the
cover of the woods when Frau Eleonore suddenly cried out:
"Stop or I'll die!"
The Count dropped into a walk. "What is it, Madame?"
"My heart! It's bursting! I must lie down or I'll die!"
"Let her die!" growled Michel.
"You still don't seem to comprehend what a nobleman is,
Michel," the Count called back. "Ride on. I'll follow later."
Michel gave spurs to his horse and galloped on into the
forest, with hamper and maid bouncing up and down, and
vanished. Father Lukas followed at a walking pace and stopped
at the edge of the trees. Frau Eleonore lay on the grass, and
the Count bent over her. We couldn't hear what he whispered
or see what he did; but suddenly we heard the hoofs of a
number of horses coming towards us at a gallop. We saw they
were Tartars, crossing the Tulln and making straight for us!
In an instant the Count had Frau Eleonore back in the
saddle, had leaped up behind her, and was racing for the cover
of the trees. A forest aisle opened in front of us, along which
the priest now urged his horse. The Count raced past us, leaping over a number of fallen pine trunks, and was already more
than thirty feet ahead of us when his horse stumbled—apparently over an exposed root—fell, and threw the Count and the
lady to the ground. While the lady got to her feet, took a deep
breath, and began to scream shrilly, the Count lay motionless
beside a tree-bole.
We reached them; I dismounted, bent over the Count, and

seized him by the shoulder. But however hard I pulled, his body remained lifeless, and behind us the Tartars were already entering the forest. Father Lukas was defenceless and unarmed; it was true I had my pocket pistol and the Count's larger ones, but I had had too little practice in shooting, and Michel was nowhere to be seen.

There seemed no prospect of saving the Count and his important dispatch!

And the Tartars were thundering nearer and nearer!

Without another moment's pause, I tore open the Count's coat, found the leather satchel, and ran with it into the trees, where the Tartars could not follow me on horseback. I saw nothing, heard nothing as I rushed blindly and dumbly up the hillside until my heart began to thump as if it would burst, the blood throbbed in my ears, I stumbled over stones, slithered on wet, slippery clay, kept charging on, getting some nasty cuts and bruises but never giving them a moment's thought, for I had to get that satchel to Stein—the fate of Vienna depended upon it. And so I kept on running, running, running . . . panting and exhausted, until, bumping into a tree, I clasped it with both arms and slowly sank to the ground.

I did not lose consciousness; I simply couldn't move. Red spots danced before my eyes, and I was struggling for breath. When I had finally recovered the full use of my senses, I listened to the sounds of the dark forest. Somewhere I seemed to hear a faint cry, but it came from a long way off which gave me hopes that the Tartars would not find me.

After I had rested for a while, I went on farther. I did not know the way or which direction to take. I only knew that my destination was Stein and that I must reach it soon.

26

In the region around Lempach quite a number of tales are current about the Haspel, and in all of them the forest plays a sinister and uncanny role. The tales tell either of murders that were committed there or of bands of robbers who carried out raids from its cover; it is also portrayed as the abode of evil spirits and ghosts. The place is spooky, and I had always avoided going there, even in daylight. Now here I was, in dense darkness, groping my way between ancient trees, making my way with difficulty through the undergrowth, clambering over mouldering, fallen tree trunks and making very slow progress. As I now was well aware of how eerie a forest sounds at night with its cracking, squealing, howling, and whimpering, I did not let myself be too alarmed by these noises; my whole attention was directed to finding a path and to calculating how I could get out of the trees into the open again.

After a short while I reached a small clearing where a shattered pine tree stood, with a jagged, splintered trunk that showed up clearly against the night sky. I crossed the clearing, struggled for about another hour through the thickets, and came then to a second clearing. Here, too, there was a lightning-struck pine tree, and I recognised its outlines.

I had been moving in a circle.

As clouds covered the entire heavens, I could not find my direction by the stars, and there was no wind that might have helped me to find the west. At a loss, I suddenly remembered a lesson at the seminary in which Father Lukas had taught us how to find our way by signs in nature. We were not allowed a compass, and it was assumed that no sun, moon, or stars were visible. Father explained that tree trunks are often covered with moss. Whenever this happened, in this region it was usually on the side facing the west because winds bringing rain usually blow from the west in our parts. I felt the trunks of the trees. At first I could not find any with moss on them, but finally I found one and then another. The moss on them was indeed thicker on one side. If Father Lukas was right, that side must face west, and that was the direction in which I must go.

So I groped my way along, feeling for moss all the way, and found myself climbing uphill. At last I reached the top, came to a path, and followed it, although it was leading somewhat to the south. As I was now proceeding more quickly, I soon struck a cart track that I recognised: it was the way from Raipoltenbach to Murstetten. I knew the Goldburg was over there and that it was possibly still in Christian hands. But as it was also quite possibly besieged by Tartars, I turned left towards the Bildstock Heights and wandered along the crest of the Haspel woods until I could make my way down through the gulch leading to Gunnersdorf.

When I left the wood, dawn was already breaking, and the sky was bright over Thalheim. The Count had told me that General Dünewald was encamped at Sankt Pölten, so that there would apparently be no danger to me from the west, and as long as the hills to the east protected me from sight, I made my way along their lower slopes. But the Count had also told me that I should ask my way: this was so far impossible, for neither in Thalheim nor in Perschling did I encounter a single soul, and if I had not happened to know these places already—I had once accompanied Doctor Voytt on a trip there—I should never have been able to make out exactly where I was.

From Perschling I went along the bank of the stream until I saw Etzerdorf lying in front of me, turned off in that direction, and finally met a young fellow of whom I asked the name of the village, in order to be quite sure that I had made no mistake.

All he replied was "Ohh?"

"Is Herzogenburg this way?" I asked, and pointed ahead.

He grinned.

"Are there Tartars there?" I went on.

"Tartars!" He screamed with laughter. "Ohh . . . !"

It was some time before I realised that I had fallen in with the harmless village idiot who perhaps kept watch over the sheep belonging to the village but who couldn't tell a Tartar from a tin kettle. So I said: "Ohh!" and went on. He laughed out loud after me.

An hour later I could see Herzogenburg before me, where the Count had told me I should find safety and help. I wondered for a while whether I should ask for hospitality, but although I was very tired, I decided to press on farther. Starhemberg's message was of the highest importance, and perhaps on the way I might fall in with a military patrol that would certainly take me under its wing. After I had crossed the Traisen bridge, standing still untouched, I passed the monastery to the right and wandered on towards Kölbling. I began to feel the pangs of hunger. I looked about me for fruit but found only bramble bushes with red, unripe berries. Nevertheless, I picked a few, put them in my hat, and sitting down at the edge of the wood in the sunshine—for the clouds had departed some time ago—ate the last portion of dripping, though I had no bread to go with it, swallowed the hard berries, and rested for a while.

I fell asleep then, and when I awoke, the sun was already fairly low.

At once I started on my way again and a little later encountered two dragoons. I waved to them; they stopped and asked me what I wanted.

"I've come from Vienna and have a message from Count Starhemberg to Count Leslie!" I told them. That this should have sounded somewhat bumptious is understandable, and maybe that was the reason why the two dragoons burst out laughing.

"You've struck lucky," one of them answered, after they had stopped laughing. "I am Count Leslie."

"And I'm the Duke of Lothringen," the other added.

And then they laughed even louder.

"But I'm serious!" I cried. "I really have a message!" I was just about to pull it out of my pocket when I remembered that the Count had most strictly forbidden me to show the leathern satchel to anyone but Count Leslie. What if the two dragoons were to take the satchel from me? Obviously they couldn't even read, and as they thought the whole thing was a joke, they might easily throw the precious document away! So I left the satchel under my coat, and the dragoons rode on, doubled up with laughter.

Ten minutes later I heard the sound of galloping hoofs, turned around, and saw a soldier of the Emperor's forces approaching. Again I waved, and he stopped. I asked him to conduct me to some officer because I had a very important message from Count Starhemberg to be delivered to Count Leslie.

"You idiot!" he cried. "It's I who am carrying the important message, not you! Don't stand there wasting my time. If you want to play jokes at a time like this, try pulling your own leg, not mine!" And he galloped away.

Obviously he couldn't imagine that someone as young as myself could have been entrusted with an important message from a besieged city to army headquarters, and this realisation filled me with bitterness. In a fuming rage, I went on; it was already getting dark, and when I once more heard horses' hoofs behind me, I stood in the middle of the road, but instead of waving, I stretched out both my arms as if to bar the way. The three men very nearly rode me down, but the horses saw me despite the darkness and shied.

136

"You stupid young fool!" the first rider cried. "Can't you look where you're going?"

"You are the fools!" I shouted back. "I have to get to Count Leslie with an important message from Vienna; but here you come charging along at breakneck speeds and leave me to go on foot! I want to speak with your commanding officer!"

"The chap's mad," declared the second rider.

"Let's get on!" the third shouted, and drove his horse forward past the other two.

"Stop!" the first rider cried. "He's serious. Nobody yet has ever called me a fool and got away with it, if it was in jest. What kind of a message have you, young fellow?"

"One from Count Starhemberg to Count Leslie."

"In writing?"

"Yes."

"Give it here!"

"I may not give it to anyone, only to Count Leslie himself!"

"Give it here!"

"You must take me to Count Leslie and not take the message away from me!"

I leaped away from them to the edge of the wood, ready to vanish among the trees and thickets at the least sign of danger.

"Leave the young dolt alone!" the third rider growled, and again spurred his horse.

"Wait!" the first rider shouted to me. "Where did you get the message from?"

"The courier, Count Alram, was overtaken by Tartars near Lempach. He commanded me to take the satchel to Stein to Count Leslie and not to let it out of my hands until I could give it to him personally."

Now even the third rider showed some interest. "Alram?" he said, astonished. "The one-time colonel now a courier?"

He stood silent for a moment while the others looked at him in perplexity.

"Come up on my horse," the first rider said. "I'll take you to Stein."

"And how do I know you won't steal my message if I get on your horse?"

"I am Baron Leisser and am myself a colonel-in-chief. I give you my word of honour that I shall not take your paper away."

"What about the others?"

He became impatient. "Am I a baron or not? When I give my word, you may be sure you can keep your paper!"

I decided to risk it and let myself be helped up on the horse. I sat behind the baron and held on tightly to the high-ridged saddle.

We trotted on for over an hour, till I got cramp in my fingers, but finally we rode across the Danube bridge, trotted through the village of Stein, then on beyond across meadows till we came to a large house where we halted. The three officers took me through the hall, up some wide stairs, and through two huge rooms with guards and officers, who sat at enormous paper-strewn tables and stared at us in bewilderment. Outside a massive door we were stopped by a guard; the baron was allowed to enter, was closeted inside for a few minutes, then came out again and led me into the room. In front of me stood a man wearing a grand, long-ringleted wig; he had a somewhat strained but friendly face and bright blue eyes.

"I am Count Leslie," he said. "If you have a message for me—you can hand it to me now in all confidence."

I put my hand in my coat, drew out the leathern satchel, and handed it to the man wearing the long brown wig.

But then the man began to turn around, the chandeliers in the room began to spin, the furniture waltzed wildly, and the whole room swam faster and faster around me until everything went black and I lost consciousness.

27

I awoke in a room such as I had never slept in before. Over the wide, low bed hung a purple-red baldachin; on the floor lay thick-piled carpets; the furniture was richly carved and upholstered with luxurious brocades, while the curtains at the long windows were sumptuously embroidered with gold thread. As they were drawn, the room was in half-darkness. Nevertheless, I noticed that outside the sun was shining brightly and that it must already be almost midday.

Someone must have undressed me and left me only in my undershirt, so I looked around for my breeches and shirt and coat; but I could see them nowhere and for a while was at a loss as to what to do now. Finally my glance fell upon a small table, which had been placed beside my bed. On this small table stood a glass of water and a tiny bell.

I rang, and soon afterwards a man came in, closed the tall gilt-studded doors with elaborate care, walked slowly across the room to me, and laid my clothes, which he carried over one arm, very neatly on the chair beside my bed.

"You are to get dressed now," he said in a voice so deep and sonorous that it seemed to come from inside an iron washtub. "His Excellency is waiting for you." With these words he turned and strode, with measured steps, back to the door, which he closed ceremoniously behind him.

I obeyed his command and, in doing so, discovered to my great joy that my coat, shirt, and breeches, which had been torn in many places, had been thoroughly repaired, cleaned, and pressed. There were new stockings and underwear, too, and my shoes had been polished till they shone like new. When I went out into the corridor, there stood the same man I had seen before. He looked at me sombrely and announced in sepulchral tones: "Pray follow me."

This was not very easy. He literally placed one foot before the other in the most measured and haughty manner, for all the world like a Spanish grandee at a coronation. As I did not dare overtake him and yet could not fit my steps to his leisurely, deeply pondered tempo, from time to time I just had to stop and stand still, until finally he paused outside a lofty door-way, gravely signalled to me to wait, entered, and a little later called me into the room.

It was the same room I had entered the evening before, only this time I came in through a side door. Count Leslie was writing at his desk, and behind him on the wall hung a gigantic map of the country. The manservant who had accompanied me left the room soundlessly; the Count stood up, came towards me, and shook my hand.

"You did a good job," he said, in his friendly way. "What's your name?"

"Andreas Thanradl."

He asked about my home, my parents, what I had done with my life so far, and particularly about my adventures between Vienna and Stein. I related everything as truthfully as I could and then inquired whether the message I had brought was after all so very important.

He smiled. "Important! That's quite another matter. I'm afraid I must disillusion you: the course of the war obviously does not depend upon it. We now know how things were in Vienna on 27th July, and that does indeed help us in our review of the whole situation. But of course we shall need a similar report within a week at least, and someone must risk his life again to lend a little assistance in the winning of the war, which God willing we shall fight out to the bitter end—and win! We are all just little wheels in some great timepiece. His Imperial Majesty is the greatest, His Serene Highness the Duke of

Lothringen is the next biggest, and so on right down to you and me, who are among the smallest. But we are all necessary if the clock is to keep going—in fact, the smallest wheel may be the most important."

I had really believed that I had decided the course of the war, and the Count must have noticed from my air of disappointment how little pleasure his reply had given me, for he laid his hand on my shoulder and said consolingly: "You wouldn't have wanted me to lie to you? After all, you're a reasonable fellow, as well as a brave one!"

His friendliness gave me courage. "Your honour!" I cried. "You perhaps do not realise what the people on the land have to suffer! I thought that now the army would be on the march, driving the Tartars from our country!"

He took back his hand, regarded me silently for a few seconds, and then shook his head. "That they will not do. They cannot do it. Our army is too small still." He turned on his heel, strode across to the map, and signed to me to follow him. "Now perhaps you'll want to know why it is so small. My dear fellow, if it had grown any bigger through all the decades of troubles we've had with the Turks—can you imagine what it would have cost? All our money would have gone into the army—and that would have meant higher taxes! But now we're calling in the men, and it won't be too late, either. Look!"

He pointed to the wall on the right-hand side of the map. "About here lies Hungary. That's where the Duke of Lothringen had gone when we learned that the Turks were coming. He has besieged two towns and then raised the siege. That was not wrong as a few too-clever fellows have claimed. It caused the Grand Vizier with his gigantic army to make a detour; the Vizier did not march on Wiener Neustadt, by which route he would have reached Vienna much earlier; instead, he marched on the Duke."

He shook his head sorrowfully at this point.

"Naturally," he went on, "the Duke's forces were defeated—he had only a tenth of the Turkish manpower! But through this manœuvre he gave Count Starhemberg time to make his final preparations and in the end was able to send him half his troops to help in the defence of the capital. The remainder he divided into divisions. Here in Krems we are gathering together the soldiers who have come from Germany and Poland and are defending the Danube bridge. The Duke himself has marched towards Pressburg, and there he came to grips with the Hungarians who have gone over to the Turkish side, so that they cannot take us by surprise from the rear. Months ago, Count Starhemberg saw to it that we should have boats enough to build temporary floating bridges. When all the soldiers have arrived, we shall construct those bridges and cross the Danube. Only by using our heads and not our fists can we beat the Turk. Initial successes mean nothing. The important battle will be the decisive one fought around Vienna. A few country villages do not count, however sorry I feel for their inhabitants."

"With the help of one squadron of armed men we could bring the people from Lempach to Stein," I replied, as he stood looking at me expectantly. "And you don't need to lose a single man."

For a moment he stared at me in bewilderment, then laughed out loud. "And you say you want to be a painter? There's no sign of it. You talk as if you'd been five years with the dragoons!"

"Your honour, my mother is probably in Lempach."

He at once became serious again. "Good. You told me that before. If your mother, as we hope, has not been taken by the Tartars, she will either be in Purkersdorf or in Lempach, and there she will be in safety. What is important to us is that these places should hold out. In the first place, if they do so, the defenders will not lose their property; just imagine how much property refugees have brought into a place like Lempach!

They would lose all that if we brought them to Stein. Secondly, they are holding up enemy forces and disrupting Turkish transports. If I evacuate Lempach, then I'll have weakened my position—and you don't even have the assurance that your mother would really come with them. She might well be in Purkersdorf."

"Give me one good soldier, your honour, and three horses! I would ride back there with him and bring my mother here!"

"Have you been reading cloak-and-dagger romances, Andreas?"

"I went all alone from Vienna to Stein!"

He shrugged his shoulders and went back to his work desk. "If he's lucky," he answered after a long pause, "Count Alram has come through unharmed. And he's a brave, careful man with much experience. It would be a crime to let you go back to that area when it's swarming with Tartars already."

I followed him to the table and stood opposite him. "Will you not be sending a courier to Vienna, your honour? Count Starhemberg needs information from you, just as you need it from him!"

"I'm sending a courier. But not a young boy."

"I could show him the way!"

"As far as Lempach? He can find that without your help."

I was just going to say that I would willingly conduct him as far as Vienna, if only my mother could be brought from Lempach to Stein, but it occurred to me how difficult it had been for me to get from Währing to the Haspel woods and how much I owed to the Count in the way of help—and so I fell silent. Go once again through that hellish nightmare in the forest? Never again.

Count Leslie stared at his papers and tried to put them a little bit in order.

"Andreas," he said, in a calm, slow voice. "You are barely fifteen years old. At your age, it is natural to want to dare everything, to escape from a city without any knowledge of the situation or of the Turkish language, without weapons and without any kind of assistance—to escape from a city surrounded by over a hundred thousand Turkish soldiers. It was madness, but contrary to all expectations all went well. It would not be like that a second time. And that is why you're staying in Stein. My servant has found a family that will take you in and in whose house you can live until we have driven out the Turks and brought your mother back to you. I'm sending you a tailor who will fit you out with a new suit of clothes. And here is some pocket money to be going on with."

He laid three ducats on the table. "Laurenz will take you to your new home; I shall be responsible for you from now on."

He held out his hand and nodded. We shook hands. Then he rang the bell. The manservant appeared and took me away with him.

The audience was at an end.

28

With measured paces we proceeded along the corridor. I was given back my hat and my knapsack, and then, still walking with ponderous deliberation, we went to the stableyard attached to the mansion's farm-house, took our places in a carriage, and set off for Stein.

We stopped outside an old-fashioned, cumbrously built house, went through the entrance hall into the parlour, and there were greeted by a red-cheeked serving girl, who on my companion's request called the lady of the house. She took me under her wing, Laurenz gravely withdrew, and the first thing I had to do was take a bath in a tub of warm water, after which I was left alone in my room.

This room contained a neatly made bed with sheets white as the driven snow and a table with a pure white tablecloth, set in a window with bright blue curtains in which one could still see the folds they had lain in in the press; there was a crucifix in the corner, a picture of the Madonna over the bed, a picture of St. Augustine and St. Monica over the table, and a picture of St. Crispin, the patron saint of shoemakers and tanners, over the door.

I wanted to sit on the bed, but it looked too spotlessly clean. The seat of the chair had been freshly polished; I pondered a moment, then decided to venture to sit upon its edge. I stared up at St. Crispin and thought of the old saying: Crispin made shoes for the poor and stole the leather to sole them with. It wasn't much help to me. Crispin had obviously also been well scoured.

There was no real reason why I should go to Lempach, for it was uncertain whether my mother was there or not. But there was no real reason for me to stay in Stein in this frighteningly spick-and-span room. It was truly a very fine room, much too fine to be soiled by human contact. I made up my mind to get away from it as soon as possible.

The master of the house was called Leonhard Stubenvoll and was a tanner. As he carried on his trade in the yard and in the two adjoining sheds, the whole neighbourhood stank of carcasses and tanbark. The smell had in a way an almost home-like aroma for me because it was not a clean smell. But Herr Stubenvoll was not the sort of person who made me feel at home. He had a gigantic stomach, ten sparse hairs on his bald, greasy pate, and not many more scattered about his upper lip and double chin; his eyes stood out so far that they could have been snipped off with shears. His wife was at least as fat as he was, so that I began to wonder why they had not had double doors built into the house; it would have made exits and entrances so much easier for the enormous couple.

Besides these two, there were five daughters from nine to fifteen years of age. They all had long, thick white-blonde pigtails and their father's blue, protruding eyes, and they all constantly sniffed and snuffled, although we were now in the middle of summer. At supper they all sat demurely together, stared down at their plates, and uttered never a word. From time to time one of them would sneeze.

"You must tell us all your adventures," said Herr Stubenvoll, and made the sort of long face Father Josephus puts on in the seminary when he tells us that we are all brothers in Christ, even though he has just given us a thousand lines to write that have made our fingers sore from the pen.

I was not much in the mood to tell anything to those two great fatties and their snuffling daughters, but I didn't want to appear impolite and so started with my escape from Vienna. When I mentioned that I had stuck my knife into a dead tree-trunk, Herr Stubenvoll waved his hand in disgust. "We'd rather not hear about that—it might have been a man."

"Of course!" I explained eagerly. "That's why I struck! I wouldn't go and stab a dead tree just for the fun of it. . . ."

"That's quite enough!" cried Stubenvoll. "It's too horrible." And he discreetly pointed to his five daughters, who were sitting with heads bowed low over their soup plates, snuffling all the time, so that it was difficult to tell whether they were drinking their soup or sniffing it up their noses.

I continued my tale, but he interrupted the account of the first Tartar attack, in which one of the Tartars was shot, at the point where I said that the Count raised his pistol to fire.

"We don't like that sort of thing in this house. We are a decent, God-fearing family and never talk about such unpleasantnesses."

I felt my anger rising. "But it's war, sir!" I cried.

"Yes, unfortunately. But war is a brutalising horror; that is for soldiers, not for the ears of my wife and daughters."

I secretly agreed with him about the brutality and horror of war, but I felt compelled to go on. "If you had been in Baaden or Mödling, sir, you couldn't have helped becoming involved in it. Your daughters, too."

"But I don't live in Baaden," he retorted in a self-satisfied way, as if it were some great virtue that was his alone, as if all the people who were unfortunate enough to live in Baaden were criminals who had to bear the consequences of their folly in living in such a place. "If you have nothing to tell us but these horrors and miseries. . . ." He shrugged his shoulders apologetically.

The remainder of the evening passed somewhat silently, but the next morning, as I was about to go downstairs, the eldest of the five daughters stopped me on the second step, pulled me into the girls' bedroom, where all the others were waiting, and begged me to tell my story in full.

"Tell us about all the murders!"

"We want to hear about blood and terrible wounds!"

"Lots of blood! And *gore!*"

"Did they torture you?"

"What did they do to you?"

They were all sniffling with excitement, and their eyes were popping out even farther than usual, a thing I should hardly have deemed possible before.

"From Hadersdorf to Lempach we marched arm in arm, singing at the tops of our voices," I replied. "Very decent and proper songs, of course, with no bad words. Once the Count happened to tread on a beetle and at once made a solemn vow that he would go on a pilgrimage to Rome to atone for the crime, although it had occurred by the purest accident. But outside Lempach, when a kindly Tartar asked him if he would come to Constantinople with him, he accepted the invitation because he didn't like to refuse a fellow human being's cordial offer. He's getting along famously, as are the Tartars and the

147

Turks. I am getting on fine, too; to-morrow will be a lovely day and the next day will be even lovelier. We work and sing, we sing and work, and as long as we don't kick the bucket, we'll all live to be a thousand, so that we can go on singing for the rest of our born days."

Thereupon I turned on my heels, fled from the room, and slammed the door behind me.

In the forenoon I bought provisions and a field bottle; in the afternoon I had my measurements taken by the tailor and then went to a quarry outside the village, where I shot my pistol three times so that I at least knew how to do it. Unfortunately, I did not hit anything. The kick was terrific. I shut my eyes tight every time I pressed the trigger, and the bullets flew every which way—anywhere but to the target.

I knew that it got light in the mornings about four, and I knew that the best time to start would be before the break of day. Then, by the time it was light, I would have before me the least dangerous stretch of road and would therefore be able to pass through Tartar-occupied regions during the hours of darkness. The only question was how I should arrange to wake up at the right time, and as I could think of no other means but a crowing cock, in the evening, when everyone in the house had gone to bed, I crept into the henhouse and laid myself down right in front of the little door to the run. It did indeed smell rather bad, but it was no worse than the putrid odour of Mr. Stubenvoll's hides.

My plan was successful. Well before dawn, the old cock with his long, sharp claws climbed upon my recumbent form, and when he began to crow, I cautiously opened the little door. It squeaked, so I left it open. While I crept across the yard, I heard above me a soft hissing.

I looked up. At a window in the first story appeared five bright patches: the faces of the Stubenvoll girls.

"Good luck!" one of them whispered.

"Come safe home!" hissed another.

"Farewell!" sniffed the other three.

I waved to them. They waved back.

Then I clambered over the fence and set off again on my travels.

29

I had not given a thought to the obvious fact that the bridges would be guarded. Dawn was already breaking when I reached them. The Danube was grey, the banks were grey, and the two soldiers on duty there were grey. Mist hung over the farther bank.

The soldiers were standing in the middle of the bridge. Each of them had built up a pile of stones, and with these they were trying to hit an old pewter pot, which they had set up on a post. They did not discontinue this occupation but simply asked me: "Where are you off to, lad?"

"Herzogenburg."

"There may be Tartars there. The villagers have closed all the gates. They won't let you in."

"They know me. I came from there."

"And why did you come away?"

"To find medicine—for my sick mother."

"Medicine? Haven't you got an apothecary in Herzogenburg?"

"He is himself severely ill."

Just then the other soldier hit the pot. "Did you see that?" he shouted to his fellow guard. "And with the left hand, too!"

"Stop that while I'm talking to the lad," the other retorted angrily, turning to me. "Show me the medicine!"

I opened my knapsack, drew the water bottle out, and gave it to the soldier.

"Hasn't got much smell," he said after sniffing at it.

"And it tastes just like water," I replied.

The other guard hit the pot again. "That makes two!" he cried.

"And you're going miles for this?" the other guard said to me. "If it were at least wine! Watch you don't get caught!"

With that he let me pass and made haste to catch up with his comrade's score. While I hurried over the bridge, I heard the pot ring three times behind me and the soldiers' triumphant laughter.

On the other bank two other guards held me up; I told them the same story, and then I was allowed to go on. Meanwhile, it had become broad daylight. In the east the sun hung like a gigantic red ball of fire in dark-blue clouds, and before me lay long scarves of white mist over the meadows. After an hour the road began to climb. I went past Göttweig Monastery, and soon after that I began to go downhill again. When I reached the plain, I took my first breather and had some breakfast. At Kölbling I found the very place where I had slept on my way to Stein and rested there for a second time. About midday I saw Herzogenburg, crossed the Traisen, and went on by way of Etzersdorf to Kapelln, without meeting a single person. It was as if I were walking all alone through the world, alone across hills and fields, wandering from empty villages to burnt-out manor houses, all alone in the warm sun and in a dreamlike atmosphere of peace. But to the south of Kapelln, smoke was rising; that must be Rassing, and if it was on fire, then the sense of peace I felt was an illusion, and Count Leslie would doubtless have called it criminal negligence to be making my way so carelessly, in broad daylight, through a region occupied by Tartars. Nevertheless, I strolled on, listening to the larks and singing myself from time to time.

When I came to Thalheim, I had already been on my way for at least ten hours, and though I had not been walking all the time, I was feeling very tired. As I would have to regain my strength by nightfall in order to cover the last stretch of the way to Raipoltenbach, I decided to rest for a couple of hours and turned off after Thalheim—not to the left towards Gunnersdorf but straight on towards the Haspel woods, where I knew there lay a small hamlet close enough to the woods so that I could escape into their cover if necessary. After only half an hour's walk, I could see the five little houses before me; they were thickly overgrown with ivy and lay in a pretty little garden. I shoved open the gate in the low lattice fence and walked through the cottage flowers to a well with a thick, round stone wall about its edge. There, under a quince tree, I sat down and opened my knapsack.

While I was eating, I heard footsteps all at once, jumped up, and was about to run when I saw that it was no Tartar but a Christian coming up to me. He must have been as old as the hills; at least he looked that way, with his long white hair and beard. His back was humped, and he helped himself along with the shaft of an old spade.

"Don't get up!" he called from afar. "You need have no fear; I won't do anything to you."

When he stood before me, he said: "I am glad to see a Christian once again. Keep on eating. If you'd like a raw turnip, you may have one."

I shook my head. He sighed and painfully, with the help of his stick, lowered himself to the ground. I, too, sat down again.

"Turnips is healthy grub, my grandmother always told me, and all my life long I've eaten turnips—raw, naturally. My grandmother lived to be over ninety, and I am eighty-two. . . ."

I explained to him why I wanted to return to either Raipoltenbach or Lempach, and he nodded.

"In any case, you're not all that safe here," I added. "Everybody's run away, and here you are sitting all alone in your house surrounded by Tartars."

He laughed. "Tartars! When I was a youngster like you, I kept thirty of them at bay single-handed with my broadsword . . . sent the lot o' them flying, I did. I can't do that sort of thing now. I'm not up to it, you know. But all the same I won't run away from the devils. It's not a question of sword and dagger. God helps them as helps themselves. Obey His will. Nobody can do more than that."

"Did you fight against the Turks?"

"Against the Turks and the Tartars. Against the French and the Swedes. Against the Protestants from Germany and Bohemia. I was a general in a war that lasted thirty years. And I won my battles more often than I lost them, which very few generals can say. The Emperor thanked me personally, made me a baron, and gave me lands. My name was famous throughout all Germany, and children still learn about me to-day in school. But what's the use of all that? You can't build things with wars and cannon and swords and gunpowder. We go on destroying, destroying people and people's work—the labour of centuries gone in a night. The only real joy is in building up. In Steiermark there's a castle—it belongs to me, for I presented it to one of my sons these thirty years ago. The house here I built myself, with my own hands. I am very proud of it, and I like the place."

I didn't know what to answer. The old man was not looking at me but at his ivy-covered house, the trees, the bushes, and the flowers in his garden. On the spade shaft lay his old blue-veined hand—a hand that once had held sword and pistol. Suddenly it let the stick fall, rose, and pointed rather tremblingly at a tree. "I planted that twenty years ago. I planted everything on this plot of ground. I am contented here. My children and grandchildren and great-grandchildren are somewhere abroad in the world; over there, that's my wife's grave.

152

I'm not going to leave that grave and my flowers for a few dirty old Tartars. Let them kill me. My wife's waiting here, in this garden, for me to join her."

As I had finished my meal, he led me through the garden, where he named the names of even the tiniest weeds as if they had been pets or human friends. He took me through the house and showed me furniture he had carpentered and carved himself. He said not a word about the Thirty Years' War but spoke a lot about flowers, buds, and fruit. And as I was leaving, he gave me a carnation and a turnip.

"God see you safe to your mother, young man," he said, shaking my hand. "And if one day you're thinking of conquering other people's kingdoms, remember what an old man told you he had learned in his long life: it's better to have a garden of your own than all the kingdoms in the world."

30

Again I went through the Haspel woods by night. No ghost appeared, no evil spirit tripped me up, no demon pinched me with red-hot tongs, and no former murderer's phantom uplifted bloodstained hands—I saw nothing of what the tales had warned me. It was not yet midnight when I reached the edge of the wood and gazed through the tree-trunks down into the hollow where the moated village of Raipoltenbach lay as I had left it.

It had not been burned to the ground and was not besieged.

As I ran down the slope toward it, I noticed that the gates were open. A man was coming out of a barn with a sack on his shoulders; he strode through the barbican, crossed the bridge, and vanished into the house. I ran after him, but when

I reached the inner courtyard, I couldn't see where he had gone. I turned about and saw a light in the gateway arch of the barbican. Another man, carrying a torch in his left hand, was just shutting the gate and putting the crossbeam in place.

"Is Frau Thanradl in the house?" I asked, going up to him.

Slowly he turned around and held the torch high in order to see me better. When he saw who I was, he nodded and said: "So the young master has come home. Welcome to the castle of your ancestors."

A smile spread over his face, which was without ears and nose.

31

I thought I was going to faint, for all the blood suddenly left my face and seemed to concentrate around my heart, making it almost impossible for me to draw breath. This petrified state lasted a few minutes; time seemed to stand still quite interminably, and the world congealed into a hideous, changeless picture of horror. Only when Kaspar Fetz made his first movement and began coming toward me did I awake from my rigid nightmare of fright. I turned on my heels and fled to the big house, the door of which I rattled in vain, unable to make it open.

Kaspar Fetz was coming up behind me.

What should I do, I thought in despair. He's between me and the barbican. I can't get out of the fortress, and even if I managed to swerve past him, I couldn't lift the massive crossbeam quickly enough from its supports—I wouldn't be able to get the great gate open quickly enough!

Then I remembered my pocket pistol, but it was in my knapsack. Try to think of something, Andreas! Something to give you a little more time to escape!

I ran to the right around the big house to the south-western corner tower, tugged off my knapsack as I ran, and took out my pistol, which, thank heavens, was loaded. When my pursuer turned around the corner of the big house, I fled to the south-eastern corner, waited a while until he was almost upon me, and then dashed to the left around the house back to the main entrance. There I took my stand and cocked the pistol.

"Stay where you are, Herr Fetz!" I called sharply. "Stay where you are or I'll shoot!"

Despite the darkness he at once saw the weapon in my hand and obeyed. "Would the young gent be feeling unfriendly toward old Fetz?" he replied, grinning. "I bid him a right good welcome, and he draws a firearm on me!"

"You see, I know your name and know what I have to expect from you. Open the gate at once!"

He shook his head slowly. "The size of it! The young people these days! You can't do anything with them—they're so wild after their bit of pride and power! Really the young gent, aren't you?"

"Come on or I'll fire!"

"No, my young sir—that you won't do. I'm a kind of folk hero, you know; people tell all manner of tales about my exploits. You can't do that to the Austrian people—the celebrated Kaspar Fetz shot down by a fourteen-year-old boy! No, young gentleman, that would never do!"

"I don't give a snap of the fingers for the tales about you. Do as I say and open that gate!"

With these words I stepped to one side and pointed across the bridge and the inner yard of the barbican to the outer gate. Fetz came a step closer, then stopped again and shook his head with the same pitying slowness.

"This is not the way to do things, young gent," he complained, grinning. "If I obey you, I'll come too close to you; but if I come too close to you, all I need do is make a little movement with my hand and that pretty little pistol's in my possession. If I may give you a word of advice, old son, the thing to do would be to go over to the barbican yourself, threatening me with your pistol if I try to come nearer, thus keeping me away from the bridge; then you goes and lifts the crossbeam, still keeping an eye on the bridge and all. That's the way to do it, young gent. Asking me to go and open the gate—that's the command of an amateur, a beginner, because you'll be in a rather embarrassing position if I don't do it."

"I'll shoot."

"That won't open the gate for you."

His jovial calm under the threat of my pistol did indeed embarrass me, and although at first I didn't want to follow his advice because obviously there was some trick he had in mind, I finally gave in and went across the bridge to the barbican. He walked to the main entrance to the big house and watched me.

"Keep out of sight!" I yelled.

"But I'm very curious to see how you go about it, young gent," he said. "And besides, I did not advise you to send me out of your sight but simply to forbid me to cross the bridge. Well, I'm not crossing the bridge, am I?"

The absurdity of my position now became very clear to me, and it made me angry. "D'you think you can get the better of me?" I shouted in my rage. "I don't want you to watch me. Go away!"

"What kind of stories then have you heard about me?"

"Go away!"

"Would it have been the one about my escape from the prison, just before they were going to string me up? Or the one about the horses belonging to the Pasha of Esseg? That was a nice episode, too, the one with the five janizaries. Well now, just think a minute: every time my opponents were more than two or three and better than one feebly armed boy. Do you really think, young gent, that I'm afraid of that ridiculous toy in the hands of a whippersnapper like yourself?"

His voice had suddenly turned sharp and nasty.

"You think I wouldn't dare to shoot. You're wrong. I'll count up to three."

"One!" he cried mockingly.

"Two!" I yelled desperately.

"Three!" he shouted defiantly.

At that instant a mighty hand seized my arm and turned it aside; another hand gripped my wrist and forced me to give up the pistol. I felt my whole body held by two strong arms that bound me tight so that I could not escape.

"Very good, Viereckl," said Kaspar Fetz, and came up to me. "We'll put him up in the tower. We'll see to-morrow what to do with him."

"This is the lad who told us about you in Vienna," the strong-armed man behind me growled. "Best thing would be to twist his neck and finish him off."

"I want no more blood spilt than necessary. He can't do us any harm here; in fact, he may be of help. It's easy to kill, but to bring to life is a miracle."

Without another word the man lifted me up. Although I struggled and threshed about with my arms and legs, he carried me as easily as a young tom-cat up to the first floor, where there were a number of men sitting under a lamp; he thrust past them, climbed a ladder, and laid me on bare boards under the roof.

"You stay here," he grunted. "If you so much as put one foot on that ladder, it'll be the end of you."

With that he turned and clattered down the ladder. I now knew who he was: it was that stubble-bearded fellow with the leather jacket whom I had seen in the Winged Bell and about whom Michel had told me, saying he was Kaspar Fetz's treasurer. And I knew something else: on the lower floor I had seen by the light of the lamp the dwarf with the night-cap and the hatchet-nosed Shiftyface, respectively the secretary and the second-in-command.

Raipoltenbach was in the hands of Kaspar Fetz and his gang of thieves!

No one willingly loses all self-respect, but one does so very easily when one is carried up a ladder with as much ceremony as a plucked goose. I raged inwardly at my humiliation, but I began to wonder how I could get away despite all those threats and tried to reconstruct in my mind a plan of the fortress.

The ground plan was almost quadratic, except that the north and south walls were a little longer than the other two. The reason it was not completely square was that the big house itself formed a long rectangle. It stood in the middle of the fortress and had three stories, a high-gabled roof with three attic windows on its longer side, and an entrance to the north. Around it lay the courtyard, which was surrounded by a six-foot wall with wooden defence platforms and four round, solid corner towers. These corner towers each had two stories, the upper one overhanging and covered with a pointed tiled roof. Outside the walls ran the broad moat.

In the middle of the north wall, opposite the entrance to the big house, was the main gate, and in front of this was a bridge, which in earlier times could be drawn up but which for the last hundred years had been firmly mortared into the outerworks of the barbican itself.

The barbican was said to be the oldest part of the fortress, and its two squat one-storied round towers were built so close together that there was only room for the outer gate between them. At the back, these towers were not rounded but were joined by a boxlike structure that rose out of the water of the moat, though the towers themselves stood on the dry land beyond it. They too, had pointed tiled roofs to which the gable roof of the boxlike portion was linked. If one looked at

158

the fortress either from the front or the side, one immediately realized that not only the big house but also the barbican would offer the strongest resistance to any attacker.

There were three gates, all facing in the same direction: the outer gate and the inner gate of the barbican and, behind the bridge, the main gate in the wall of the fortress. The outer and inner gates were connected by a passageway from which two doors, to right and left, led to two storerooms. In the left-hand storeroom was a wide stairway to the first story, which extended in the form of a single room over the towers and the additional boxlike structure behind, as well as forward over the outer gate, where there was a slit in the wall for pouring down boiling pitch and another slit for shooting.

The corner towers had always served only for defence; perhaps in earlier days there had been bows and arrows, crossbows, buckets for molten tar, and other war materials stored in them, perhaps even doss-downs for the guards when they were relieved. But for a long time now they had stood empty.

In the big house there were the cellars and storerooms in the basement; on the ground floor my mother and the steward and his family had lived, while the first and second floors were reserved for the use of the gentry whenever Count or Countess Palffy wanted to spend the night here. The servants could be accommodated in the third floor, and in the attics under the roof there was all sorts of old junk that I liked to play with during the holidays. For years now the barbican had only been used as a storehouse for the steward's private possessions, but in the top story there were still cannon-balls, rusty halberds, and a few old helmets—useless and worthless rubbish that had been shoved up there just to get them out of sight.

A wooden draining system supplied the fortress with drinking water from the Langenberg hills; there was one outlet in the barbican and one in the big house. The well in the yard produced only brackish bog-water now and for a long time had not been used.

That was how Raipoltenbach looked that night as I lay under the conical roof of the left-hand tower of the barbican and racked my brains to think of how I could escape from the situation in which I had so shortsightedly landed myself.

32

The conversation of the robbers in the room below me had been getting louder and louder, and suddenly Kaspar Fetz's voice broke into my musings, angrily roaring for silence.

"Mutiny, would you?" he yelled. "Who was it spied out the nicest titbits for you? Who was it got you so much booty that each of you can live for a couple of years like lords? Who was it found the cannon and the four muskets at Unterthurn? Who was it what brought the powder from Murstetten? You're not petty thieves now, but you would still be if you hadn't had me!"

"Don't work yourself up!" the second-in-command answered. "We only want to know what sense there is in lying here in this filthy hole of a place and not even a drop of wine to drink!"

"Wine! Wine! Do you perhaps want to run through the Tartars' lines with your money and booty? We must wait here until either Vienna is delivered and the Turks give up and withdraw or until Vienna's taken and the Turks move on to Linz. This is a good fortress. We're safe here. As soon as we set foot outside, we'll be snapped up by the very first lot of Tartars as comes along."

"All right then, we'll stay here. But we want the wine from the big house."

"I'll get it for you soon. When the lads over there are hungry enough, they'll trade their wine against our bread."

"We should set fire to the place!" the treasurer cried out wildly.

"Shut your mouth, Viereckl! You've got one good eye, but there's straw in that head of yours. Set fire to one's own fortress!"

"Why not? The house isn't any good! And we ought to freeze the marrows of all those in this fortress who don't belong with us!"

"Freeze their marrows!" the chief said mockingly. "Freeze their marrows! Freeze their marrows—that's about as far as your intelligence reaches."

"Then tell us what use the kid upstairs is?"

"What good would he be if he were dead?"

"Then he'd not be able to betray anything. I'm a bleeding nun if that lad didn't betray us to the city watch in Vienna! If we hadn't hopped it good and quick, we'd be sitting under lock and key to-day!"

"So you're afraid of a fourteen-year-old boy?"

Perhaps the other was going to reply, but the second-in-command broke in and said: "Enough of that, Viereckl. It was our own fault that we didn't twist the little varmint's neck in Vienna. For the moment, let him live; if we have to go, he'll certainly not stay here alive—I know the chief too well for that. All I want to know is, why we don't go and fetch the wine!"

"You're looking for a hole in your belly," Kaspar Fetz replied. Then in a different voice he asked: "Who's that groaning all the time?"

I, too, had been struck by the groans that had been heard from time to time during the foregoing talk and now had become so loud that I could hardly hear what Kaspar Fetz was saying.

"It's Schainckherl," somebody said in a voice I didn't recognize. "He's snuffing it."

The sounds from below indicated that the robbers went to stand around the dying man, asking each other what they should do. Again and again there was mention of a doctor, and I couldn't think where at this time and in this place they were likely to find a doctor, but finally one of them went downstairs and came back with someone a few minutes later. In the meanwhile, I had crawled cautiously to the hole in the floor so that I saw the new arrival plainly when he entered the circle of lamplight. It was no other than Doctor Voytt, and he seemed rather reluctant to try his arts on the sick man.

"You keep me prisoner in a tower, lying on wet earth," he protested. "How can you expect me to give you any help?"

The second-in-command pulled a knife out of his belt and set the blade across the doctor's throat. "How?" he repeated scornfully. "Here's how!"

It was a remarkable picture I saw from my peep-hole. The sick man lay on the floor; beside him stood the dwarf with the lamp, next to him the doctor, the second-in-command, Viereckl, and Fetz; and around these other faces formed a circle.

The doctor squinted at the knife laid along his throat.

"Take that dirty instrument away," he said somewhat hoarsely.

Kaspar Fetz nodded, and Shiftyface lowered the knife.

"If you please!" Fetz said in friendly tones, pointing to the sick man.

The doctor kneeled down, examined the man, felt his pulse, and stood up again. "Overeating," he said brusquely. "Let him go two days without food, and he'll recover. Now why must I lie on damp earth in the tower? I'm not used to it, and I'm not as young as I was."

The robbers were silent.

"It might so happen that the Tartars pay you a visit," he

162

went on. "It might so happen that one of you gets an arrow in his chest. It might so happen that you would require my services again?"

Kaspar Fetz thought for a while. Then he put his head on one side and laughed. "If the big house will give us a barrel of wine, you may go in there and sleep on a bed."

"Then let me speak to the people in the big house."

At that moment I was unable to restrain myself any longer. I leaned forward and called: "Herr Doctor, if my mother is in the big house, tell her to send out a second barrel of wine so that I can be taken in, too! I'm Andreas! They want to kill me!"

They all looked up at me; Viereckl foamed at the mouth with rage and was about to run up the ladder, but Kaspar Fetz held him back with a movement of the hand.

"Your mother is not inside, young gent," he said, grinning. "If she were, she'd have had to give me not just one barrel for you but the entire cellar. But you can try your luck, Doctor. Come with me."

He seized the doctor by the arm and dragged him down the stairs with him. Barely was he out of sight when Viereckl began to run up the ladder. Terrified, I started back and tried feverishly to think what I should do to run away from him; but then I heard the voice of the second-in-command, who was obviously keeping Viereckl from climbing the ladder.

"Stay down here," he growled.

"I'll split that young tinker's head wide open!" Viereckl shouted.

"You will not. The chief's right. A dead boy's no use at all. But if he's alive, we can do business with him."

Viereckl grumbled and complained a little longer, but he did not come up to me.

33

Probably the groaning lasted a little longer, probably the robbers went on talking, but I must have immediately fallen asleep out of sheer exhaustion. After all, I had been on my way since before five o'clock that morning, had put many miles behind me, and on my arrival had been treated to not a few surprises. Though I was anxious to know what the doctor would do for me, I could no longer keep awake, and when I opened my eyes again, the sun was twinkling through the gaps between the tiles, and I could hear someone playing the fife outside.

The melody he was playing was one I knew only too well: it was the saraband from the suite by Froberger.

At once I was on my feet, dashed to the tiny window in the roof, and tried to discover where the sounds were coming from. I could see no one. When I went to the opening in the floor and looked down, I saw at the foot of the ladder the dwarf with the night-cap, who had probably had his attention drawn by my footsteps and was now looking up at me ill-humouredly. Confident of my superior agility and strength, I might have had a set-to with him; I could have taken him on alone but not with the knife he was holding in his hand. So I abandoned the opening, set myself at the window in the roof, and yelled as loud as I could: "Count! Count! Count!"

"Hold your noise," the dwarf below snarled at me. I paid him not the slightest attention.

In the big house there appeared a figure at the window over the main door; it was really Count Alram, and behind him I could make out the burly shape of Michel!

"Andreas!" they both shouted.

"I want to be with you!"

"Be patient; we'll fetch you!" Michel yelled back.

At that moment someone seized me from behind by the shoulder and spun me around. It was, of course, the dwarf, and of course he put his knife against my chest, but my recently acquired knowledge that the Count was really inside the fortress made me feel so carefree that I gave the fellow a good hard kick in the shins, shoved him aside, and ran to the window again.

"Help! Help!" the dwarf shrieked. He was lying on the floor and had lost his night-cap. His head was completely bald and shone like a freshly shelled hard-boiled egg.

I clambered down the ladder, ran down the stairs, and was in the passageway before I encountered anyone. The crossbeam was still in place on the massive outer gate, but I no longer wanted to escape; I wanted to get into the big house, and so I ran into the courtyard and straight into the arms of the second-in-command.

"Stop, you dirty little spy!" he said, and gave me a punch over the ear. He twisted my arm behind my back and kept on twisting until I cried out with pain.

"Leave the lad alone!" someone shouted. I recognized Michel's voice, turned my head, and saw him standing at the open door of the big house with a naked sword in his hand. But as he stepped forward into the courtyard, the robbers who had hurried up from left and right formed a circle around me, and Kaspar Fetz jumped up with a long sword in his hand.

The second-in-command's grip had relaxed a little. I was no longer preoccupied with my own pain and felt only great pleasure at the thought of the punishment the chief would receive at the hands of Michel. Unfortunately, the fight started off not at all as I had imagined it.

Kaspar Fetz attacked with deceptive swiftness, danced lightly to the right and then to the left, parried every thrust his opponent made, kept going in to the attack, and finally drove Michel back into the big house. Fetz remained standing with

165

lowered sword about two yards in front of the door; he was panting a little but he succeeded in keeping his voice level and in speaking as if it had all been a joke.

"So you know the boy," he said. "You wouldn't like to watch us lame him a little, now would you. You don't like to hear him yelling for help. You were given the doctor in exchange for a barrel of wine and my fife—which I am still waiting for by the way. You can have the boy for the rest of the wine in the cellar. Roll the barrels out and we'll send him in to you."

A hand seized Michel by the shoulder and pulled him into the house. The Count was now standing on the threshold.

"You are mistaken," he replied. "I did not exchange a barrel of wine for the doctor, for I don't do any kind of business with gallows' birds like you. It was expressly agreed that as you had the doctor in your hands, we might deliver you—if it so pleased us—a barrel of wine. It did so please us. Now it pleases us no longer. Give us that boy or I'll skin you alive!"

"Don't talk so big!" Fetz said mockingly, but at once he became somewhat more courteous, bowed, and thereupon turned to his second-in-command. "Let's hear the lad give us a song, Clauss! His honour says he'll have our hide—we'd like to put him in the mood for it!"

The next instant I thought my arm would break; I cried out and the Count whipped his sword from its sheath.

Then something happened that for a second filled even me with horror. Michel was hanging on to the Count's belt. All at once there was heard the strangest rattling, snoring sound; between the two figures in the door of the big house there appeared a strange, squat shape that hopped, in a most sinister way, up to the robbers. This weird creature was a gigantic frog more than a foot in height; its powerful eyes were rolling in its revolting and terrifying head, and again and again it opened its mouth in movements so uncanny and fearsome that I was not surprised when the robbers fled back over the bridge into the barbican. The second-in-command let me go, and even Kaspar Fetz turned pale at the daunting sight. He stood irresolute for a while; then he, too, turned and fled.

After the first second of surprise, I had at once recognized the Iron Frog, which my father had built and which my mother must have stored away somewhere in the house. I knew that it was only a harmless automaton and so profited at once by the opportunity to run past the snarling, snorting, quaking monster into the house. At the same moment Father Lukas ran out and disappeared around the corner.

In the meantime, the frog had reached the bridge and was solemnly hopping across. The robbers had disappeared into the barbican, but Kaspar Fetz remained standing by the inner gate. I could see distinctly how the sword trembled in his hand and with what difficulty he fought down his fear. With distended, fixed eyes he watched the frog's advance, watched it hop past him, saw how the automaton jumped witlessly against the door at the end of the passage, fell back, jumped again, and finally rolled over on its side, lying helpless with jerking legs.

Now Fetz began to give a choking laugh. "Hah!" he gasped. "Hah, hah—the ghost! Hah! Just look at it, men! There's your ghost for you!"

He ran up to the frog and kicked it over. Shiftyface peeped through the storeroom door; behind him gaped Viereckl, and then the rest of them ventured outside again.

"You've been running away from a pile of old scrap iron!" Fetz laughingly mocked them.

In his triumph he had forgotten us, and that was well, for Father Lukas now reappeared with two men whom he had freed from the corner tower and led them into the big house.

"A barrel lasts quite a long time!" the Count shouted to the robbers. "When you've finished it, you may come and ask me for another. Perhaps we may see fit to grant your request!"

Fetz turned around. His eyes had gone very small. Then he

laughed evilly. "You've got the whip hand this time," he snarled. "But now there are not just three of you. There are seven. Not much bread for seven men. You'll be coming begging on your knees for bread. Perhaps I may see fit to grant your request. Perhaps not! Perhaps I'll just leave you to rot!"

The Count put back his sword in its sheath. "Let's go in," he said to Michel. "The matter's finished, and the fellow's too vulgar for a decent conversation." In the door he stood for a moment but did not turn around; instead he called over his shoulder: "Oh, yes, your fife! My man will throw it from the window to you—we are pleased to grant you this. Even your fife's a bad one."

34

Michel locked the big doors, laid the crossbeam in its iron sockets, and then pushed a massive wooden chest that had been in the steward's rooms against it. While we were going up to the first floor, the Count asked me: "Where is my satchel?"

"In Stein, your honour," I replied. "With Count Leslie."

He stopped in the middle of the flight of stairs and stared at me. "You mean you got the message through to Stein and delivered it to the right person?"

"Yes, your honour."

He shook his head, went on up the stairs without a word, and when we reached the top, strode along in front of Michel and me into the great corner room where the doctor, Father Lukas, and the two men who had just been released from the corner tower were waiting. One of them was our blacksmith Mangg, the other a certain Hans Althammer, a farmer from Inprugg whom I knew by sight.

After I had greeted them all, the Count drew me into the bay window, settled me in one of the uncomfortable Gothic chairs, sat down opposite me, and made me tell my whole story. He kept breaking in with questions; in particular, he wanted to know exactly what Count Leslie had said, and when I had finished, he heaved a sigh and declared: "You carried out your task faultlessly, and the Emperor can be well satisfied with what you have done for him. As for myself, I'd like to put you across my knees and give you a hearty thrashing."

I gazed at him in stupefaction. "Your honour," I stammered. "Y-your honour . . . but I . . . I thought I . . ."

He nodded curtly. "Yes, yes, I know. You were diligent and brave in the performance of your duty and you were successful. You were perfect; that's the most one can say. But have you stopped to think what your diligence and bravery and success signify for me? Didn't you overhear the conversation between me and the Chamberlain, Aichbichel, on the balcony of my house in Vienna? Don't you know why I undertook this mission? Don't you?"

"Yes, your honour."

"Why? Tell me that!"

"Because your honour wanted to have his regiment back and to be its colonel-in-chief once more."

"Exactly. I take on the commission; I make my way into the Tulln Valley. From there on everything should be plain sailing, but instead a fourteen-year-old boy takes over my commission in his perfectly sincere enthusiasm to help me, all because I fell from my horse and was unconscious for a few minutes. He it is who brings the message to Count Leslie; he it is who deserves the Emperor's thanks. But Count Alram, on the contrary, has lowered himself to the position of a mere courier . . . and all for nothing!"

"Your honour!" I cried in horror. "What else could I have done? There you were lying on the ground without sign of life, the priest was wounded, and Michel nowhere to be seen—

and on that very day you had ordered me to carry out the commission if you or Michel were unable to do so!"

Again he fetched a sigh. "I know. I'm not reproaching you. If you had been a little older, you obviously would have realised that Michel does not leave me in the lurch when we are attacked; you would have remembered that not long before we two had fought off a company of twenty Tartars. You would have realised that it was only because of the women that we fled into the woods, since we didn't want to expose them to a fight in open country. But you—and your youth is your only excuse—thought that the situation was hopeless."

"Your honour . . ."

"But of course we drove the Tartars off," the Count went on imperturbably. "And of course afterwards I was as furious as the devil to find that my satchel had vanished."

He stood up. "Well, never mind. It was just bad luck. I've had rather too much bad luck lately."

With these words he turned and left me alone. I sat there for a while feeling stupid, at a loss and desperately useless. Here I had thought I was doing the Emperor, the city of Vienna, and—not least—the Count himself a great service, and it turned out that I had harmed, not the first two indeed, but certainly the third, a man whom I wanted so much to convince that even someone who wants to be a painter can also be an out-and-out fighter.

When we've won the war, I'll go to Count Leslie and explain everything to him, I thought. He was such a gentle and friendly man, he would understand and speak to the Emperor and ask that Count Alram be given back his regiment.

Apparently Michel had noticed how downcast I was, for now he came over to me, sat down opposite me, and began to tell me what had happened after I had left them.

He had ridden into the wood with the maidservant but had halted behind the first trees to wait for the Count. He, too, had heard the Tartars gallop up, had dismounted, drawn his pistols, and thrown himself down behind a mound of earth while the maidservant sat on the hamper behind some bushes.

"The Tartars had no way of knowing how many of us there were in the wood," he said. "A few shots, that's all we fired, and they thought they were surrounded by an entire company."

He saw clearly what happened to the Count—how his horse caught a hoof in a hole in the ground and fell—and saw me bending over the Count's senseless form. Then all he could see were Tartars, took good aim, and with his first two shots brought down two of their leaders. The remainder halted, turned their horses, but did not ride far away; they stopped some way off and debated what they should do.

Meanwhile, the priest had succeeded in reviving the Count, and Michel had reloaded his two pistols. When the Tartars came on for the second attack, they were met by four shots, of which only one met its mark but which convinced them that the woods held more of the enemy than they cared to face, so that they did not renew their attack but turned and galloped away.

Then Father Lukas told Michel and the Count that I had made off with the latter's leather satchel. At first the Count refused to believe him, but in the end had to admit that the message had indeed disappeared and began to curse and swear at the top of his voice. All three of them shouted after me, and while the priest held the horses, the Count and Michel searched the surrounding woods but without finding any trace of me. I must have been running too hard to hear the shouts. I remembered hearing distant shouts, but in my excitement and distress I had attributed them to the Tartars and therefore had not thought of answering them or making my way toward them.

When the pair returned to Father Lukas, the two women were nowhere to be seen. Eleonore von Hauenstich had stopped screaming after the first shots rang out and had crept away silently on all fours into the wood, where she probably had found her maid and run farther away with her. Only the hamper stood there abandoned under a tree, and as neither the Count nor Michel had any use for women's finery, they just left it and rode on along the forest aisle down into Raipoltenbach.

They reached the moated fortress, found the gates open, trotted into the courtyard, dismounted, and tied up their horses at the iron bridle rings attached to the side of the big house. As there were no lights to be seen and they could find no one in the darkened rooms, they assumed that the fortress was deserted. The Count wanted to stay there because he was now without his satchel and was hoping that on my headlong flight I might have taken cover at Raipoltenbach. As they went back to the courtyard to unsaddle and water the horses, the fortress still lay silent and deserted in the moonlight, but the horses had disappeared.

Michel wanted to go and look for them, but the Count restrained him. "It's no use looking for them in the dark," he advised. "Who can have taken them? It must be either peasants or Tartars. Whoever it was, they're now over the hills and far away or else are lying here in hiding. If the former, you have no hope of overtaking the thieves; if the latter, you'll run straight into a trap. Our one hope is that Andreas will come here. We'll spend the night here and take turns in keeping watch."

They locked and barred the door and went up to the first floor. There was always one of them on the lookout at the window from which they commanded a good view of the bridge; but none of them noticed anything, except the Count, who had taken over the first watch and heard the barbican's outer gate being closed. The next morning there was Shiftyface standing in the courtyard; he said he was the commander of the fortress and ordered the three men to open the door of the house. The Count saw that this was a ruse but nevertheless opened the door; at once he was set upon by the five robbers who had been lying in wait on either side of the entrance, and he had the greatest difficulty in getting back into the house.

"Obviously they must have seen us coming," Michel ended his account. "They decided that they could make good use of our horses and therefore had opened the outer gates. We rode straight into a trap. In any case, they must have been in the steward's apartments not long before we arrived, for the lamp on the table was still warm, there was a big jug of wine and a lot of full and half-full glasses standing around it, and Kaspar Fetz's fife was lying on a chair."

He paused for a moment and then went on.

"The next morning they tried to kill us so that we should not be able to betray them. But they didn't succeed, and ever since then we've been sitting here in the big house, with them in the barbican. We shot at them twice but missed—they're too crafty. Twice we tried to break out but without success, for that Fetz fights like the devil himself, and that skinny one with the shifty face is not much better. They won't give up the fortress, and we can't get out. That's how it's been for the past four days."

"They intend to stay here until the Tartars withdraw," I told him. "Will our supplies last that long?"

"That long?" Michel echoed. "Father discovered the store-rooms in the basement. If the Tartars don't clear out of the country pretty soon, we'll all die of overeating."

35

I gathered that the robbers had not discovered this part of the cellars, for it did not lie next to the wine cellars but under a trap-door in the china closet; I further gathered that Father Lukas had remembered where it was, for on a previous visit my mother had conducted him over the entire house. And I knew why Michel had talked about dying of overeating, because this place was where the smoked hams and bacon and salted meat for the inhabitants of the entire fortress were kept.

There wasn't too much bread, and this was noticeable at the evening meal, at which everyone received four enormous slices of salted meat and a large piece of smoked ham but only two mouthfuls of bread. Naturally Michel, on the orders of the Count, had had to set the table in the most formal manner possible. We had damask table-cloths and napkins and silver dishes, used silver cutlery, and drank out of silver wine beakers. Old Althammer had at first refused to sit at such a sumptuously arrayed table and during the meal obviously felt ill at ease with all the silver, but the Count insisted that we all eat together, for here we were all soldiers in a besieged fortress. "We must share and share alike," he said, smiling. "For better as well as for worse; that must be our common motto here."

"I'm amazed that there should be any 'better' at all," the doctor answered. "Here we are with robbers in the place, and yet we're eating off silver platters."

"It's heavy to carry and not as valuable as gold," said the priest, who had now almost recovered from the wound on his arm, although he still wore a bandage under his clerical attire.

"As the Church certainly has possession of quite a pile of noble metals like gold and silver, you obviously know what you're talking about," the doctor answered somewhat sharply. "Anyhow, after those three weeks in the tower, I'm only too glad to have my share of the 'better' things of life. I must say, Count, that for your stay here you have picked the most civilised part of the fortress."

"Now there you're wrong," the Count retorted. "I did not choose this part and should never have done so if I'd had the choice. The really old and therefore good and civilised parts of this fortress are the walls, the corner towers, and above all the barbican. Obviously here, in the centre of the fortress, there was once some kind of dwelling house in the old style, but later they pulled it down and set up this elongated box of a place and covered the whole with tiles—a great folly, in my opinion, when you consider the danger of fire. A house is for living in; a fortress is for fighting in and can only secondly be thought of as a home. What's the use of eating off damask and silver when I could be shot dead in my chair through those great glass windows? I'd rather have loopholes and embrasures. No, Doctor, if I'd had my choice, I'd rather have been in the barbican!"

"If I had my choice, I'd rather be at home in my own bed," the doctor remarked somewhat sourly. "Unfortunately, that is no longer possible."

He then told us his story. He had been called out to visit a grievously sick patient in Johannesberg just before the arrival of the Tartars and had had to spend the night there. Towards morning the sick man had died, and when the doctor had wanted to start back home, he had been dissuaded because the Tartars had burned down Lempach and murdered the Franciscan monks who had stayed behind there; they were still, however, laying siege to the fortress. He at once made his way toward Raipoltenbach, where he ran straight into the robbers' arms and had been shut up by them in the tower, where the blacksmith was already imprisoned. Althammer, who had also sought refuge here, had run into the band two days later.

"There's a lot to be said for a good bed," said Michel. "But I once slept in one in Hungary in which a fire worshipper had been snatched away by a devil. After lying in it only half an hour, my body burned so that I felt as if I was a martyr at the stake. But the spirit of the fire worshipper sat on the end of the bed and wouldn't let me get up."

"That's all sheer imagination," the doctor retorted. "There are no such things as spirits and ghosts." He spoke quite testily.

The priest laughed. "One of the curious cases in which the Church and the medical profession are in agreement. But we can both be thankful, all the same, that the robbers were superstitious enough to take our Iron Frog for a phantom!"

At that moment we heard from the direction of the barbican the strains of the bagpipes and the fife and the stamping of boots on the floor, which I had heard before. The robbers were singing their song:

> "The raven croaks, the gallows creak,
> And blood down the steps runs black;
> When the wind blows over the waves, my lads,
> Your captain'll call you back."

We fell silent and listened. Then we stood up, walked across to the window, and gazed out into the night. The barbican lay like a solid block of black stone on the dark sky, but its loophole window slits blazed with golden light. "The raven croaks, the gallows creak . . ."

The song broke off, someone bawled out rough words, and then they all roared with laughter.

"We should have given them the wine earlier," the priest said quietly. "And not just one barrel, but three."

The Count nodded. "You're right, Father, I didn't think of that. But probably one barrel is enough for thirteen men. Let's wait an hour or two."

In order not to arouse suspicion with our own lights, we drew the curtains on the windows again. After midnight it got quieter over at the barbican, and we thought our best moment had arrived; but suddenly the racket broke out again, the bagpipes squealed, the fife shrilled, the stamping shook the boards, and again the song of the raven was bellowed through the night.

It was the same at two and also at three o'clock. Morning was beginning to break when we finally made ourselves ready. Michel pulled the chest back and opened the door. There in the grey light of the new day lay the courtyard; at the main gate was the guard whom the robbers had set there for the night. He was lying down and snoring loudly.

Cautiously we crept past him along the passageway of the barbican. Michel lifted the heavy beam from its slots.

Then we heard a thunderous noise. The ground shook under our feet, and the air itself seemed to shudder.

Uttering a soft curse, Michel dropped the beam back into place, and we all ran back to the big house. From the second floor we gazed out over the countryside.

At least a thousand Tartars were roaming the fields, about a hundred of them were galloping around the fortress, and all of them were swinging their sabres and brandishing their cross-bows and yelling as if they wanted to knock down our walls with the sheer force of their combined voices.

36

This hullabaloo would have awakened the dead, but for quite a while we saw nothing of our robbers. The Tartars whirled through the dairy and farm buildings, which obviously held nothing of interest for them; in the smithy they found the horses that had been taken from the doctor and the Count, and they roared with triumph when they found that the barns had still not been plundered. Then a number of them crept up to the main gate, tried to open it, in which attempt they were not successful, and withdrew, only to return soon after that with axes.

But if the robbers had still been sound asleep earlier on, now Kaspar Fetz had them well in hand again, for hardly had the Tartars reached the outer gate than we heard yelps of pain and saw them running away. Apparently they had been attacked by stones or halberds from the loopholes and so had suffered losses;

what had really happened we couldn't know because the barbican hid all the action from sight.

When the Count noticed that this encounter produced no further results, he left his place at the window and called us together. "They will attack us now," he said. "It is just possible that they might have withdrawn if they had found the fortress defended. They're not withdrawing, so they'll be attacking again soon. But their attempt will have no success, so they'll throw in firebrands, as is their custom. We must take protective measures against that." He turned around. "Are there any buckets?"

I nodded. "There are two in the kitchen. And there must be one in the steward's rooms."

"Good. Are there any empty barrels in the cellars?"

This question was directed at Michel and Michel replied in the affirmative.

"Then carry the barrels up to the roof and fill them with water, which you will carry up in the buckets. If the roof is set on fire, we must try to prevent it spreading by all the means at our disposal; we don't want the big crossbeams to start burning. The Father will stand at the water tap. Michel, the blacksmith, and Althammer will carry the buckets; the doctor will be up aloft to receive them. I shall stay here and keep the enemy under observation."

"And what shall I do?" I asked.

"You will give a hand wherever it's necessary."

He cast a glance out of the window, beckoned us to his side, and pointed down into the courtyard, where we noticed two robbers digging up the ground with rusty old spades. Others came with boxes and jars and carried the earth into the barbican.

"Yon Kaspar Fetz is a proper louse, but a louse with brains," the Count declared. "He's having soil taken up. Obviously he's going to stuff the roof of the barbican with it so that the beams and planks of the roof don't burn through. A good idea; I

178

only wish I could get out into the courtyard and do the same. Soil is better than water."

While the others went to their posts, I stayed beside the Count and watched the walls, the robbers, and the Tartars. I had been hoping that we'd soon have the gallows' birds under control and then set out on the road to Lempach to set my mother free; now we were not only the prisoners of Kaspar Fetz, but also prisoners of the Tartars, and when I thought of the vast number of men out in the fields, I couldn't possibly imagine that our situation would have a favourable outcome.

The Tartars had dismounted, tied up their horses in small groups, and were looking across the walls at us. All at once one of them stepped out of the crowd, approached the moat, and waved his cap at us.

"Hey, you there!" he shouted.

I watched Kaspar Fetz come out of the barbican, run along to the west wall, stumble up the steps of the defence platform, and peer over the breastwork. "Well?" he shouted back.

"We know that you're not on the Emperor's side!" the Tartar yelled back. He spoke as good German as we did and had certainly not been brought up in Tartary. "You are robbers, the peasants told us! And you have money! Give us the money and we'll let you alone!"

What Kaspar Fetz replied, I cannot write here. None of the dozen or so words he employed could be set down without setting fire to the paper they are written on.

"If you don't give us your money, we'll come in and slice your heads off!" the Tartar shouted.

Once again Fetz replied in a manner that cannot be transcribed in writing.

The Tartar went back, informed the others of the outcome of his conversation, and then began the assault on the fortress. But it didn't even reach the outer gate; as soon as the first groups with their axes were in some sort of battle order, a cannon shot

thundered out and knocked a number of Tartars flying; the
others fled from the danger area. Soon after that the whole of
the northern side was free of the enemy, and the succeeding
assaults all came from other directions, but never from the
north.

In the courtyard four robbers were now hard at work with
spades and picks, while four others were carrying the soil away.
One man stood at each of the east, west, and south entrances.

The doctor came and asked me if there were any ropes in the
fortress. I remembered that my mother kept her good strong
washlines in the cupboard in the room next to the kitchen, and
I told him so. He disappeared again; but a little later the smith
appeared, went up to the Count, and declared that he would not
go on working any longer, as the priest wasn't doing his fair
share of the defence work. "It's these Jesuit rotters we have to
thank for this war with the Turks," he said angrily. "And now
we have one of them sitting up there twiddling his thumbs!
Yes, he's not only sitting around doing nothing; he's getting
himself mixed up with that scum!"

"Mixed up with what?" the Count inquired.

"With those who arouse the wrath of God through their
greed, their shameless words, and their sinfulness! While we're
wearing ourselves out carrying water, he's making a pact with
the robbers!"

The Count shook his head in perplexity; the three of us went
upstairs and found that now only Michel and the farmer were
working. The doctor had invented a new method of bringing
water from the kitchens to the roof without having to carry it
up the stairs: the buckets were tied to a washline, let down from
above, and hauled up after being filled at the tap. Althammer
was filling them down below; Michel was pulling them up and
emptying them into the barrels. The doctor was thinking out
new and quicker ways of getting the water up. The blacksmith
had become rebellious, but the priest was sitting at a window

in the steward's apartments discussing with Fetz's second-in-command the concept that twenty fighters were better than only thirteen against the Tartars. When the Count appeared, the second-in-command disappeared and Father Lukas turned around.

"Why are you trying to negotiate with that rabble?" the Count asked. "Are you afraid?"

The priest smiled. "My lord, what is the most important thing at the moment? That we should drive the Tartars away. We can do that easier if we are united rather than divided. Once the Tartars are driven off, then we'll see."

"And is that why you are prepared to collaborate with the representatives of the devil? You, a servant of the holy Christian Church?"

"We have to work every day with evil, my lord, for we are all of us sinners; that is our nature. God alone is the judge of good and evil, not we."

"All the same you've burned at the stake as witches people who were true Christians!" the blacksmith protested. "That's what they're like, the Jesuits! And to think we have to protect a pestilential worm like this against the Tartars! We are tested in the fire because we are not upright and honest and God-fearing! But these creatures, these Jesuits, are like the slimy snakes we are told about in the first book of Moses! I'll have nothing to do with you; I'll have no part in this battle if it's not going to be conducted decently, in the true spirit of the Almighty!"

"Father—I shall decide what we shall do here."

"Count, you don't know how to bargain," Father Lukas answered. "You might even comply with these rogues' suggestions. It's the very fact that they are making certain proposals—that's why I'm sitting here at the window."

"You Antichrist!" howled the blacksmith, and threw himself upon Father Lukas. The priest stepped back and stuck out a foot. The blacksmith went sprawling over it and fell to the ground.

"It was the evil in me made me do that," Father Lukas said contritely. "I am very sorry."

The blacksmith jumped up and swung his fist at the priest, but the Count stepped in between them.

"Will you use your common sense!" he shouted at the blacksmith. "Outside there are robbers, and farther out there are heathens—and here we have two Christian men fighting with each other! Father, you go back to the tap! Blacksmith, you help with the buckets!"

The door burst open at that point and revealed a smoke-blackened Michel on the threshold. "Your honour—they're shooting burning arrows! The south-east tower and our own roof are on fire!"

37

In between the various floors, the staircase led past small windows that gave a view of the southern part of the courtyard, and I looked out of each one as I ran past. The left-hand corner tower was burning; two robbers were carrying pails of water to it and throwing the contents over the wooden defence walk, which at that point, extending from the east wall, followed the rounded outline of the tower for a short way before joining the south wall. Even though it lay a good twelve feet under the roof, there was still the danger that it might catch fire from falling pieces of red-hot tiles or blazing wood fragments. And once the defence walk was destroyed, one could no longer reach the top of the wall, and so the fortress could only with difficulty be defended.

Meanwhile, the greater part of the Tartars had departed with their horses out of range of our shots. They let the horses graze on the fields to the south-west, near an encampment of those leaf huts that I was already familiar with and were obviously busy getting ready for a siege. One could see a few of the Tartars felling large and small trees along the wood's edge; others were standing around three fires to the east, south, and west of the fortress, igniting arrows, while yet others passed these blazing weapons to the attacking forces who surrounded the walls in a half circle; from their crossbows shower after shower of blazing arrows fell upon our roofs.

Most of the shots missed their targets, falling either in the courtyard or against the walls or the windows of the big house. Of those that struck home, only a small number remained sticking in their objectives, and as, to our great delight, there was that day not the slightest trace of wind, most of this small number went out, so the roofs took fire only in one or two places. The barbican and the three other corner towers were untouched; the big house was burning fitfully along the long southern flank; but the south-east tower had received three direct hits all very close together, and its roof was well alight.

The danger to the big house was soon averted, but on the Count's orders we went on flooding the wooden floor copiously with water so that the planks would remain damp enough to withstand flying sparks and the falling embers of any freshly ignited portions of the roof. The robbers in the same manner were assuring the safety of the defence walk around the three other towers.

Our water supplies had been used up, and we were just going to start carrying up more in buckets when the Count called us to the banqueting hall, which ran the whole length, from east to west, of the building's second story. He had opened a couple of windows and was pointing down at the Tartars who, however, at once discovered our presence there and began to shoot. One of the arrows actually whizzed through my hair and stuck, quivering, in a ceiling beam; another ripped through the shoulder of Michel's shirt sleeve. We ducked at once and peeped cautiously over the window sill while the arrows rattled like hail against the outer walls or whistled over our heads into the hall. Though I was tempted to go to a room on the more tranquil northern side, I remained at my post and even moved frequently from an eastern to a western window and back again. In my intense curiosity to know what was happening, I could not refrain from watching all the preparations the Tartars were making for their assault.

The attacking forces' half circle still stood around the southern part of the fortress, but they were no longer using burning arrows. Apparently they had been given the task of making the defenders of the fortress keep out of sight. Behind these men, twenty horses to the east and twenty more to the west were hauling two recently felled but untrimmed trees with their tops pointing to the walls. Before they reached the moat, they divided, twenty going along the north bank and twenty along the south bank. But the trees moved straight on toward the water, into which their tops soon dipped. Behind them came storm troops with larch saplings whose branches had been lopped off but leaving stumps, so that one could climb up them.

The foe's intentions were clear: they wanted to cross the moat by means of the two large trees, then lean the larch saplings against the walls and thus enter the fortress. If I could grasp this simple piece of strategy, then the robbers must have grasped it, too, and must be wondering how to defeat the move, for once the Tartars had managed to get inside, all resistance was useless.

Viereckl and his cannon were powerless—the horses never entered their line of fire. But why Kaspar Fetz didn't bring his four muskets into play, I could not understand; I asked the Count.

184

"Apparently he has only a little ammunition," the latter replied. "Besides, even with the greatest luck, he could only kill one horse with one shot; when you know how long it takes to reload such a musket, you can reckon that this sort of fire would not hold up the Tartars or prevent them from erecting their saplings against the walls. If you also know how cowardly the Tartars are and how they seldom will start a siege when there's any resistance then it's obvious that you have to shoot, not at horses, but at men. And that's exactly what Fetz will do when the trees are fixed against the walls."

As the assault came from two sides, the robbers had divided. I counted three men with the leader to the east and three men with the second-in-command to the west. That Fetz looked upon himself as superior to Shiftyface could be seen from the fact that he had kept the dwarf for himself. Of the other five, Viereckl seemed to have remained at his post by the cannon, while one man, carrying a musket, covered the enemy from each of the four corner towers.

When the treetops reached the walls, the horses were unharnessed and led away. For a while the Tartars consulted with each other. Then once again they began to yell as loudly as they could, and at the sound of these yells the storm troops crawled over the large trees carrying their primitive ladders, leaned the larch saplings against the walls, and apparently began to climb up them, though this was something we could not see from where we were. At the same time they were covered by the bowmen, who also watched to see that none of the defenders showed his head above the walls.

None did show, but as the corner towers stuck far out from the walls and their loopholes made flanking shots possible, there suddenly burst forth four shots in rapid succession. Even from the burning tower to the south-east, a white cloud of smoke came from the lowest window loophole.

I learned later that three of these shots had hit their targets;

the second-in-command had bagged two Tartars, the chief only one. But while to the west two of the three larches overtopping the wall wavered and disappeared, on the chief's side all three remained visible, and soon after that the first Tartar head appeared over the top. Fetz was crouching right underneath him. His sword flashed upward; the Tartar threw both hands in the air and tottered helplessly backward. Almost at the same time a second had appeared alongside him; this one was struck by another robber. The Tartar did not fall backward but over the breastwork; yet another Tartar jumped from the third improvised ladder on to the defence wall. With his curved sabre he hacked down Schainckherl, the man who the day before had been groaning with stomach trouble, and turned to face the next robber.

Already the fourth Tartar was appearing over the top!

"How do things look on your side, Michel?" the Count called out, who was crouching with me and Father Lukas by the east window.

"The second-in-command is standing his ground!" Michel yelled back.

The Count handed the priest one of his pistols. "Aim at the second one!" he said. "Give a flying prayer and perhaps you'll hit him!"

The Count stood up, took aim, and fired. The Tartar who had jumped down from the wall grabbed at his breast, staggered a couple of steps, and fell from the defence walk down into the courtyard, where he writhed abominably and then lay still.

The priest, too, had stood up, but hardly had he appeared at the window than an arrow tore through the lobe of his left ear. All the same he fired. I had only known him as a teacher in the seminary, where we once had pinned a notice on his gown: "*Stultus itaque bonus sum*," which means, being translated into the vernacular, "I am stupid and therefore good." Never had it entered my head that he knew how to handle a pistol; never would I have believed that, at this distance, he could have hit a Tartar.

But he did!

The Tartar jerked back from the top of the wall and in falling obviously carried a number of others with him, for his larch ladder disappeared. Meanwhile, Michel and the blacksmith had come across to us; they aimed at Tartars, who were coming up over the dead one and whose body lay across the breastwork, and their shots rang out almost at the same time. I don't know if they hit both of them—at any rate one of the Tartars fell forward over his dead comrade.

We now could see the rest of the storm troops crawling back over the tree laid across the water, and from the west the doctor announced that the Tartars were also in retreat.

The attack had been beaten off!

Streaming with blood, Father Lukas stood in the middle of the room, but looking with an almost mocking smile at the Count, he said: "Well, now, Count—even you come to the help of the robbers."

The Count stammered something; then he, too, laughed. "Devil take it!" he answered, and did not for an instant think of begging the priest's forgiveness for the mild oath. "Devil take it—it's certainly not a pretty thought, that we must go to the aid of robbers to defend the West! But what else were we to do?"

38

An ear lobe is certainly a very minor part of the human anatomy, but if it is damaged, then the resultant flow of blood is more difficult to staunch than that from any other wound. Moreover, though the doctor had taken his little black bag with him on the journey to Johannesberg, he had left it behind in the coach when he was taken prisoner by the robbers; and now the coach was standing outside among the Tartars, in the blacksmith's shed. Fortunately, I remembered that my mother had somewhere a rough kind of domestic medicine chest; I looked around her room and found it finally under the tumbled pile of things the robbers had thrown on the floor when they plundered her chests and cupboards.

"A pity there isn't a big pair of scissors," the doctor said, as I showed him the chest and gave him a roll of bandages. "I'd have gladly cut off Father Lukas's entire left ear. The Jesuits are reputed to be such good father confessors, and a confessor needs good ears; he might have had to leave the Jesuits, and that would have given him a chance to become a reasonable human being."

"Are you a reasonable human being, Doctor?" the priest asked.

"I try to be a rational one."

"Then I prefer to remain a Jesuit."

Instead of answering, the doctor wound the bandage around the priest's head, in the process of which both ears were covered and the mouth partially. "The argument is concluded," he grinned as he sewed up the loose end with a needle.

At that moment someone knocked at the door downstairs, knocked so hard that we could hear it above our laughter at the doctor's last sally; someone was shouting for the doctor. We all went downstairs. Michel pulled the big chest to one side, drew his sword, and opened the door. Outside stood the second-in-command and asked if the doctor and the priest could go with him. Josef Radolt had been badly wounded, and they didn't know how they could succour him. But Schainckherl was dying and was asking for a priest.

"They'll go with you," the Count replied. "But you're getting a doctor who has no instruments and a father confessor who can't hear—or say—a thing."

"Thank you," Shiftyface courteously replied, and added: "The chief would very much like to speak to you as well."

"He would, would he? Why, I wonder?"

The second-in-command looked at the Count for a moment in bewilderment, then said again: "He would very much appreciate a word with you."

"I can well believe that. But would I appreciate it, too?"

The priest, who had already stepped out of the doorway, turned around, tapped the robber on the shoulder, and said in a friendly way, muttering through the bandages: "Is your chief asking for an interview?"

"Yes—that's it. He's asking for an interview!" cried Shiftyface, greatly relieved.

"Then let him come," the Count replied. "I shall wait upon him here."

Saying that, he put on such a grand manner that Shiftyface found himself giving a deep bow before he departed with the priest and the doctor in the direction of the barbican. About a minute after he had disappeared, Kaspar Fetz appeared with the dwarf and two other robbers. He had buckled on his sword and wore his three-cornered hat; with measured tread he advanced at the head of his small entourage, stopped in front of us, and with a grand gesture swept off his hat without lifting his left hand from his sword hilt.

"I beg your honour for an interview," he said.

"It is granted."

"I came here from the barbican—would your honour be so good to come two paces to meet me?"

I noticed that the Count was about to respond at once by stepping forward, but Michel held him back by the arm.

"Allow me," the Count insisted, and stepped into the courtyard; Michel and I followed and remained standing behind him.

Kaspar Fetz waited until we had taken up our positions and were standing quite still; then he made a brief bow and began his speech.

"We find ourselves in a difficult position. In the past we may not always have been of the same persuasion, but life seldom gives us the opportunity to be of the same opinion as all those we encounter. The struggle for daily bread arouses animosities, creates enemies; nevertheless, these do not affect our immortal souls and disappear when greater things make such a struggle seem unwise. Such an eventuality has now come about. Your honour finds himself with five men in this house, while I with only ten men have to defend a fortress whose preservation is for you too of the utmost importance. With a very proper awareness of this bond between us, you entered into the recent battle and gave it a decisive turn in our favour. I thank your honour for this and hope that I demonstrate my thanks by making the first step, as I have just done, and coming to meet your honour considerably more than half-way. I believe I am speaking also to your need when I venture to propose a collaboration of our forces. I am persuaded that we shall reach a settlement and an agreement that will considerably improve our position with regards to the enemy without making promises that would offend our respective sense of honour."

The Count made a sign of impatience, and Kaspar Fetz piously raised his hand.

"One moment, your honour! My secretary, Herr Scher-häggl, before he was compelled by the vicissitudes of fate to earn his daily bread by manual labour, once studied law at the respected University of Vienna. He is skilled in the making and understanding of the laws of jurisprudence and is also extremely adroit at drafting contracts and the like. He has had the goodness to draw up a few points for us to study at our leisure."

When I had met Kaspar Fetz for the first time, he had played the goodhearted old soldier; later I had seen him as the leader of a band of murderous thieves, and now he was giving himself out to be a king who wished to sign an advantageous treaty with his royal neighbour. The whole episode reminded me of many a play we had put on at our Jesuit Seminary, in which we witless boys had played Roman emperors, bishops, or great generals. A little later the doctor told me that in the most difficult situations people always resort to theatrical devices. I have not forgotten this and have noticed its application to events and persons in my later years. But at that time I didn't understand.

If Kaspar Fetz seemed to be acting strangely, I thought the Count was acting even more strangely when he went right up to him and asked: "What sort of points have you in mind?"

Without turning his head, the robber chief gestured behind him, flicking the fingers of his right hand; the left hand still lay unmoving on the sword hilt. The dwarf, at this signal—his name, I now knew, was Melchior Scherhäggl—sprang dutifully to the fore, unrolled a piece of paper covered with small handwriting, and began to read:

"Agreement between his Serene Highness, the Count von Alram, and the honourable Kaspar Fetz, given into my hand this Maria Nives Day Anno Domini 1683. It is herewith declared that, *primo*, both parties, having the same rights and of their own free will are prepared to . . ."

He didn't get any further, for the Count told him to stop.

"What's all this about equal rights?" he demanded. "Either you and your cronies bow to the ground or I go back into my house."

"Your honour!" hissed Scherhäggl. "If your honour would be so kind as to peruse the text—we quite understand your honour's attitude! We are basically in agreement, I trust. It's only the form—the form, your honour!"

"It is I who decide on the form! I think you might, under my leadership, fight against the Tartars; I should have accepted your agreement in writing, if necesssary—but I will conclude no treaty with gallows' birds and dishonourable scum like you who insist that we are on an equal footing. . . ."

All at once Kaspar Fetz was no longer a king on his dignity. He went red as a turkey cock and shrieked: "Shut your mouth, you overdressed monkey!"

This courteous appellation was accompanied by several other remarks I cannot reproduce here.

As Fetz at once pressed forward to attack the Count, the latter also drew his sword. Michel leaped to his master's side, but the Count commanded him to keep away and watch the movements of the other robbers so that the duel might pursue its course without unseemly interruptions. While the Tartars outside were getting ready for their next assault, the Count and Fetz danced about all over the courtyard, making their sallies and sorties and parries and altogether behaving as if the salvation of the entire world depended on the outcome of their fight.

To our relief the priest suddenly appeared at the main gate, took in the situation at once, and dashed between the two contestants, paying no attention to his own danger.

"Folly! Sin and folly!" he cried, and if his voice was a little deadened by the bandage over his mouth, it was loud enough for us all to understand what he was saying. When the two opponents disengaged, he turned first to the Count.

"Did you not yourself forbid my altercation with the blacksmith?" he said. Then, turning to Kaspar Fetz: "Have you taken complete leave of your senses?" Then to both of them: "Schainckherl has just surrendered his soul to his Maker, and Radolt is in a bad way. We are two men short already, therefore; we must work together, whatever we know and think about one another!"

"He shouldn't talk to me like that!" Kaspar Fetz shouted.

"I refuse to sign agreements with such a . . ."

"Stop!" The priest raised his arms reconcilingly. "If you both go on talking, it will finish up with one of you slitting the other's belly open. We don't want any slit paunches here; we need live men. From now on the fortress will remain under the Count's command—because he was educated to wage war, and you were not, Kaspar Fetz. For the length of the siege you will promise to obey Count Alram's orders—is that understood, Kaspar?"

For a moment there was utter silence in the courtyard. The doctor had appeared in the main gateway, together with those other robbers who were not stationed on the defence walk, while the blacksmith and the farmer leaned in the door-way of the big house. In the middle stood the priest with the bandages around his face, trying to bring about peace on earth.

The long seconds ticked by; then Kaspar Fetz thrust his sword back in its sheath. "I promise," he said hoarsely. "But if all goes well . . ."

"If all goes well, you can thank the Count or slit his belly open; and he for his part can either thank you or let you go hang. That's not my worry. Count, it all depends on you now! Give your orders! We shall obey them!"

39

The Count gazed around him, looking from one to the other; at last he, too, sheathed his sword, beckoned Fetz over to him, and said: "Have the three guards stay on the defence walk; call the others in here, Kaspar; in the meanwhile I'll see what the Tartars are up to."

He disappeared into the big house, and very soon we could

see him upstairs moving from window to window. Kaspar Fetz had no need to call anyone because his treasurer had also appeared in the courtyard; and so we waited until the Count should come down to us again.

"As I see it," he told us on his return, "at present we need have no fear of another attack. But I think they'll try it again, probably during the night. If they don't bring it off then, they'll have disappeared by morning. Night fighting has this advantage—our roofs will not be threatened, as a fire would create too much light. But its disadvantages are greater than the advantages, and so we must prepare ourselves very carefully. Let us begin with the counting and division of weapons and ammunition."

We discovered that, besides the four-pounder in the barbican, we had five suitable cannon-balls, ten rounds of cartridges packed in linen, and also a sufficient number of cartridge cases filled with gunpowder. There were twenty for the four muskets, for the four pistols belonging to Michel and the Count no more than six, and for my pocket pistol eight shots.

Apart from the treasurer, the secretary, and myself, all had sabres or swords, and moreover there were ten old halberds in the barbican. As there was far more powder in there than we should need for our few shots, the Count ordered a number of pewter platters to be placed on the walls and filled with gunpowder; if these were lit at dangerous moments in the action, they would throw out for a few minutes a bright light by which we would be able to take stock of the situation. The rest of the powder we poured into glass bottles we had found in the wine cellars, provided these primitive hand grenades with fuses, and laid them in readiness on the defence walks and in the barbican. The straw mattresses from the servants' quarters were also placed on the defence walks and in the barbican: in the event of an attack they were to be set fire to and thrown under the Tartars' feet. Near the loophole in the barbican a great vat full of water was placed, so that a possible attempt to set fire to the outer gate could be dealt with.

The Count sent four robbers into the corner towers, together with the priest, Michel, the blacksmith, and the doctor, each man carrying a musket or a pistol. A guard stood at the main gate in case the Tartars chose to attack the bridge. Viereckl and the dwarf stayed by the cannon; I was sent up to the second floor to observe the field and to report significant movements. Fetz with two of his men took over the western side, while the Count with Althammer and the second-in-command took the eastern side.

"The first thing is to be prepared," the Count had said. "The second point is to keep our preparations secret."

Therefore, we had done everything as quietly as possible and were feeling in some security because we had thought of all the enemy's possible moves and taken measures to counteract them, which the enemy knew nothing about.

Unfortunately, the situation worsened in the afternoon when the Tartars began to use their horses again to pull two freshly felled trees up to the south wall and thus make new temporary bridges across the moat. This did not promise a very successful defence, but we could not waste bullets, and so the Count ordered that some of our home-made hand grenades be thrown under the horses' hoofs.

Two were sufficient, for the Tartars' horses were not accustomed to explosions, shied at once, and could not be calmed. On the next attempt, with fresh horses, a single grenade brought about the desired result, and the trees were left lying there in front of the moat. We had certainly got rid of this danger, but our enemy now knew that he had to reckon with hand grenades.

As night began to fall, every man was at his post and all awaited the attack with great excitement. I was alone in the vast banqueting hall. I would stand for a while at the east window, then run across to the west window, trying to make out in the dark the movements in the Tartar encampment. I felt like a tower watch in the Middle Ages or the days of chivalry, and I would have liked to shout down below from time to time directions about the approach of enemy attacks; but,alas, the sky was overcast with heavy clouds, and thus I could make out only the outline of the walls. We would be able to find out more of what was happening in the fields by listening, and for that purpose those on the defence walks had the best place, for they were closer to the enemy.

Time dragged. I peered out of the eastern window, then peered out of the western window; nothing was stirring, either inside the fortress or outside among the Tartars. There was only the croaking of the toads in the moat, and on the meadows the crickets were singing. There was no clock in the tower and no night watch to call out the hours. Suddenly everything seemed remote, like a dream. Was this banqueting hall real? Were the Tartars, the Count, Kaspar Fetz, and the squinting dwarf creatures of flesh and blood? Should not Father Lukas be in his seminary schoolroom, where we had pinned the absurd notice on his gown? There was nothing all around me but darkness. Nothing else. It was just a mild summer night with croaking frogs and chirping crickets.

I noticed how heavy with sleep I felt. Still nothing happened. I began to count up to a thousand; I nipped my calves; I knocked my sleepy head against the wall. My eyes kept closing.

Suddenly a ray of light fell through the west window. I was just then at the east window, so I dashed across the room and stared out. Someone had lit the powder in a pewter platter. The flame stood out harsh and white against the blackness, but I could see nothing because it was burning between me and the moat, and its brilliance made everything behind it invisible.

Then there was a flash from the east. I ran across the room again. Still nothing.

There was stillness. There was only the croaking of the frogs and the chirping of the crickets. My situation seemed to me more and more unreal. Had I been standing at this window for minutes or hours? Again and again I had to fight against the desire to run downstairs and ask the Count what was happening or to go to Michel in his tower and ask him to tell me more of his ghost stories—anything to make me feel that I was not alone in time that seemed to have come to a stop.

And then they came—and that at a moment when, despite all my efforts, I had dozed off. I heard them yelling, saw the lights blaze up in the pewter platters, and ran from one window to the other. Shots rang out, blazing straw mattresses tumbled over the walls, and hand grenades exploded. It was an uncanny, strangely exciting, and yet once again an unreal picture that I gazed on from above.

Just as swiftly as the outbreak started, it died away. As if at one stroke, everything was still again. I could hear nothing more, could see nothing more; and now even the frogs and crickets were silent. I ran down into the courtyard; it was empty. I climbed up on the defence walk along the east wall. The Count was leaning against the breastwork.

"What are you doing here?" he asked crossly. "Why aren't you at your post?"

"The attack—!" I stammered. "The attack—was *that* the attack?"

"Yes. That was it," the Count replied, and sighed. "At least, I hope that was it."

"Was anyone wounded?"

"No." He turned to the second-in-command, who was standing beside him gazing out into the darkness, and said: "Divide the men into watches. One man to the south, the east, and the west, at the main gate, and in the barbican. The others can get some sleep—all together downstairs in the big house. I'm going there myself."

"Very well, your honour," said the man, saluting in a very military manner.

The Count nodded to him, signed to me to follow him, and stepped down from the defence walk. In the steward's apartments, he lay down on the bare boards, turned over on his side, and at once fell asleep.

When we awoke, it was light outside; Kaspar Fetz was standing in the door-way looking somewhat scornfully at the Count.

"Good morning, your honour," he said. "Would you not like to say your prayers? It could do no harm."

The Count drew his sword. "So you're getting cocky because the Tartars have fled, is that it?" he cried. "You're not going to catch me again—!"

Fetz raised both hands in a deprecating manner. "Why should I want to catch you? To lock you up? And who says the Tartars have fled? Think you're a prophet, do you? Well, they're still there. And there's somebody else, too."

He stood silent.

"Who?" asked the Count, lowering his sword.

Kaspar Fetz's smile vanished as easily as it had come.

"Turks," he replied. "Regular Turkish soldiers."

40

There were about fifty foot soldiers, but no janizaries, and they were camped in five groups along the road to Lempach, obviously in the same formations as they had marched in. The soldiers were sitting on the grass; the group leaders were standing nearby looking at their captain, who was speaking with a few of the Tartars outside the dairy yard. Kaspar Fetz had stated that they were regular troops, and I noticed this to be so at once. The difference between their behaviour and that of the Tartars would have been apparent to the most uninstructed person. Until now we had only dealt with cowardly plunderers; but this was a disciplined company drawn up against us, and certainly it had not been simply scorn that had made Fetz recommend us to pray.

The captain noticed our heads above the breastwork, interrupted his consultations, beckoned to a man who had been waiting two paces behind him, and gave him an order. The man came towards us, raised both hands, and stood like that some distance away.

"We want to parley with you!" he shouted in somewhat rough German.

"Very well!" the Count replied.

The man lowered his arms. "Send us a man of rank with whom we can negotiate!"

"You send one to us!"

"No. He must come to us. We do not want your fortress; we want something else. We shall speak about it. Send us the man or else we'll take the place by storm."

"Just try it!"

The Turk hesitated a moment. "It will cost a great deal of blood on both sides," he called.

"We're not afraid. If you want to negotiate, come here to the wall or send someone in to us; I give you my word that he shall be allowed to depart unharmed."

The interpreter shook his head, turned, and went back to the captain, who was still standing outside the dairy yard. While the two were deliberating, the doctor came up beside us on the defence walk, turned to the Count, and said: "Those aren't mere incendiaries, Count—they're professional Turkish soldiers. If you do not wish to do so yourself, then I will go out and parley with them."

"Why should you risk your life unnecessarily? These fellows

could just as well come up to the wall and tell me what it is they have on their minds."

"Apparently they're mistrustful and are afraid we'll shoot at them when they come near enough."

"I don't trust *them*."

"But how can we come to a rational settlement if nobody trusts anyone?" the doctor cried heatedly. "I have never believed the atrocity stories about the Turks—they are human beings like ourselves, and if we show we trust them, they will trust us, too!"

The Count pondered this for a while. "But we don't know yet what they want," he said at last. "I like your spirit, Doctor, but I'm not quite sure if you don't feel brave simply because you don't realise the danger. I know how dangerous it would be, and so I think it better you should stay with us."

Meanwhile, the interpreter had received fresh instructions from the captain. He came toward us again and waved. "We'll give you quarter of an hour!" he shouted. "If your representative has not come out to us by then, we shall attack and take the place by storm!"

"Good luck to you!" the Count muttered.

He gave his orders for the defence, then went with me up into the second story of the big house to observe the enemy's moves. Two groups of Turks placed themselves at the east and two at the west; the fifth marched into the dairy yard and was apparently to attack the barbican, while the Tartars again formed their semicircle in order to keep the defenders at bay with their arrows. "If they change this formation, give me a shout," said the Count, left me alone at my post, and went downstairs again to take up his position on the defence walk to the east.

At first, all I noticed was a certain amount of movement among the soldiers near the dairy yard; they were all looking in the direction of our barbican. Then their group leader left them and moved out of my line of vision. After a few seconds he reappeared, and beside him walked—the doctor! I later learned that he had persuaded the robbers to open the outer gate for him, and they had obeyed only too willingly, because thus they would avoid being attacked and the Count's forces would be weakened by one man.

The captain, the doctor, and the interpreter parleyed for some time under one of the linden trees next to the dairy yard; then the doctor turned and was about to return to the barbican when he was prevented by the interpreter and sent toward the east wall. He stopped on the banks of the moat, and as the distance between him and the wall caused him to shout at the top of his voice, I could hear quite clearly what he was saying.

"The Tartars have captured a column of refugees and handed them over to the Turks. The Turks examined the refugees and discovered that there was a courier from Vienna on the way to Krems who, a few days ago, asked the way to Raipoltenbach and who apparently was attacked by Tartars in the valley of the Tulln and taken prisoner. The Tartars outside Lempach know nothing about such a captive; they only recall an encounter with such a man and believe that he has taken refuge here. Now this courier is said to be a count, and as counts usually do not carry out the duties of couriers, the Turks assume that his dispatches must be of the greatest importance and may reveal the weak points in the defence of Vienna."

"What did you tell them?" the Count cried.

"That the courier was here but has now gone on."

"And—?"

"The Tartars said that this fortress was occupied by robbers but that they heard someone inside addressed from time to time as 'the Count.' And so the Turks do not believe me. If we hand over this Count, they are prepared to withdraw without meddling in the fight between us and the Tartars. But if we do not hand him over, they will take the place by storm."

The Count was silent for a moment. "You can tell them again that the Count is not here but that we know where he went. Say we are ready to reveal his hiding place if they will let you return unharmed into the fortress."

The doctor nodded and went back to the dairy yard. I heard the captain's voice raised in anger and saw the doctor turn to come back to the barbican.

He didn't get very far. Two soldiers knocked him down, tied him up, and laid him under a linden tree. I thought he might call out to us, but he was silent.

41

Following the orders I had been given, I shouted down to the Count all that had happened, but he simply waved to me as if he already knew what I was reporting. Kaspar Fetz, who had also heard my news, ran along the defence walk to the east wall and asked the Count what he was going to do now.

"We'll use the cannon and fire on the dairy yard, make a sortie, and bring the doctor back," the Count retorted a little sharply, as if he were surprised that anyone should have to inquire about something so obvious.

"Shall a nobleman allow an innocent man to suffer for him?" Fetz angrily countered. "Why don't you go and give yourself up so that the doctor may be set free?"

"You've got the wrong end of the stick," the Count said in a bored voice. "I no longer have the message I was entrusted with—it's been in Stein these last six days. If I go over to the Turks, they'll ask me at once for this message. I cannot give it to them, and they will assume that it is here in the fortress; not only will they then not let the doctor go—they will attack the fortress all the same. Your only gain would be to have one man less here."

"You've thought it all out, haven't you! But as I see things, our worries are over if we deliver you and the boy to the Turks. You can then tell them everything, the boy will back you up, the Turks will withdraw—and the Tartars have had enough of us, anyhow; they would soon depart also."

"So you'd kill three birds with one stone: you'd be rid of the Turks, the Tartars, and myself. But I shall not grant you the pleasure."

Kaspar Fetz stared at the Count for a while; then he suddenly put two fingers in his mouth, gave a shrill whistle, bent over the breastwork, shouted something in Turkish, and then turned around to the Count again. "If you haven't got enough common sense yourself, we shall assist you to perform your duty as a nobleman should. You will leave the fortress at once or we'll drag you out, bound hand and foot like a pig!"

A number of the robbers had appeared in the courtyard. Kaspar Fetz shouted to them: "Cover the entrance to the big house and the door of the barbican!" And to the Count he said: "Now, Count! A nobleman's word . . . the Turks are waiting!"

And the Turks were indeed waiting, as I could see from my upstairs window. As soon as the doctor had been made secure, the captain had given a sign, and the groups were marched away. After Fetz had called out that Turkish phrase I could not understand, the attack was called off by the captain. The soldiers now were standing about in the fields looking up at us.

On the eastern defence walk were the Count and Althammer, Fetz and his second-in-command. Down in the courtyard were two robbers; in the door-way of the west tower a third appeared with his musket trained on the Count.

I knew that he could not hit him at that distance if he didn't want to run the risk of accidentally shooting Fetz or his second-in-command; but on the defence walk it was still two against two, for Michel, who had appeared in the doorway of the tower with the burnt-out roof, was prevented from moving by the robbers, who had kept him company there, while the robbers in the opposite tower on the east side were likewise holding back the priest.

I heard the Count muttering something to the farmer. Althammer shook his head and stepped aside.

"Are you mad?" the Count yelled at him.

"Your honour must excuse me," Althammer answered. "I have nought against ye, but I am not for you neither, for you're a landed gentleman and I'm a nobody. As far as I can make out, the Turks will leave us alone if we give you up. I don't feel like dying yet, so I would rather you were handed over."

During this exchange the second-in-command had crept noiselessly behind the Count. I shouted to give the Count warning, but it was then too late. Shiftyface put out his foot and gave the Count a shove, making the latter lose his balance, stumble forward, trip over the foot, and tumble head over heels into the courtyard. The second-in-command immediately jumped down after him, and obviously things might have gone badly for the Count if Michel had not then thrust the two robbers aside and dashed to his master's assistance. He arrived just in time to kick aside the second-in-command, who was about to land on the Count, and to deliver a well-placed punch in the belly of Kaspar Fetz, who had jumped down at the same time. They both went sprawling for a distance of several feet.

Perhaps Fetz was the better swordsman, but he was not used to fighting with his fists. He fell to the ground and made no further move, while the dazed second-in-command tried to scramble to his feet. He rose to his knees, but Michel gave him a knockout blow, and he lay down peacefully beside his master.

The Count had got up, but he was limping, and Michel had to support him as they both, with drawn swords, turned to face the next two robbers. They fought inch by inch back to the north tower, where the priest was still struggling with his two opponents, and were already around the corner when the man on the other side decided to let off his musket. I saw how the Turks in the fields outside were nudging each other and laughing; then I left my post at the window because it occurred to me that I could perhaps free the entry to the big house so that the Count and Michel could fight their way inside. So I seized a candlestick that was standing on the table, ran out of the banqueting hall, went down the stairs two at a time, and crept along the ground-floor passage toward the treasurer, who had taken up his position in the main door-way.

With all the strength in my body I struck him across the back of the head with the heavy candlestick, but either I had aimed badly or I was simply not strong enough—or perhaps his skull was abnormally thick! Viereckl just staggered a little, then turned, and grabbed me by the arm.

At the same instant the Count and Michel rushed by outside but did not attempt to charge the entrance to the big house; instead they thrust aside the sentry at the main gate, dashed over the bridge, and disappeared into the barbican.

Fortunately for me, Viereckl noticed this move and, releasing me, ran after the Count. As there was nothing more for me to do in the big house, I too ran out into the courtyard, saw the robbers from the north-east tower just running through the main gate, and heard Father Lukas calling to me: "Come here, Andreas! Come in here with me!"

I hesitated for an instant, for I saw that a fight had broken out on the steps of the barbican; then I obeyed and joined the priest. As soon as he had seen that I was coming, he had vanished into the tower, holding the door open for me; when I arrived, he slammed the door shut and bolted it. Now his head bandages were all askew, so that one ear and his mouth were free and he could speak clearly.

"Thank God you came in here," he said with a sigh. "You can't be of any help to the Count, and perhaps they might have decided to torture you in order to make him give in. He's safe in the barbican, and here we'll do our own part to keep the Turks at bay as we did the Tartars."

"But how can we?" I asked, quite bewildered.

He saw my bewilderment, then calmed down and even managed to smile. "My friend has left his musket behind. I'll use that and the pistol, and you can be loading for me. Things haven't changed outside all that much. Instead of Viereckl and the dwarf, it's the Count and Michel who are now in the barbican—otherwise everything's as it was before, as the Count planned it. If the Turks attack, I shall shoot—and I hope I shall not miss. Remember what the Count advised me to do? Give a flying prayer! Well, God is on our side."

42

As I've already mentioned, our tower was round and had two stories, the upper one of which overhung the lower. There was only one door below into the courtyard, and in order to reach the defence walk from the tower, one had to use a ladder. It could be placed in the upper room of the tower so as to reach a square opening in the ceiling. While in the lower story of the tower there were only five long, thin loophole windows, the upper story was larger and had several holes for pouring boiling pitch and twelve small windows from which one could fire on the defence walks if the enemy should happen to occupy them.

It was to this upper room that we repaired. At first, we felt rather nervous as everything was so quiet in the fortress. But by now Kaspar Fetz had recovered from his knockout blow and had gone back on the defence walk. I stood at the hole right above him and heard every word he said, but his conversation was no use to me because he was talking Turkish, and the only word I could recognise was "barbican," which occurred again and again. As he kept pointing with his left arm in the direction of this structure, I realised that he was advising the Turks to attack this part of the fortress, where the Count had made his new stand.

One of the group leaders ran to the captain, who just then was standing near the dairy, and told him what Fetz had said. The captain thought for a moment and then gave his orders. Shortly after that the groups to the east and west moved toward the north while the Tartars took up their positions again.

The assault began thus: six Turks brought dry wood out of the smithy and straw from the barn and crawled along the moat to left and right of the barbican, where they laid their burdens down before the outer gate. I saw only those three who approached from the east, and then not even those after they had moved around the tower of the barbican. Immediately afterward a shot rang out. I recognised the sound—it came from my pocket pistol, which the day before had been distributed to Scherhäggl. He must have left it up in the barbican, and it was now being fired by either the Count or Michel.

On my side, I saw only two Turks crawling back, but soon one of them ran back with a blazing torch and threw it on the piles of wood and straw outside the main gate. Observing the clouds of smoke that instantly began rising, I realised that he had hit his target with the torch.

The conflagration lasted only a few seconds; then I heard the Turks give a shout of rage, and I knew that the Count had poured water from the vat and put the fire out.

The soldiers were looking at the captain, who yelled something, pointing. Now muskets were handed out, and the group that had been waiting by the dairy marched, with their muskets levelled, to the bushes opposite the gate in order to take up positions there and apparently to cover an attack that was to be launched by the four other groups. But scarcely had they raised their muskets than a charge of shot met them from the cannon in the barbican, which left only one man unwounded—the others were all dead or severely hurt.

In order to understand the success of such a small cannon as a four-pounder, you have to realise that a charge of shot from one of them is composed of many bits of iron, big nails, or sharp-edged stones, which are placed in a box or a bag and shoved down the barrel of the cannon. The particles of sharp iron spray out of the mouth of the cannon like water from a hose, and if the enemy is not too far away, the effects can be horrible.

In this case they were; the sight of the wounded men was ghastly, and their screams were even worse. Although I had already witnessed similar scenes during the siege of Vienna, I now staggered back from my peep-hole in horror. Father Lukas, who had been standing behind me, laid his hand on my shoulder.

"I know; it's terrible," he said softly. "And men have known for thousands of years how horrible war and violence are, but the devil is in them all, and from time to time they listen to his evil counsels and not to the reconciling voice of God that is in them also. It is horrible, and yet we cannot change it. We have no choice: if we spare their lives, we can be sure that they will destroy ours. The fifth commandment says that thou shalt not kill—but that applies to us, too, for our lives are of no less worth than those of our enemies. And as they have descended upon our land, as they threaten us and wish to kill us, we must defend ourselves. Perhaps the men who are dying down there are innocent; perhaps their Sultan is the one who alone is guilty— that is something he must answer for to God Himself. But outside there now are men who, whether innocent or no, wish to kill us. And we ought to defend ourselves; we must defend ourselves against them."

I didn't quite follow the priest's logic. Was it so absolutely necessary to defend ourselves? Was it not simply because we, too, were using violence that violence was being used against us?

When I went back to the observation hole, the Turks had dragged their wounded away and were continuing the attack. I could see how one group (and probably a second group to the west) was creeping along the moat toward the barbican. They were pulling along larch saplings, the same as those with which the Tartars had endeavoured to scale our walls, with the intention either of battering down the main gate or of clambering up those improvised ladders to the loopholes. Without encountering any defensive shots, they reached the gate, where I could see no more of them. Probably they were trying to lean their tree trunks against the barbican; but as the two holes there were small, the defenders were at an advantage, and the Turks had to abandon this attempt. Now they were placing the larch trunks vertically against the gate and came once again into view; they were now within very close range of the cannon, which the Count, as I later learned, had managed to shove forward so far that he and Michel had been able to tilt the barrel downward.

Even before the first assault of the battering ram, the second charge of shot thundered out, and it, too, had a devastating effect.

The Turks fled—those who could—called off the attack, and again gathered in the fields along the highway to Lempach. If they had been Tartars, we should not have expected another attack, for after the loss of more than a quarter of their men, the Tartars would certainly have withdrawn. Eight men started marching towards the south, something that boded no good for us, and on the orders of the captain the Tartars again began to shoot burning arrows at our roofs.

All the same, it was to be assumed that there would be no fresh attack before the eight men had returned, and it occurred to me that the Count might now make his attempt to rescue the doctor, which he had previously planned to do and which—as I well knew—he could certainly only have temporarily postponed.

After observing for some time the activities of the Turks in the east, I went back to the northern loophole to see what was going on in the dairy yard. I saw then that from the iron pulley we had used to haul the hay up to the loft there hung a motionless figure.

It was the doctor. The Turks had hanged him.

43

There is a great difference between experiencing the death of some nameless soldier—whether Austrian, Tartar, or Turkish—and the death of a person whom one has known well, whose manner of speaking, drinking, and blowing his nose is as familiar as one's own habits.

I had met the doctor for the first time when we had come to Raipoltenbach almost four years ago from Vienna and my mother had fallen ill shortly after taking over the direction of the dairy. Then he appeared in the middle of the night, bringing medicine with him, was gruff and grumpy but willing to do everything he could for her. He knew everything about the Khainacher family and scolded my mother gently because she had not looked after her health better.

Later he had helped me prepare for my examinations for the

high school, taught me my first Latin declensions, and made me conjugate "*laudo, laudas, laudat*" for him. His wife had died ten years before, his son two years, and his two daughters four and five years ago; he lived alone in a tumble-down house on the square in Lempach, played chess in the evenings with the apothecary, was always arguing with his housekeeper, and never spared himself when a sick man called for his assistance.

Now there he was hanging from that pulley, dead.

I did not tell the priest what I had seen. I leaned my forehead against the wall beside the spy-hole and stared sightlessly at the plaster. After a while I heard him calling me, but I gave no reply. He came up to me, shook my shoulder, cast a glance out of the spy-hole, and discovered the reason for my silence. He took me by the arm, led me to the rickety old bench that stood against the east wall of the room, sat me down on it, and placed himself beside me.

He didn't speak. He just looked at me, and after a while I raised my eyes but didn't know what to say and weakly shrugged my shoulders.

Down in the courtyard the second-in-command was yelling for wine: "If we have to die like dogs, we'll die drunk and happy at any rate!"

Father Lukas laid his hand on my knee. "Yes, it's hard. It's hard for me, too. He was a freethinker and always believed that he could grasp the meaning of existence with his reason alone. He always inveighed against the Church and often in fun inveighed against me; but at heart he was a believer, as he would be the first to admit, in his own strange way. It is hard for you, and it is hard for me because we thought a lot of him. It's not hard for him. Not any more."

Again I shrugged my shoulders.

"You see, Andreas, it's as if he had gone back home. We come from God and we go back to Him, to our one true home. Dying often hurts, but death never. And if we realise that dying is simply a return home, why should it hurt us? There, where we all go, we are reunited with all those who went on before us and left us feeling sad. The doctor is meeting his family again. Already. He is happier than we are."

From outside came the yells of the robbers, who were rolling a barrel out of the big house; they cheered as they burst open the bung and let the wine bubble out into their tankards. A flock of crows flew screeching over the buildings, and as if in mocking defiance there came up from below the robbers' song:

"The raven croaks, the gallows creak,
The blood down the steps runs black;
When the wind blows over the waves, my lads,
Your captain'll call you back . . . my lads,
Your captain'll call you back."

Father Lukas smiled. "They know not what they do. They have never known. The world knows their captain as Kaspar Fetz. But one day their real Captain will call them back . . ."

44

The roof of the big house was on fire, and also the roofs of the towers that until now had been spared were ablaze. As we had no water, we went down to the first floor. After a short while the rain of burning splinters would set the floor alight, so that we would have to go down another flight and finally abandon the tower if we didn't want to be roasted alive.

Obviously this did not worry the robbers at all. As the glowing tiles and the burning spars from the roof of the big house were now falling into the courtyard, they had crept under the defence walk, where they just lay and drank and sang their songs.

"Perhaps there's still a guard on the main gate," the priest said. "Or perhaps he's now quaffing wine with his mates. We ought to see if we can't fight our way through to the barbican."

He pushed the bolt back, cautiously opened the door, and peeped out. "The guard's still there," he announced, somewhat reluctantly, as he stood up again. "You take the musket—I need the pistol. If I start to run, you stick close behind me and make sure you get into the barbican. Call to the Count; he will open up for us."

I put the musket over my shoulder and stuffed the rest of the ammunition in my pocket; with his left hand Father Lukas seized his sabre and pistol. When we were once again standing in front of the tower door, he made the sign of the cross, took the pistol in his right hand, kicked the door open with his foot, and ran for the main gate. I followed.

The guard noticed us rather late but at once shouted loudly and placed himself in our way. The priest cast a swift glance at the roof of the big house, ducked in pretended terror, and yelled: "Look out!" As there were, in fact, blazing beams falling here and there, the guard jumped to one side for shelter, and before he realised that he'd been tricked, we were already running across the bridge and along the passageway into the barbican.

"Open, Count! Open up!" I yelled.

"Bang at the door!" the priest shouted. I obeyed and thundered with both fists on the locked storeroom door, while he levelled his pistol at the approaching guard. "Stop where you are! If you come any closer, I'll shoot!"

"Open quickly! Open up, Count Alram!"

It seemed to me an eternity before I heard footsteps on the stairs. In the meantime, the guard had halted, but the robbers had roused themselves from their drunken carouse, were coming after us, and were only about four yards away when the

213

door opened. I shoved Michel aside; he grasped the situation at once, made room for the priest, slammed the door shut, and dropped the crossbeam into place with a great thud.

"It's good to see you here!" said Michel, smiling jovially all over his face. "We're very comfortably placed inside here. Enough provisions for a month, a good cannon, solid walls, and first-rate morale."

"The doctor—" I stammered.

He became serious and rubbed his cheeks. "Yes," he muttered sadly. "That was rotten bad luck. I've seen it happen before. Once in Croatia I knew a tax collector; he was really a stargazer, an astronometer y'know, and could reckon up sums like a professor. One day I meets him at the tavern, and he's sitting there with his tankard, clerking away. 'What you writing there?' I asks him. 'My last will and testament,' he says. 'What's the hurry?' I asks, joking-like. 'To-day I saw in the stars,' he says, 'that to-morrow I shall quit this earth.' Well, bless me, you'll hardly credit it, but the very next day in his barn he falls out of the hayloft bang on the threshing floor and breaks his neck. Dead he was. When they opened the will, it turned out he'd left all his money to the biggest spendthrift in the town— so that it would benefit the common people quicker."

He put his foot on the first step, but the robbers rushed against the door and yelled that we had to come out at once or else they would blow the barbican to bits. I hesitated, and even Father Lukas looked anxious.

"Leave them to their blathering," Michel said. "They're drunk. The door is solidly secured; it can't be lifted off the hinges and can't be rammed in. Let's go up."

Although the robbers continued their threats, he went calmly upstairs, and we followed him. "I don't see what your tax collector has to do with the doctor," I remarked.

"Oh, that's easy!" he answered, not turning around. "The stars never lie. That man had reckoned them up, but I can do it without ciphering and clerking; I can feel the future in my liver because I'm a child of Mary. It was all up with the doctor —God rest his soul. I knew that soon as I set eyes on him. But we're all right; I can promise you that. And if it's not all up with us yet, why should we complain?"

The Count was lying on the floor next to the four-pounder, chewing a straw and peering through a spyhole at the outside world. When we appeared, he turned his head and nodded to us. "I was going to fetch him," he said. "I had loaded and was going to shoot—but then it had already happened. Did you say a prayer for him, Father?"

"A silent one."

"Well, it's all quiet outside just now. If it gets lively again, you take the loophole over the bridge, Father; Andreas, you will take the west one and Michel the east. Meanwhile, we can have a little chat. Michel told me about the stars. I would gladly talk with you about Aristotle, Father. What do you think of his ideas about entelechy?"

As Aristotle played a great part in the formation of Christian theology, we had heard about him a lot in school, and I knew more or less what the Count meant by his question. But that one should even entertain the thought of discussing a Greek philosopher and his writings in a fortress besieged by Turks, with drunken robbers at the door and the big house on fire, seemed to me so crazy that I laughed out loud.

The Count paid no attention to my rudeness, but the priest lay down on the other side of the cannon and looked through the spy-hole; he formed a complete contrast to the Count, and both of them looked like two stone statues at the edge of a fountain. Michel pulled me to one side and talked again about the stars, putting all the blame for our situation on the planet Saturn and setting all his hopes of salvation upon Mercury. The Count and the priest lay there talking philosophy.

Meanwhile, our own roof had begun to burn.

"This is my idea of European civilisation," the Count said, getting to his feet at last, "and that is why I feel so happy here in this barbican. It suits me; it's like a home to me with its two massive round towers, its recessed gate, and the cannon up above. It is a symbol."

Michel was preparing a meal, which we later ate with enjoyment. Over us the flames prattled in the roof. Despite the thick layers of soil on the loft floor above us, the fire sent out so much heat that the sweat stood out on our foreheads, and the smoke that penetrated the cracks clutched at our throats. We paid no heed. Michel was telling us about the Bektashy dervishes in Bosnia, who with a single word could turn a man into an ape.

"Circe turned them into swine," the priest said, "but with us it only needs a word and they become wolves—"

Outside, a sentry sounded the alarm, and we dashed to the loopholes. At first we could make out nothing unusual; but Michel called us over to the eastern side, where, between the northern corner tower and the right-hand side of the big house, there could be seen a part of the hill and the highway to Lempach. Along this highway were marching the eight Turks; behind them came two horses. The horses were pulling a small limber, and on the limber lay a cannon.

"I was expecting that," said the Count.

45

The small procession stopped some distance away; one could see the captain and a few of the group leaders going toward it and discussing the management of the cannon with the Turks. The captain sent them to our eastern moat, which they approached so closely that they were hidden from our sight by the wall. After some time the Turks pushed the cannon, which they had meanwhile unloaded from the limber, forward towards the wall and again disappeared from our sight.

We had almost no means of observing the proceedings outside the wall to the south, east, and west, and this was an extremely unpleasant situation; but for the same reason, however, we could be sure that we could not be shot at from that position. But things looked differently when the Turks pushed the cannon farther to the north and indeed set it up so that it could hit our towers but could not be hit from our own loopholes, which were set too far back in the walls. The Count, therefore, thought we should try to break two larger apertures in the towers by using the halberds, making one on the western and one on the eastern side. As I was physically the weakest, I was given the task of following the proceedings outside as far as I could and of announcing any unusual movements while the other three set to work.

What until now had seemed to us the barbican's greatest advantage, its massive walls, which made it the strongest part of the fortress, now became our greatest trouble. The halberds did have iron spikes but only wooden shafts, which very soon began to splinter when they were used as levers. The three men worked away like galley slaves, and as our roof was still in flames and the heat constantly increased, they gradually threw off coats, waistcoats, and shirts, and the priest even cast off his robes in the end—creating a picture that all my fellow students would have found extremely comical but that didn't bring the smallest smile to my lips then. On the contrary, the fact that my teacher worked, panting, to pull down part of the wall and was working in his underclothes demonstrated to me once again the seriousness of the situation.

Meanwhile, the Turks had fired their first shot. I merely noticed that it must have met its target because a cloud of dust rose up. It was obviously not a charge of shot but a cannon-ball intended to make a breach in the east wall. While I was considering how strange it was that now both attackers and defenders were engaged, though with very different intentions, in smashing up the old fortress, the eighth halberd broke, and the Count tossed it away from him in a rage and cried that he'd rather use gunpowder.

It then occurred to me that I had once seen down below in the other storeroom a breaching iron, but this storeroom could not be reached from the first story—only from the passage. So I asked the Count if I might venture to open the door down below and bring the handspike.

"Our robber friends will certainly be having other troubles to contend with now," he answered, "but we'll come with you all the same."

The three men took up their empty weapons, and then we went downstairs; the priest stayed by the door, Michel kept a lookout in the passage, and the Count crept with me across to the other storeroom. No robber sentry was to be seen.

We broke in, found the handspike, and turned to go back; but as we were crossing the passage, I happened to cast a glance at the bridge and there noticed to my great astonishment through the upper right-hand corner of the open inner gate the tip of a pole, which slowly lowered itself on to the breastwork. I jerked the Count by the arm; he gave a momentary start, then stormed across the bridge with Michel close behind. I could hear them hitting and stabbing at someone whose face I could not see from the passage. Immediately afterwards a musket shot rang out; the Count let his weapon fall and grabbed his shoulder, but then he picked up his sword again and fought on.

Meanwhile, Father Lukas had run with upraised sabre to the help of the others but arrived too late to do any fighting. Together with Michel and the Count, he pulled the pole on to the bridge. It was one of those larch saplings that the Tartars had felled to scale the walls with. We closed the inner gate of the barbican, put two crossbeams against it, left the sapling lying in the passage, and went back upstairs.

When we reached the next floor, the Count nodded gratefully to me. "That time you saved the fortress from defeat, Andreas," he said earnestly. "If you had not seen that tip of the larch sapling, the Turks would soon have surprised and disposed of us. It was my fault and your great service. I should have thought that they would try to catch us unawares while they were trying to breach the wall outside in readiness for their assault."

"But how did they get on the bridge?" I asked, for I still couldn't quite follow what had happened.

"They crept on the barbican from the west while you were observing preparations for the attack on the east. They laid a tree trunk across the moat right under the western tower, in fact slanting towards the main gate. It was too short, but from where that first tree lay in the water they were able to prop up another against the crown of the first and lean it against the bridge, which it just reached with its tip. Thus a way across was created, and the first two Turks were just going to swing over the breastwork on to the bridge—when we appeared, at the right moment."

While he was speaking, Father Lukas had come up to him and examined the flesh wound that the stray shot had made in the Count's shoulder. "If Michel is a child of Mary," he said, "then you are at least the luckiest fellow alive. A fraction of an inch deeper and you'd have been a hospital case."

"An officer who never has any luck ought to become a parson," the Count answered. Then it struck him that the sooty, sweaty man who stood before him in his underclothes was indeed a parson of kinds, a priest in fact, and he made him a slight bow, adding: "A soldier needs luck; a priest needs faith."

"No offence intended, I'm sure, and none taken," said the priest, seizing the handspike.

"You keep your eye on the bridge," the Count told me. "But from time to time go to the other loopholes and spy-holes. They might very well try to set fire to the main gate again."

At that moment a heavy beam from the burning roof dropped with a loud bang on the floor above us; dust trickled down over us through the floorboards, and it was hot as red-hot iron. As the Count's back and shoulders were naked, he cried out, tried to brush off the blazing dust with his hands, and burned them, too. I brushed it off with my neckerchief, but his shoulders obviously hurt him more than the flesh wound.

The Count gritted his teeth in pain; then he said: "Go to the loopholes!" and went to help Michel and the priest.

Outside, in the meantime, several shots had been delivered. Now we could hear other explosions, and I remembered that that was how our hand grenades had sounded. When I looked through the south loophole, I saw Kaspar Fetz and Veireckl lying against the breastwork of the east wall's defence walk and throwing the bottles of gunpowder high into the air towards where the enemy's cannon must be standing. I could follow the flight of these primitive projectiles until they disappeared behind the wall; whether they hit their target or not was something of which I knew as little as Fetz or Viereckl.

The chief of the robbers was just lighting a fresh fuse; he waited a long time, then slung the grenade over the wall. We heard the dull thud it made on the grass. Then Viereckl threw another but obviously threw it too soon, for no sooner had it disappeared than it reappeared, flying back the same way! One of the Turks must have noticed that the fuse was not completely burnt out and had caught it and tossed it back. It broke on the cobblestones of the courtyard but did not explode.

I wondered if the Count had realised that a glass bottle

would remain unbroken on turfy ground but would break on stones and whether that was why he had ordered us to make these grenades. Michel, meanwhile, had succeeded in pushing the most deeply embedded stone in the breached wall outward, creating a hole that was sufficient to receive the muzzle of our four-pounder. The three of them gave an exclamation of joy but immediately carried on their work in the west tower.

Only a few minutes later the fortress's east wall shuddered beneath a shot, the freestones in the middle fell out, the wall sank, the upper stone courses followed the lower ones, and all at once there was a great hole gaping in the wall.

I heard the triumphant yells of Turks and Tartars and saw Fetz and Viereckl jumping down from the defence walk, seizing their swords, and posting themselves to left and right of the smoking breach.

They stabbed the first Turk and the second; as they were hidden by the wall, they could not be hit by arrows or musket fire from outside; moreover, they had firm ground to fight on while the attackers had to clamber painfully over piles of rubble. Then the third Turk appeared and stumbled over the two dead bodies till it looked as if the Turks would block the entire hole in the wall with their bodies.

Perhaps Fetz and Viereckl could really have held their position, but the robbers had not thought about the Tartars to the west. Instead they stood in readiness at the eastern corner towers, waiting to go to the help of their chief. Only two shots rang out on the western side (as I later learned, they had been fired by the smith) before the first attackers swarmed over the breastwork, slashed down with their sabres the one guard on the defence walk, and leaped, yelling, down into the courtyard.

Behind them came others, and yet others . . . more and more and more and more. . . .

46

I had at once informed the Count of what had happened. All three of them rushed across to me and tried to look through my loophole. As this was only a few inches wide but two feet high, I was the one at the bottom gazing through, with the Count above me, above him the priest, and above the priest Michel.

Fetz at once realised that any further resistance was useless, abandoned the breach, and ran to the north wall; the rest of the robbers followed him, and after a short while we saw them appear in the main gateway, where they must have discovered that the inner gate of the barbican was now closed. Nevertheless, they stormed over the bridge and there were met with a rain of arrows from the Tartars, who meanwhile had occupied the northern corner of the moat. One of the robbers fell.

"Open up!" yelled Fetz, and sprang back to the main gate. Viereckl followed him. They were both defending the narrow bridge against the oncoming Turks and Tartars, while the others lay on the ground behind the breastwork and hid themselves from the arrows. The blacksmith and his companion were firing their muskets. Fetz, who was thus granted a little breathing space, turned around and yelled: "Inside!"

I could see how the men who had lain on the ground half stood up and bent down to run to the inner gate; how Fetz and Viereckl, who had covered the withdrawal, also suddenly turned tail and followed their men. Immediately after them the Turks and Tartars came storming across the bridge. At the same time I heard a sharp report behind me. The Count had fired the priest's musket, and there immediately followed the report of the pistol in Michel's hand.

Dazed, I staggered back from the loophole. In the next instant Michel sprang to one side, ran past me, raised the ladder, and thrust open with it the trap-door in the ceiling, which we had shut because of the danger of fire. A rain of sparks streamed down; Michel dodged them, grabbed a halberd, climbed up, and vanished through the hole. I could hear his footsteps; I heard a roaring and a shoving. Suddenly something whizzed down outside past the loophole. I caught a glimpse of falling flames, and then the blazing joists of wood crashed down on the swarms of Turks below.

When I next looked through the loophole, the bridge was covered with burning fragments and empty of invaders, but Michel went on throwing fiery beams over the edge until between the inner and outer gates a smoking heap of rubbish had accumulated. The Tartars began to shoot arrows at him; he kept it up another few seconds, then drew back, appeared once again by the trap-door, and before he clambered down laid the trap-door on top of the ladder's end, so that, when he had come down, it closed of itself when we drew the ladder away.

The priest had opened the inner gate to let the fleeing robbers in and shut it behind them. Now they came upstairs: Fetz and Viereckl, the second-in-command, Althammer and the blacksmith, along with the robbers, four more of whom came up behind these—Huetstocker, Gurttner, Teubel, and Grim.

"Viereckl, take over the cannon!" the Count cried. "Kaspar, take the east; Clauss, the south; Heutstocker, the west! Give us a shout as soon as you see anything! You others, help us break a hole in the west wall—we've already made a start! Muskets at the loopholes! Father and Andreas will load for you!"

Michel sat in the middle of the room pulling off his boots, whose soles were completely charred. His hands were covered with blisters from his burns; his hair and eyebrows were singed, his clothes burnt and torn.

The robbers said not a word; each one silently obeyed the

Count's orders. He, for his part, behaved as if there had never been any quarrel between them. I wondered anxiously how long this state of affairs could continue; then Fetz announced that the Turks had hauled their cannon around to the north and brought it into position on the edge of the moat. So we dragged our cannon from where it had stood to the newly made opening. Viereckl called for a cannon-ball, we rolled it over to him, he loaded it himself, and we shoved the barrel out.

The Turks shot first, and their ball hit the tower on the ground floor. I thought that it must crash down under the force of such an impact, but Viereckl didn't bat an eyelid. He aimed the cannon with the utmost care, lit the fuse and shoved it in the flash hole. The cannon leaped backwards, but our cannon ball bored into the earth barely half a yard in front of the Turkish cannon.

The Turks fired another shot. Then they shoved the cannon back, almost fifty yards away into the fields.

Meanwhile, Tartars had appeared bearing a larch tree and were attempting to batter down the outer gate. We loaded a charge of shot and rolled our cannon back to the loop-hole. Viereckl swiftly aimed and primed it, and the iron fragments sprayed downward. The trunk was left lying there; the Tartars fled.

But one more ball came flying from the east, and under its impact the whole tower trembled.

"I can't hit them at that distance if we can't raise the barrel higher!" Viereckl panted. "You must dig out at least one more stone from the top!"

Michel brought the handspike from the west tower and thrust it again and again into the opening until a stone was loosed from the top, bringing a second with it. At once we loaded again and shoved the cannon into the enlarged aperture. Meanwhile, Viereckl had been searching the room and came back with the lid of a box; he grabbed a charred stick and drew a quarter circle on the lid, then divided it into twelve equal parts. This he placed at the side of his cannon, raised the barrel in accordance with the markings on the quarter circle, and lit the fuse.

The shot was dead on the mark: the Turkish cannon was destroyed.

"Huh!" was all Viereckl said, and though his action had lifted a load from our hearts, no one felt like raising a shout of triumph—our situation was still far too desperate.

The Count ordered work on the west tower to be abandoned. Instead we were to make a hole directly over the bridge, at a height recommended by Viereckl. We dragged the cannon back to the hole in the north wall.

At every moment we were expecting the next attack, but it did not come. Time went by; the enlarged hole in the south wall was ready. Now we could even meet an assault from inside the fortress with a charge of scatter shot.

But no one appeared. It began to grow dark.

Suddenly we heard hammer blows from the smithy and glanced up uneasily. Were they attempting to repair their cannon? Viereckl shook his head, scratched his red stubble beard, and knitted his low brows into extraordinary wrinkles and furrows.

"I know now what they're making," he said at last. "A petard."

"What's a petard?" the priest asked.

"It's a board to which a metal capsule is fixed," the other explained. "Inside the capsule is gunpowder, and at the other end of the board is a hook. You light the thing with a fuse and hang it on a door or gateway. The charge explodes and blows the door to bits."

"We're always learning." The priest sighed. "I know the writings of Saint Thomas Aquinas and of Saint Augustine; I know Pythagoras and Leibnitz, Francis Bacon and Descartes or Cartesius. But I'd never heard of a petard until now. And so this daft thing is to decide our fate?"

The Count said: "Don't bother your head about it. Time works wonders. Place guards and keep changing the watch. The Turks arrived at five o'clock this morning and now it's seven in the evening. Every one of us could do with some rest."

The guards were posted, and the rest of us sat down on the floor in the middle of the room; we ate and lay down but were unable to sleep.

Kaspar Fetz took his fife out of his pocket and was about to put it to his lips when the Count asked if he might borrow it.

Thick night hung over the fortress, whose burnt-out roofs were still glowing red.

The Count played his saraband.

In the smithy the Turks went on hammering.

47

At some time or other I must have fallen asleep. When I awoke, they were all on their feet, and the grey light of dawn was creeping through spy-holes, loopholes, and cannon slits.

"No!" shouted the Count.

My teeth were chattering with the cold. I got up, but my feet were numb, and I had to stamp a few times on the floor before I could walk and go over to look through a spy-hole. Below stood the interpreter.

"Another attack and it'll be all over with you!" he called.

"I have no message—and if I had one, it would have been burned long ago," the Count replied. "Give up this siege— it's not worth the lives it is costing you!"

The interpreter spat and departed.

"Everyone at his post!" the Count ordered.

But again we waited in vain for an attack. Almost two hours passed thus, and we might have thought that the besiegers had withdrawn if we had not seen their horses grazing and the smoke rising from the camp-fires beside the leaf-covered huts.

Then all at once single Tartars, as well as as groups of them, appeared, creeping cautiously up to the barbican. Although we could hardly believe that they were attempting another frontal attack, we watched them with considerable anxiety until Kaspar Fetz at his southern loophole uttered a loud cry, raised my pocket pistol, and fired.

"Damn it!" he shouted. "Just missed! Now the thing's done!"

"What's the matter?" asked the Count.

"He's hung the thing up!" Fetz bawled. "The door'll be flying off the hinges in a minute!"

"Downstairs! Viereckl, stay by the cannon—all the others come with me!"

But the Count was not the first. In front of him the blacksmith was bounding down the stairs; when we got down, he was already heaving the beams out of place.

"Away from the gate!" shouted Fetz.

The blacksmith paid no heed to him, opened one wing of the gate, shut it again, opened the other—and there hung the board with the metal capsule, from which a fine smoke was rising! With a single movement the blacksmith ripped the board from the gate and slung it across the bridge into the court-yard, right among the Tartars who were standing there with their bows drawn. The petard exploded and felled two of them; but before that the arrows had been let fly and five of them hit the blacksmith, who sank groaning to the ground. Fetz dragged him to one side, slammed the gate shut, and with Huetstocker's help put up the crossbeams.

We hurried up the stairs; once up there we saw that Viereckl had somehow managed alone to shove the cannon to the southern opening in the wall and was just then loading it with a charge of scattershot. The first Tartar had barely appeared at the main gate, trying to storm the inner gate despite the failure of the petard, when he set fire to the fuse.

The shot made a devilish crack; immediately afterwards the Tartars to the north began an attack and shot seven arrows through the loopholes, one of which hit Gurttner in the shin.

"Cannon to the north!" yelled the Count.

We all bent our backs to the wheels. Then there came a dull thud from the outer gate, another from the inner gate, another up above in our loft: the Turks had not only prepared a petard but also several hand grenades, which they were now tossing at us from all angles. Two of them tore holes in the floor of the loft above where we were, and the still-glowing rubbish cascaded down upon us but injured no one very seriously. A number of Turks showed their heads above the outer wall of the fortress. Muskets were trained on our loopholes and firing slits, and soon the bullets were raining down on the barbican.

It was like a fevered nightmare.

I rolled cannon-balls; I helped Viereckl aim the barrel; I cleaned out the barrel with an old jacket and burned my fingers on the ironwork that was becoming increasingly hot. I saw the robber Grim hit in the head, just beside me, by a musket shot and felt no worse about it than if I had swatted a fly. I had my toes crushed when Viereckl rolled a cannon-ball over them; yet I did not notice it. The smoke from the gunpowder blackened our faces, and through this bitter soot the drops of sweat made rivulets and ran burning into our eyes, while the stink of the powder grew almost suffocating.

I could hear nothing beyond the crash of explosions, forgot myself entirely, did unthinkingly whatever seemed necessary, all the time silently praying that this hell-on-earth would come to an end sometime.

And then it suddenly became quiet, almost uncannily still.

The Turks and the Tartars had disappeared; the fortress seemed to have been abandoned. Nothing stirred.

Grim and Althammer were dead, Gurttner and the blacksmith were lying severely wounded in a corner. We had a few more charges of shot, but no more hand grenades, no more ammunition for muskets or pistols.

"Has everyone got his sword?" the Count inquired calmly.

48

But we didn't need our swords.

For a time we heard and saw nothing of our besiegers; when they reappeared, they were unarmed. About thirty Tartars went across to the smithy and the dairy, filled baskets with kindling, dragged them in front of the barbican, and in a half circle piled a great wall of wooden fragments from one side of the moat to the other. As we could not fire, we had to look on helplessly as the wall of chips and shavings and kindling and logs grew higher and higher.

Viereckl cursed long and loud, then added: "They're going to try and smoke us out!"

When the entire apparatus for smoking us out was erected right around the fortress, the Tartars brought green wood and dead foliage, as well as old clothes, bed linen, rags, old mattresses, and sacks of rank straw, as well as other kinds of unpleasant stuff that they routed out of the surrounding houses, and threw everything pell-mell on the piles of kindling.

"Very artful, and as well laid as an old woman's morning fire," said Michel. "And the wind's coming from the north. In a couple of hours we'll be running out on the meadows, and we'll be stuck like pigs."

"We shall leave only one guard up here, to be relieved every half hour," declared the Count. "All the others are to go down to the storerooms, where we can seal ourselves off easily from the outside. There'll be enough air to last us a good long time."

"Then what?" the priest asked.

"Then we shall see."

"With all that smoke?"

The first stinking clouds of it were already pouring through the room when we picked up the blacksmith and Gurttner and carried them downstairs. In the storerooms it was pitch dark, and although we had lamps and candles, on the Count's orders we might not strike a light because it would have used up the air. We could see nothing outside, and we couldn't see who was next to us inside. Through the chinks in the ceiling and the door there drifted fine wisps of smoke that made us cough. The guard on the first floor could hardly keep a further lookout, so thick were the clouds of smoke around the barbican, and our only hope was that in these circumstances the Turks could not attack.

Somewhere in the blackness the smith was moaning. The priest sat beside him, praying. He was praying this time not in Latin but in German. And the smoke kept pouring in through the cracks.

The Count had not given me guard duty, but as I did not want to stay behind, I accompanied him when it was his turn and laid myself beside him next to the cannon at the southern opening in the wall, where there was the least amount of smoke and from where we could see the bridge and the main gate.

For a long time we lay there together, hearing only the crackling of the flames outside and the sound of our hoarse coughing. But after a while we suddenly heard something else: a voice rising from the courtyard, a plaintive, thin voice singing the robbers' song about the raven, repeating itself again and again. We stared out into the billowing smoke but could see nothing. Only after some time did the voice become louder, and now there emerged from the dense grey clouds the outlines of a strange figure. We saw it was the secretary, who went tottering through the main gate and along the bridge, stopping only in front of the pile of rubbish Michel had thrown down.

"Fire!" he said, swaying. "Fire," he repeated thoughtfully. "And the gate is shut. Gate shut." Then he laughed aloud.

He was hopelessly drunk. Apparently he had hidden himself in the cellars when the fortress was attacked and had consoled himself with wine.

"Fire!" he growled again. "All alone in the fire. Melchior Scherhäggl is like a salamander in the fire!" And again he started singing: "The raven croaks, the gallows creak, and blood—"

He didn't get any further. An arrow struck him in the back; he stood there for a while as if dreaming, staring in front of him. Then his knees gave way. He fell over and never moved again.

Almost at the same time we heard a dull thundering in the distance. I thought it must be a fresh Tartar horde coming to overwhelm us, but the thundering stopped and then started again a little later. It grew nearer and louder—thunder, real thunder. We looked at one another. Neither of us dared say a word.

Finally the Count whispered: "A storm!"

"A storm," I repeated softly.

Soon after that it began to rain heavily.

49

It was a cloudburst such as I have seldom experienced. At once
the fire was put out and the smoke disappeared. All of us mounted from the storeroom to the first floor; even Gurttner came
with us, and only the blacksmith remained lying down there
because the priest said that the smallest movement would cause
him great pain and that he was likely to die in a very short space
of time. He stayed with the wounded man in the darkness,
while the rest of us stood at the firing slips and loopholes and
breathed in the fresh air with wide-open mouths. Outside, the
rain fell so fast and thick that it covered the stink of the charred
rags; this was very nice, but on the other hand we could not
see any better than we had through the smoke.

"Why don't we simply run away from here?" I suggested.
"Before the Turks have time to notice it, we'll be away in the
woods."

Fetz gave a scornful laugh, and the Count shook his head and
said: "There are over a thousand of them, and we couldn't get
very far. We must hold out here in the fortress—this is our
only hope. Once outside, we're lost."

"And what shall we do if they attack again?"

The Count looked from me to Fetz. "What do you mean,
Kaspar? Do you still want to hand me over? To give yourselves
up? There are five of you, not counting the wounded. We are
only four; but the priest is sitting downstairs with the blacksmith, and Andreas is a fourteen-year-old boy. That means
five against two. Did that occur to you?"

Fetz nodded. "It occurred to me, but there's no point in
sending you outside. We've killed too many of their men. They
don't grant pardons."

"Agreed. But you must also consider that I shall hand you over to the first judge we meet if we live through this siege."

"You stuck-up swine!" Viereckl shouted. Michel moved closer to the Count, and I really thought that now, after we had escaped the danger of choking to death in the smoke, there would be fighting in our own ranks again; but Kaspar Fetz merely laughed and sat down on the floor.

"I thought of that, too, your honour," he replied. "A count is always a count, and you can't take milk from an ox."

He snickered, then went on.

"If I'd managed things as well as your honour, so that I could steal things and yet remain within the law, then I should be all for the sanctity of the law. I understand you because I have all the assets of a nobleman: courage, intelligence, recklessness, and a healthy desire for accumulating money—greed, in fact. A little civility and courtesy—I leave that to my grandchildren. And no one can expect me to be my own descendants."

"So you'd let me take you to court?"

"All in good time, your honour. We still have the Turks and the Tartars outside. Just like me and my men, you have to fight for your life, and you know, your honour, as well as I do, eight men are better than five. As long as the Tartars are there, you are no danger to me and I am no danger to you."

"But when the Tartars go . . ."

Fetz slapped his hand on the hilt of his sword. "Then we have our irons, I think, haven't we, your honour? I am not one to be quite so easily dragged into court."

Now the Count sat down, and we others followed his example. "It's nothing to do with unity of purpose," he said with a sigh. "As we happen to be for the moment on the same side, you must accept my commands in the future."

"I have nothing against that—your honour gives his commands very nicely."

"How did you bring the cannon into the fortress?"

"We used the doctor's horses to drag it into the passage. From there we pulled it into the storeroom, tied a rope around it, laid the rope along the stairs, and hauled it up through the trap-door. We took about an hour to get it up."

"Is the rope still there?"

"It's lying under the stairs."

"Then we're going to bring the cannon downstairs again. We still have some powder left, enough for three more charges of shot. We shall break up the old halberds and use the metal for shot charges. If the Turks invade the passage, we'll fire a salvo at them. If despite that we cannot hold them back, we'll haul the cannon back into the storeroom. The gates will not be defended, but the doors will be. As there's not likely to be anything more than hand-to-hand fighting, everyone will sleep down below. Up here we'll keep only two guards: one of our men and one of yours."

Fetz stood up and bowed. "As your honour commands," he replied, and it wasn't very clear whether he meant the expression seriously or jokingly. The Count apparently decided to take it seriously, stood up, and went to work with the rest of us.

We passed the rope around two beams from the left floor and tied one end to the axle of the cannon while five of us gripped the other end. Next Fetz and Michel shoved the cannon to the top of the steps and let it roll down step by step, taking care not to roll down themselves, while the five held on to the rope with all their might. It was easier than I had expected. But the halberds would neither bend nor break at first, for we had no tools apart from the handspike, the spade, and the pick, and it was a long time before Viereckl found a way to chop up the defiant metal and thus acquire material for three charges of shot.

As dawn began to break, we were ready. We could hear nothing from the Turks and the Tartars; we could only see their horses on the meadows, and once we glimpsed a man running across the courtyard.

"They will surely come during the night," the Count said. "You had better sleep now—we need to conserve our strength."

He divided the men into watches, and we lay down to sleep. The rain had stopped, and it was quite still outside. Across the way, the blacksmith was groaning. He was still alive.

50

Michel turned over in his sleep, and in doing so gave me such a hefty push that I woke. I sat up and looked around me. There were no loopholes in the storeroom, but enough daylight entered from the trap door over the steps to the upper story for me to see that the Count, Michel, and I were alone. I got up and pushed open the passage door. I went outside, where the cannon was standing, looking strange in the full light of day.

The outer and inner gates were standing open.

At first I thought that Fetz had betrayed us to the Tartars. But then they would have come inside and slain us in our sleep —so that couldn't be the reason. I wakened the Count and Michel. We first of all shut the gates and then climbed up to the first floor. We found there only the priest, lying asleep beside his spy-hole.

The Count bent over him and shook him by the shoulder. The priest started up, grabbed his sabre and stared at us wildly. We asked him where the second-in-command was who had shared the watch with him but he didn't know. He knew nothing.

And the robbers had vanished.

We looked through the south loophole across the meadows. The leaf-thatched huts were still there, but we could see no horses.

The Count didn't say a word, but Michel talked without stopping, speaking about treachery and defection of the watch and miracles and madness and ambushes. We all went downstairs, cautiously opened the inner gate again, clambered over the pile of rubble, and crept into the courtyard. There was no one there. We climbed on to the defence walk and gazed in all directions.

There were the leaf-thatched huts, but no Turks, no Tartars.

"They've gone," said the Count. "And the robbers have gone, too, without killing us before they left. We've been luckier than we deserve."

"I'm sorry I fell asleep . . ." the priest began but the Count dismissed this with a wave of his hand.

"You're exhausted, like the rest of us. Let's forget the matter. I don't know why the Turks have withdrawn, and I don't know why the robbers have left—but that hardly matters now. They have both gone away, and that's all we need to know. We are free, and the sooner we disappear from this region, the better I shall like it."

We went to look at the blacksmith, who must meanwhile have died. To our astonishment, he was still alive, though unconscious. There could be no thought now of a hasty departure, for we could neither leave the wounded man there alone nor carry him on our backs. So Michel ran along the highway towards Lempach, to the top of the hill, and came back with the news that there were no Tartars to be seen outside Lempach either.

We cut down the doctor from the pulley and laid him with our other dead, for whose burial in consecrated ground we trusted the people of Lempach would be responsible. The priest uttered a short prayer.

We constructed a stretcher of boughs and rope and straw and laid the blacksmith upon it. The Count and Michel carried the stretcher; I went on in front, and Father Lukas walked behind. And thus we left the fortress.

It was a strange feeling to be able now to pass tranquilly through the gate that yesterday we had had to defend so desperately, to be able to move freely in the fields from which in the last few days all our troubles had come. We marched past the dairy where the Turkish captain had given his orders, past the place where the Turkish cannon had stood, past the camp sites of the five Turkish groups. When we reached the top of the hill, we rested a while and looked back towards the fortress. The roofs were in ruins; the windows of the big house gaped blackly; in the east wall was the hideous breach the Turks had made. It was a ruin.

"My lovely barbican," said the Count with a sigh. "I liked the place."

We set out on our way again, reached the village an hour later, and walked between empty, burnt-out houses along the main street to the fortress. The gates were still shut but were opened when we explained who we were, and a little later we were standing before Countess Palffy, who was waiting for us in the castle yard. She had not buckled on a sword and had no musket in her hand, as the peasant from Kogl had said, but she looked just as a real lady ought to look. All the same, we knew that it was she who had led the defence of the castle fortress and, in doing so, had saved the lives of many people.

There was no doctor but a number of old women who understood how to treat wounds, and we handed over the blacksmith to their ministrations. This done, I asked about my mother.

The Countess shook her head and said: "Your mother went to Vienna. That's where you should be now—at least, that's what she assumed."

237

My voice failed me at these words. The Count explained for me. "She is bound to be in Purkersdorf," he concluded, "and you'll just have to wait patiently until we've defeated the Turks. Then you'll be able to see her again."

It was not as simple as all that, for my mother might well have fallen into the Tartars' hands, and though I didn't like to think so, this possibility seemed considerably more likely than Purkersdorf.

The Countess must have been thinking the same thing. She suddenly put her hand on my shoulder and became very friendly, something she had never been before, because she had always looked upon me as a lazybones and a good-for-nothing. "That's the way, Andreas," she said, smiling. "You shall stay here for a while until your mother sends for you."

After I learned that my mother was not in Lempach, the place lost all interest for me, and I didn't want to be left behind by the Count and Michel, with whom I felt safe and at ease wherever we were.

"I should very much like to stay, your ladyship," I answered, "but I still have an important journey to make."

She looked at me in astonishment. "What journey?" she asked.

"To Stein. To see Count Leslie."

Obviously she did not believe me.

"What business can you have with an Imperial general-in-chief? And do you imagine that in times like these you can stroll around the countryside in such a carefree manner?"

"He knows the way and has made the acquaintance of the Count." Count Alram spoke up in my defence. "In fact, a week ago he took an important message from Vienna to Stein, from the city's commandant to Count Leslie."

"Yes, but all the same . . ." she stammered, confused.

"He's no longer a mere boy, you know." The Count smiled.

238

"What is it you have to see Count Leslie about?" he asked, turning to me.

"I have to go there myself."

Obviously he didn't want to leave me behind with this woman, who was, perhaps, a very brave specimen of her sex but who would almost certainly lock me up with a volume of Livy as soon as he had gone. So I dug Michel in the ribs and quite unashamedly smiled at the Count.

"In any case," the Count continued, "one thing must be considered, your ladyship. Andreas's mother expects her son to be in Vienna. So when we have freed the city, she will not go to Lempach but to Vienna. We must spare her the shock of not finding him there. I think, therefore, it would be better if I took Andreas with me and let him join the army of liberation on its march to the city. In that way he'll meet his mother again at the earliest possible opportunity."

The Countess gave her consent and left us with a most gracious inclination of her noble head.

As Father Lukas, too, did not wish to remain but to go with us to Stein, we decided to set out again at once after paying a final visit to the blacksmith. He was in a pleasant room, lying on a soft white bed, sound asleep. The old woman who was tending him told us that he was indeed in a bad way but that, in her own opinion, with proper attention he would pull through. "He's got the constitution of an ox," she said," and I'll soon have him on his feet again. It's not the first time I've looked after him. The best way to deal with this one is to treat him rough."

"Do you know him?" the Count asked.

"Know him! He's my nephew! When he was just a lad, no bigger than this young fellow here, he had his head split open in a street fight, and nobody ever thought he'd live. But just look at the man he's grown into! It was *my* nursing did that. . . .

No, your honour, as they say in these parts, 'Ill weeds grow apace'!"

She laughed, and we left her with the feeling that our wounded blacksmith would soon recover, as he was in the best possible hands.

51

We passed by Raipoltenbach on our way to the Bildstock Heights, turned west there, and rested in the small house in the Haspel woods where the old man lived who had given me a turnip and a carnation. To my great astonishment the Count knew him; the strange old fellow really was a baron, and I had indeed learned his illustrious name at school. He led us into his living-room, related to the Count an episode from the Thirty Years' War, told Michel how to plant a birch tree, assured the priest that God prefers to grant immortality by turning us into trees and flowers, and on our departure gave each of us a turnip.

We went on to Herzogenburg and spent the night there in the monastery. We overslept the next morning and only set out again towards noon, so that we did not reach Stein until after night had fallen.

At this point I missed the way that Colonel Leisser had shown me, and by the time I had discovered my mistake it was, in the Count's opinion, too late to present ourselves to Count Leslie. As Stein and Krems were overflowing with officers, the Count could not find quarters anywhere and finally had to content himself, as we did, with a hayloft that Michel discovered on the outskirts of Stein.

I was very tired but tried to keep myself awake by every

means possible. While the others were sleeping, I cautiously got up, left the hayloft, and within a short while found the right road. A little later I was standing before the house in which little more than a week ago I had spoken with Count Leslie.

The sentry stopped me, but I asked for Laurenz, and as I proved myself familiar with the name of Count Leslie's valet, I was allowed into the hall of the house. Soon afterwards there appeared that solemn gentleman's gentleman, walking towards me with slow and measured steps. He at once called me an ungrateful scamp because I had abused Stubenvoll the tanner's hospitality by running away. I said I wished an immediate interview with Count Leslie, to which he replied loftily that it was now ten o'clock and hardly a Christian hour for a formal visit.

"The Count promised me that he would receive me at any time!" I retorted, and as Leslie was still awake and working at his desk, Laurenz took me to him.

He was sitting before the map of our country, and at first his manner was none too friendly. He asked severely why I had run away from the Stubenvolls and why I had dared disturb him at this ungodly hour.

"Count Alram has not been taken prisoner," I replied eagerly. "We were besieged for a whole week by Tartars and Turks at Raipoltenbach, but we fired at them with our old cannon, and they withdrew yesterday. Count Alram is a hero; he brought his dispatch as far as the Tulln Valley and would certainly have delivered it to you himself but for the misunderstanding that caused me to take it from him. The Lord Chamberlain himself, Aichbichel, advised the Count to take on the role of courier, even though the Count's a colonel-in-chief, so that he could get his own regiment back, and now that it was I who brought the message, the Count still can't get his regiment back and that's not fair!"

I paused, choking for breath.

"Well, what do you want?" Leslie asked me. He shook his head at me, obviously at a loss what to think. "Where is Count Alram? What are you doing here? Can't he come here himself?"

"He's sleeping in a hayloft because he thought it was too late to disturb you, but I ran away as soon as they were asleep to ask you to let him have his own regiment back! The whole thing was no fault of his—it was easy enough for me to get here from the Tulln, but before that was the worst part, a very difficult and dangerous part, and that's where *he* was carrying the dispatch, not me. Don't you understand? You should have seen him at Raipoltenbach! A regiment is not sufficient for him! He ought to be in charge of the entire army, I'm telling you!"

Leslie stared at me in perplexity for a moment. Then the corners of his mouth began to twitch until finally he burst out laughing.

"You young rascal!" he cried, as soon as he had recovered. "Don't you realise that you very nearly did more harm to Count Alram than you could ever have done simply by taking over his message? An Imperial colonel-in-chief who sends a fourteen-year-old whippersnapper like yourself not only is unworthy of having a regiment; he doesn't deserve to lead even the smallest company!"

"Count Leslie—!"

He signed to me to keep quiet. "All right, I know all about it. I can't make any decision about the regiment—that concerns His Majesty and can't be settled now or even by to-morrow morning, you know—"

"But the battle for Vienna!" I broke in very rudely, without thinking that high-placed gentlemen are not used to being interrupted. "You can't just let him sit and watch things from a suitable distance! A man like the Count! Before you leave for Vienna, give him his regiment back!"

Leslie burst out laughing again. Then he rang his bell. "You can't buy regiments like breeches' buttons—but as it happens, there is one at the moment without a commander. Alram will come to see me early to-morrow morning, and I shall tell him what an enthusiastic if not always very polite young mediator he has in you. I shall send your petition to the Emperor, and within a week your hero shall once again be Colonel-in-Chief. And now go and get some sleep!"

The worthy manservant had entered when the bell was rung. Count Leslie nodded to him, shook my hand, and conducted me to the door, where Laurenz took me in charge.

We strode along together, step by step, in the most dignified way, until we reached the same room in which I had slept before.

"If I were your father—!" Laurenz began, but remained silent about what he would do, though I gathered a good thrashing was involved.

"Take off those filthy clothes!" he said, in quite another tone of voice, which almost made me think he was inwardly laughing, if laughter could possibly be associated with this solemnsides.

When I was finally in bed, he pushed the little table with the bell to the bedside, brought a glass of water, placed it beside the bell, put out the light, and silently disappeared. I was dead tired, but for a long time my thoughts would not allow me to sleep. The barbican, the Turks, Kaspar Fetz, my mother, the Count . . . .

Again and again they whirled through my mind.

Finally everything became confused with memories of my early childhood . . . and then at last I knew nothing more.

52

Next morning when I had awakened and been called to the Count, everything had been settled. The two counts were sitting at a small round table on which was a flask of wine and seemed to have come to a very amiable understanding with one another; as they wanted to drink a toast with me, Laurenz unwillingly brought another glass for me. Leslie drank to my health and declared it was a crying shame that I should want to paint pictures when I would make such a good soldier.

"The last word has not been spoken on that subject," Alram replied. "In about two years' time I shall offer him a place as cornet in one of my squadrons, and devil take me if he doesn't throw away his paint-brushes then!"

Leslie assured me again that he would always be willing to speak in my favour but added: "I would, however, prefer to receive you in daylight next time—you seem to have a preference for the night hours that does not accord at all with your tender age."

Meanwhile, Michel, with Count Leslie's recommendation, had obtained good quarters for us in Krems, where we could all, including Father Lukas, be accommodated. Count Alram had a large room on the first floor of a nobleman's house, the priest a room on the second floor, while Michel and I shared an attic from whose steep roof a look-out turret rose. From the turret windows we had an uninterrupted view over the spires and towers of the entire town. This was where we were to put up until Count Alram could join his regiment.

As we were no longer vagabonds of the highways and byways, Count Alram's behaviour altered. He did not play sarabands on the harpsichord. He ordered a new wig and a new suit of clothes, as well as a sparkling new uniform, shaved every day, and seemed to me as remote as he had seemed in the house in Vienna. Michel had to see about obtaining fresh equipment for his master and so had little time for me, while the priest had meetings with priests who had fled from Vienna and also had to prepare for his journey to Innsbruck. I sat in the attic, stared at the passing clouds, and felt bored.

I sat for two days, then turned to the man who by rights should not have been disturbed by outsiders, namely Count Leslie. Again I was granted an interview with him and in the course of it asked him for paper, pencils, and colours, which I had not been able to find anywhere in Krems. At first he seemed a little embarrassed by my request. Then he called one of his aides and gave him orders to find what I wanted. The aide at first didn't know what to do, but he treated the matter as a military action that must be successfully carried out, and within a few hours I had my materials.

Then what exciting days I spent at my table in front of the attic window! My happiness was clouded by uncertainty concerning my mother's whereabouts and by my longing to see her again; but how different were those days from the ones I had spent in the barbican! With enthusiasm I threw myself into this work with pen and brush!

After a time the pictures made a strong enough impression upon Michel so that he gathered them together and took me downstairs to the Count, who was just then busy writing to Field-Marshal Dünewald, under whose command he would be if his officer's commission were restored to him. The moment was not a very favourable one, and the Count looked a trifle impatiently and absent-mindedly at the first drawings he saw. In them I had portrayed his duel with Kaspar Fetz. Suddenly he grew enthusiastic, pointed to Kaspar's legs, and said, marvelling: "But that's exactly how he stood—the right foot a little turned inward when he was on the defensive, and outward when he was attacking! You've got a good eye, Andreas!"

The next picture showed our banquet in the big house, where Althammer had felt so embarrassed by the display of silver and crystal, and it made the Count laugh out loud. He was just as pleased by the portrait of the Mayor of Kogl and one of Black Kate from the charcoal-burner's hut. The painting that showed him and Father Lukas lying side by side near the spy-hole, discussing Aristotle, he held for a few moments silently in his hands, then cast me a sharp look and said: "Lying by the cannon, we couldn't see that our roof was on fire! Why have you painted the flames?"

I shrugged my shoulders—rather impertinently, perhaps. But it had really seemed to me that the two were philosophising while the roof burned. The flames represented my own view of a reality more real than the event itself.

The Count looked through more of the drawings and paintings, and when he took up the one of the drunken secretary at the moment when the arrow hit him in the back, he shoved his letter to the general to one side, laid the painting on the desk in order to examine it more closely, and for a while said nothing. At last he looked up.

"I'll have to find myself another cornet," he said. "As soon as we've liberated Vienna, you're going straight to Italy, Andreas. I'm going to settle an allowance on you—in your own name, for even colonels-in-chief can fall in battle. But whatever happens, you are going to Italy to study painting. I know now that you're as little cut out to be a Jesuit scholar as I am. You *are* painting, just as the priest *is* theology. Perhaps, after all, there are people who are not cut out to be soldiers but who are nevertheless real men. You're going to Italy. Only this one thing you must promise me: don't let yourself be spoiled down there. Be a man and not a drawing-room hero!"

"Your honour—!" I stammered. "How could I—what do I want with drawing-rooms?"

"Good," he answered. "We're in agreement. You're going."

We went up to our attic again. Michel brought the priest up, and he, too, looked through my pictures, at first with a teacher's condescension, then with growing interest. "You young scamp!" He laughed. "Those days at Raipoltenbach have turned you into a man!" He gave the pictures back to me. "Before, you painted yourself, even if the picture was just a stable, but now you are painting the lives of others even when you are present there yourself. At last I've had a pupil to whom I've been able to teach something more than just Latin!" But at once he corrected himself with: "But obviously you had it in you already, and I suppose that after all the only thing I taught you *was* Latin."

Once again he leafed through the paintings. Then he nodded and said: "There's one missing. Do it for me: the barbican."

"But why . . ."

He smiled. "The way I see the barbican, it isn't just a building made of stones and mortar. Remember what we went through inside it. It is a parable, a portrait, in fact, perhaps of Vienna, or of Austria, or perhaps of our whole tradition. It may even be a portrait of man himself as he is at present; and as I cannot entirely forget my theology, which looks at our existence here as a reflection of the beyond, perhaps it is a portrait of our life on earth, of our whole being."

I stared at him uncomprehendingly. "But, Father, how can I put all that into a painting?"

He waved his hand impatiently. "Don't try," he said. "Just paint the barbican for me! It will always be a symbol to me of how senseless and yet sense-making human life can be. I know you don't understand that. Never mind. Just do me a picture of the barbican."

I did it and presented it to him as he was starting for Innsbruck, which he wanted to reach in accordance with the orders that had been given him, though now he possessed neither the altar plate nor the five hundred ducats nor the letter he had been entrusted with. He was going simply to fulfil a duty that he had taken upon himself but that in the meantime had lost all its meaning in earthly terms.

"Never forget the barbican," he said to me when he had mounted his horse. Then he rode away.

53

After his offer to send me to Italy, the Count began to find more time for me—partly because he was still waiting to be transferred to his new regiment, partly because it took time to assemble his equipment. He told me things about the preparations for the relief of the siege that I should hardly have credited. He also told me that the Elector of Brandenburg was not helping us against the Turks because he (and his wife also) received a yearly allowance from the French King on condition that he should not offer any assistance to Austria; but if we had paid him more than the French were doing, he would willingly have come over to our side.

He told me also that the Saxons had received only half a million Gulden for their auxiliary forces and that no prince would ever dream of sending troops without first being paid for them; that Hanover, despite the best will in the world, could send us no troops because it was forced to prevent the Elector of Brandenburg from attacking Sweden. And he told me that the Emperor was not with his army because otherwise the Polish King, Sobieski, would feel there was no renown for *him* and would withdraw his regiments.

248

It was just the same as at Raipoltenbach—the folly of war and violence, only on a larger scale, an equally tragic scale.

On 24th August the navy was instructed to build a bridge across the Tulln. The next day the Count was finally given his regiment, and we left Krems. On 5th September we crossed the Danube at Tulln and assembled on the plain to the south. There I saw for the first time the King of the Poles and the Duke of Lothringen. Sobieski made a wonderful impression, and I liked him at once. But the Duke of Lothringen was a disappointment to me. He was pock-marked, had a huge beaked nose, and was somewhat crouch-backed. His blond wig was barbarously made, his grey field uniform was without the slightest sign of decoration, and his shabby old hat did not boast a single feather. His riding boots, too, seemed down-at-heel, and his saddle and bridle were of the most dismal inelegance. Could it be possible that such a man, with such Gothic accoutrements, could be called the first field-marshal of the West?

Count Alram explained to me that Sobieski's command was really only a formality and that it was the Duke of Lothringen who had worked out the plan of attack. The Count knew that these matters depend upon a field marshal's intuition and knowledge, but to me the plan of attack seemed much less important than the way things were conducted on the field of battle. The grey-clad Duke may well have worked out his victory on paper—but it was Sobieski, in all his magnificence, who would really carry the day!

Yet it worked out otherwise.

As the baggage train remained behind in camp, on the night of 12th September I slipped away and climbed the Kahlenberg. In the ruins of the burnt-out monastery there, I found a place that commanded a fine view of Vienna and its environs, and thus I actually saw more of what was going on than if I had been with the troops themselves. Of course I didn't understand it all, but one thing was quite unmistakable: the Duke attacked early in the morning, while Sobieski did not put in an appearance until noon.

It was the Duke of Lothringen who made the move that decided the conflict when he overran the Turks at Nussdorf and pressed on toward Döbling. Unfortunately, he had to stop there because the Poles under Sobieski had still not arrived on his right flank! They came along about two o'clock and very nearly were forced to run away, had not the Imperial Army come to their assistance. The Count had also told me that Sobieski was thinking in terms of a battle lasting several days, while the Duke had reckoned it would take one day at the most —in which assumption he proved to be right. It was finally quite apparent even to me that this victory was due to the sombrely clad general and not to the magnificently attired King of Poland.

My first insight into the ways of the world was therefore that big things are achieved mostly through the judicious laying out of large sums of cash; my second was that a plain exterior and a modest demeanour are more likely to be the attributes of real ability than arrogance and fine clothes.

Towards evening the Turks fled; we occupied the suburbs and set up our bivouacs. As we still had to reckon with a possible counter-attack from the Turks, we were strictly forbidden to remove ourselves to any great distance from the encampment. All the Imperial troops obeyed this order, but the Poles were singing and dancing through the Turkish camp, stealing and plundering. I learned later that they had acquired booty amounting to over six million Gulden—of which their king received the lion's share, that is to say, everything—of what had formerly belonged to the Grand Vizier. But the Imperial troops got nothing, and Sobieski made fun of Lothringen because he had not even received the smallest token of appreciation from the Emperor.

He didn't want it, and the Emperor knew that.

Soon afterwards I received my third insight into the ways of life when we had actually liberated the city. I then learned something that during the siege had not been apparent while the Count and Michel and I were still in Vienna. I knew that our troops were courageous from my experiences on the defence works. It was only now that I heard half of them had perished in the fight. I also knew that the guild companies, which had not taken any part in the actual fighting but had performed their duties as watchmen and labourers and, in doing so, had often exposed themselves to enemy fire, had also given proof of their courage. But what about the others? I was told that many citizens had engaged in profiteering by raising the cost of living to unheard-of heights; that many reverend gentlemen had only agreed to tend the wounded in their monasteries after a good deal of prodding; that sacks of straw (for mattresses) could only be obtained for their unfortunates by main force; that the apothecaries had put exorbitant prices on the simplest of medicaments, on ointments and bandages; that the commandant only four days before the liberation had had to conduct a house-to-house search for able-bodied men to serve in the labour units and had unearthed thus over six hundred strapping fellows who until then had remained in comfortable hiding; and that finally the soldiers during attacks on the fortress and the Löbel bastion by the Turks had been afraid lest the citizens might open the gates and let the enemy in.

Then came the final revelation.

Although the Emperor had pleaded with Sobieski to wait and although the Emperor had remained well away from his own army, the Polish King had made his entry into Vienna the very next day after the siege was raised. The German soldiers and their officers refused to follow him: they stayed outside the city. But he had himself proclaimed victor in a battle that someone else had won.

While Sobieski was riding into the city, Bishop Kollonitsch was moving out, with all the carriages he could find, into the deserted Turkish camp. He, too, started plundering—though not gold and jewels. He brought back to Vienna five hundred of the children taken prisoners by the Turks, gave them into devoted hands, and saw that they were all looked after.

I saw this terrible procession and once again realised all the dismal horror of war. War meant good business for certain people, from Sobieski down to the lowest candlemaker, who in times of national emergency had sold his wares at the highest price—and it meant the most wretched poverty and degradation for all the rest.

And there were others, loyal ones!

If that was how life was—a life in which Sobieski could accumulate renown and money, while a Duke of Lothringen was used merely as a tool—how was it that, if I were offered the choice between the two, I would most certainly have chosen the lot of the Duke of Lothringen?

Though I knew that war and violence meant untold suffering, useless suffering, why should I have thought myself so poor in experience and so deficient in feeling before the events I endured in the barbican, events that I would have so gladly escaped?

It was not until much later that I realised that Father Lukas, in speaking about the senselessness and the sense of human life, had been referring to this very problem. Who can solve it? Only God.

54

For a few days we once again lived at the house in New Square. I had left word with the Langseisen family to send my mother straight to me as soon as she came to Vienna. I had given up all hope of seeing her again and was convinced that she had been among those whom the Turks, before their withdrawal, had slaughtered like cattle. Then one day I was called by Michel down to the first floor and led into the Count's reception room.

There sat my mother.

I threw my arms around her and kissed her. She held me tight. An eternity seemed to have passed between that moment and the day when she had showed me the Khainacher treasures —and yet the time had been so short! What has time to do, anyway, with the love of a child for his mother, the love of a mother for her child!

When we were at last quite sure that we were once more together, that we were both alive and healthy, I sat in the chair opposite her, and she said: "We can thank God that a good-for-nothing like yourself has been able to spend all this terrible time in safety here in Vienna. At least your otherwise useless and senseless approaches to the Count have had some result."

I looked at the Count. The Count was smiling.

"And what makes you think my approaches were so senseless and useless, Mother?"

She stammered: "But it was about your painting, wasn't it?"

"Yes."

"I can hardly imagine that his honour would come to your assistance—"

"He has!" I shouted. I could contain myself no longer. The Count nodded.

My mother looked from one to another, shaking her he doubtfully. "Does your honour really—"

"Andreas is leaving for Italy," the Count replied. "The agreement is drawn up. After his second conversation with Count Leslie in Stein, nothing else was possible."

My mother stared at him. "Count Leslie? What's Andreas got to do with Count Leslie? And what's this about him being in Stein?"

Once more everything had to be explained. It was a good thing that Michel came along just then, for he was able to fill in the pauses wonderfully well, to increase the suspense and make my story even more exciting with tales of limping demons, flying wolves, and witches astride burning broomsticks!

55

All I have to do now is to bring my story to an end.

Within a week after Vienna had been delivered, the Count was on the march again with his own regiment for Hungary, and Michel of course went with him. In Hungary there was proof, if proof were needed, of what Alram had already told me —namely, that Sobieski was perhaps a clever leader of cavalry but was certainly no general. He was ignominiously beaten at Palanky. But Lothringen won a victory, and because of his bravery in this fight, Alram was made a general.

The reason the Turks had withdrawn at Raipoltenbach was told me by Count Leslie one day when he paid a visit to New Square. In the night of 3rd to 4th August, the Turks outside Vienna had succeeded in making a definite breakthrough in the moat. It no longer seemed important to them to learn about secret messages carried by the Austrian courier. They were of the opinion, too, that the Burg ravelin was the right place to launch their attack. Therefore, they called in the small commando group from Raipoltenbach, and the Tartars disappeared, of course, as soon as there was no captain to give them orders.

Our blacksmith, despite his five arrow wounds, recovered perfectly. Father Lukas soon returned from Innsbruck and began teaching again at the seminary, which, out of gratitude for his deliverance, gave old Black Kate enough to build a new cottage for the charcoal burners.

Kaspar Fetz was never seen again—apparently he had fled abroad. But the second-in-command and Viereckl were apprehended in Wiener Neustadt almost a year later. It came out at their trial that Viereckl had wanted to murder us before they left the fortress, but Fetz had been all for a swift and silent flight because he wanted to have our family jewels all to himself. The judge pronounced them both guilty, and they were sent to the gallows, which they had so often sung about in the robbers' song.

Our family jewels never reappeared. Kaspar Fetz must have gradually converted them into money, and sometimes I wonder if I may not find them again in the possession of some quite honest and respectable citizen. My mother would have been happier if I hadn't had to be indebted to the Count for my studies in Italy, but from my own point of view it was better that way. The Count's kindness was something I had never expected, and the fact that in the end he did help me and that I had to prove my worth in the most difficult situations, first by showing I had some spunk and then by my painting, were things greater than all the money in the world. So, I can truly say I achieved my aim not by virtue of my forefathers' wealth but through my own efforts.

Count Palffy could not decide whether to restore Raipoltenbach or not, and so that fine moated fortress is gradually falling to pieces year by year. My mother was made housekeeper at the castle in New Lempach. And by November I was already on my way to Florence. My mother took me to Vienna, and Father Lukas came, too, to say farewell before I climbed into the coach in the Big Market. When the horses drew away, they both waved to me, and I waved back. Then I started travelling through the city and left it by the Carinthian Gate, and as I went, I cast a last look back at the walls and domes, spires and towers of Vienna.

The road lay downhill, and the kingdom of my childhood vanished.

Many years have passed since then. I learned my trade in Italy and after my return to my homeland found some recognition as a painter. It's a long time since I thought about fortresses, sieges, sword fights, and charges of shot from four-pounders. But always when I hear a bagpipe or a fife, the old robbers' song about the raven begins to ring in my ears. I seem to see the robbers squatting there in the lamplight and stamping on the floor with their heavy-booted feet. I see the grin on the mutilated face of Kaspar Fetz, the Count with drawn sword, Michel with a primed pistol in his great fist, and Father Lukas incongruously loading his musket. I see the blacksmith, the doctor, Shiftyface, and Viereckl aiming his cannon. But behind all the clouds of smoke and dust rise solid and impregnable, squat and invincible, the towers of the barbican.